The redhead fished approached. When she sto out one of his business Danny Tarantino?"

He stared. A breathtaking mountain lake was right outside his back door, but the blue didn't compare to the color of her eyes. A flawless complexion with a hint of freckles didn't hurt either. It had been a long time since a beautiful woman had affected him like this.

She cleared her throat and gave him a knowing look. "Are you finished with the inventory?"

Embarrassed, he put on his best smile. "Sorry. What can I do for you?"

She gave him a mild appraisal in return. "A blackjack dealer at Suttons handed me this when I asked about a high-stakes poker tournament. He said to tell you hello from Rick."

He raised an eyebrow. This woman played high-stakes poker? He looked down at his card as if he could find the answer there.

Praise for DeeAnna Galbraith

"DeeAnna Galbraith's *GAMBLING ON THE GODDESS* is a hot winner for any romantic suspense lover. Galbraith deftly deals thrills and surprises the reader won't see coming. Highly recommended!"

~Melinda Rucker Haynes, Author

Gambling on the Goddess

by

DeeAnna Galbraith

This is a work of fiction. Names, characters, places, and incidents are either the product of the author's imagination or are used fictitiously, and any resemblance to actual persons living or dead, business establishments, events, or locales, is entirely coincidental.

Gambling on the Goddess

COPYRIGHT © 2020 by DeeAnna Galbraith

Cover Art by *Abigail Owen*

The Wild Rose Press, Inc.
PO Box 708
Adams Basin, NY 14410-0708
Visit us at www.thewildrosepress.com

Publishing History
First Crimson Rose Edition, 2020
Print ISBN 978-1-5092-2994-9
Digital ISBN 978-1-5092-2995-6

Published in the United States of America

Dedication

For my husband, Reed.
Stick with me, kid.

Chapter One

Exasperation tightened Pallas Mulroney's jaw. "We've covered this already, Charles. It's my fifty thousand dollars, and if I lose it, I lose it."

Charles Wyatt stood firm across the small, nondescript, Lake Tahoe, Nevada, hotel room, his stiff shoulders telegraphing disapproval. "The idea is appalling. You can't want the partnership very much if you're willing to gamble your inheritance." He set his jaw. "Of course, your father would no doubt support your decision."

Pallas gritted her teeth and counted to ten. Charles viewed her father's occupation as a professional gambler as an aberration and brought it up whenever he wanted to make a negative point. He hadn't figured out it just served to tick her off. This time she wouldn't take the bait, and be damned if she'd tell him how much the partnership meant.

"You're being stubborn on purpose," he continued. "How is it going to look if the person I recommended can't deliver on the half-million-dollar buy-in?"

The line separating her patience from her temper disappeared. She crossed her arms, glaring. "So bottom line is how *you* would look if I fail to come up with the money."

He backed up a step but kept his rigid posture. Clear gray eyes regarded her as he pushed straight, mouse-brown hair back from his forehead. "Perception is part of it. When I made the short list at the start-up, I emphasized your business skills and education. Otherwise, you mightn't be under consideration."

She thought about counting to ten again, then dismissed it. "The 'otherwise' meaning my father's background. Fortunately, you and the other partners are allowing me to bring a half million dollars to the table." She paused. "Not to mention the Baxter-Dolan Project. You forgot to list that along with my business skills and education. I happen to know, however, it's a big part of why I've been made the offer."

He rubbed his index finger up the bridge of his nose. It was one of Charles' tells. A giveaway that meant he was about to whine. "Don't be like that. I care about you, and I'm trying to help."

She picked up her purse and strode toward the room's door. "No, you're not, Charles. I'm not changing my mind, so you're wasting your time. Be sure the door is closed when you leave."

Charles had the good sense not to follow her to the elevator crowded with Japanese tourists. Tahoe drew travelers from the Pacific Rim, sports enthusiasts, and gamblers, as well as those taking in the shows and beautiful scenery. Charles had insisted on coming with her "as a friend." Now she knew why. He'd spent the entire trip from San Francisco on a singularly annoying lecture about financial responsibility.

She sighed. Charles wasn't obnoxious all the time. He was an old friend and had been her mentor at Stanford. They now worked as principals for the same venture capital firm. She owed him big for the partnership recommendation at a prestigious new firm, but that obligation didn't include a say in how she used her money or the closer relationship he kept hinting at.

As a venture capitalist, Charles should understand risk-taking, but it was becoming clear he was blind when it came to her. Telling him she'd inherited her stake money had been a white lie. Her father, Jack Mulroney, believed in being generous in the here and now, so he'd given each of his daughters fifty thousand dollars when they reached twenty-five. Pallas meant to turn that into the money needed to buy the partnership by winning it in a poker tournament.

Thoughts of her father reminded Pallas of the second reason she'd come to Lake Tahoe to gamble, an agenda Charles knew nothing about. Twenty years ago, Jack Mulroney had been banned from gambling casinos at Lake Tahoe. For cheating. She'd been six at the time.

When she was in high school, a classmate who'd had too much beer at a kegger confided his uncle was the security guard who had escorted her father out after he'd been caught.

Pallas had come home in tears. Her parents wouldn't talk about it, except to say the story was true, but the allegations weren't. From that point on, she'd wanted to know why he'd been falsely accused. Her father had never cheated in his life. He didn't have to.

She took a deep breath and strolled around the casino. As long as she was going to take half a million home to San Francisco, she might as well take the truth about her father's ban, too.

The dealer at the blackjack table she chose was a tall, handsome man, probably in his mid-fifties, who looked like he enjoyed his job, a plus in her book. His nametag read *Rick* with *Nevada* underneath, proclaiming this as his home state.

She tuned out the clangs of bells from slot machines and hoots from craps players. Quiet surroundings worked best, but Pallas made do by concentrating. Within a half hour she was up five hundred dollars. Things were definitely going her way.

Collecting her chips, she smiled. "Do you know where I can find a no-limits poker tournament? I thought it would be easy, Tahoe being a place with lots of casinos, but I haven't been able to find a location where I get a good feeling about the tables."

He raised an eyebrow. "Vibes not right?"

Pallas nodded and passed a fifty-dollar chip across the table. "Not so much. You were lucky for me. I thought you might have a suggestion."

The dealer tapped the chip on the table to indicate to the "eye in the sky" observers that it was a tip. "Thanks. We're hosting a tournament day after tomorrow to open a newly remodeled area." He winked. "The cosmos might align for you in there. If you don't want to wait, I know of another place." He pulled a business card out of his vest pocket and slid it to her. "This is a new casino and dinner club. They might have a player slot open. Tell the owner Rick said hello."

Pallas took the card. "Over the Moon. Sounds interesting."

The dealer nodded to some new arrivals, then gave her a two-finger salute. "Promise to come back and give me a chance to get even?"

Pallas grinned. "I'll be back, but I can't promise you'll get even."

****

Danny Tarantino walked into the dining room at

Over the Moon, pleased with the size of the lunch crowd. He entered a short hallway that led to the gaming area, and the undercurrent of chatter let him know it was even more packed.

As he emerged, his glance fell on a roped-off corner where his poker tournament entrants played. He frowned, remembering the note tucked under the wiper blade of his car two days ago. It railed against the evils of gambling and threatened punishment if he didn't cancel the event. Danny hadn't taken it seriously until last night. One of his players had crashed his rental car and suffered a compound broken leg. The man had insisted his brakes had failed.

Danny had taken the note to the sheriff's department and turned it over to an officer who opened a case but told him casinos received threats regularly from dissatisfied customers and zealots. Danny already knew that from his previous job as a security specialist at one of the big casinos. He wanted something on the books just in case he had to cancel the tournament. The officer had agreed to send a man to interview the player and have the brakes on the car checked.

As Danny scanned the crowd, one of the spectators talking to a stunning redhead pointed at him. Her gaze followed, and she started in his direction. Whoever she was, her clothes and the way she carried herself spelled class and confidence.

Though a little above average in height, she didn't fit the showgirl mold. Danny had never been wrong about that. His father was a dealer, so he'd grown up around women who worked in the hotels. Showgirls and cocktail waitresses led far from glamorous lives, and although not immune to their charms, Danny didn't have time to get serious. He had been, and still was, too busy fulfilling his dream of owning and running his own club.

The redhead fished in her small purse as she approached. When she stopped in front of him, she held out one of his business cards. "You're the owner, Danny Tarantino?"

He stared. A breathtaking mountain lake was right outside his back door, but the blue didn't compare to the color of her eyes. A flawless complexion with a hint of freckles didn't hurt either. It had been a long time since a beautiful woman had affected him like this.

She cleared her throat and gave him a knowing look. "Are you finished with the inventory?"

Embarrassed, he put on his best smile. "Sorry. What can I do for you?"

She gave him a mild appraisal in return. "A blackjack dealer at Suttons handed me this when I asked about a high-stakes poker tournament. He said to tell you hello from Rick."

He raised an eyebrow. This woman played high-stakes poker? He looked down at his card as if he could find the answer there.

The redhead was tapping her foot. "*Hellooo*. About this tournament you're hosting. Do you have any openings, and what does it take to buy in?"

His attention snapped back to her face. He didn't want to tell her about the possible cancellation in front of his customers, so he tipped his head toward the back of the club. "Why don't we go to my office? We can discuss the entry requirements there."

She nodded and in that quick action conveyed agreement but on her terms. He liked that. The bluish, silky shirt and matching pants she wore outlined a nice figure. Shiny hair caught up in a couple of gold combs swung against her shoulders. His concentration was so complete he had to stop quickly to keep from running into her. She studied the displays hanging in the hallway.

"What are these?"

He grinned. "Some of the finest examples of card cheating devices anywhere."

The notion dawned on her, and she threw back her head and laughed, exposing a beautiful slender throat. "I love it. What a great idea. Just steps from the gambling." She pointed to the one she'd been looking at, a thin, hinged, metal circle with what looked like tweezers attached to a tiny spring. "How does this one work?"

He held up his arm. "The circle fits above your wrist, and the clamp holds an extra card. When you bump it against your leg, the spring activates, and the card slides past your cuff into your hand. It was very popular until they started randomly changing deck colors."

"And that one?"

He leaned in to see the object of her interest. Fragrance immediately enveloped his senses. Not too strong, but sexy as hell. "That one's a little cruder. It's made to look like a sock garter, but a third piece of elastic secures an extra card or two. I imagine the other players got suspicious when he kept leaning down to scratch his leg."

She shook her head. "They were in the wrong business. If you can't depend on your brain when you gamble, you may as well pack it in."

He grinned. "That's always been my philosophy. Unfortunately, depending on your brain would exclude about ninety percent of my customers."

The beautiful woman turned toward him. "Brains, and of course the room has to be right."

He laughed out loud. "Of course." He'd given up arguing with gamblers and their superstitions. He'd heard it all, from lucky underwear to a locket with a snippet of a beloved pet's hair.

She cocked her head. "He's a relative, right?"

Danny was lost. "Who, the sock cheater?"

"No, Rick the dealer. You look like a younger version."

He nodded. "My dad."

"So why isn't he dealing here?"

"Actually, I asked him, and he turned me down. Said he was more at home in his big casino. What I really think is Suttons made him a better offer."

She grinned. "I wouldn't be surprised. He's good."

"The best."

They continued down the short hallway between the gambling area and the bar/dining room. Danny caught a subtle thumbs-up from the bartender. Bru was an extraordinary mixologist who favored streaked platinum hair and electric tans. He looked like he'd gotten lost on his way to a surfing beach. The guy used to make a fortune working private parties and now tended full time at Over the Moon. He appreciated the ladies and was giving his endorsement of Danny's companion.

The redhead stopped in front of the door marked *Private*. Danny pulled out his keys and opened it. He followed her in and closed the door, indicating a chair across from his desk.

"This is nice," she said, trailing her finger along the rounded edge of his desk. "Your father mentioned the casino was new. How long have you been open?"

"About a month. We're still in shake-down mode."

"It's got a lot going for it. Sage, dove gray, and dark lavender are not colors you expect to see in a casino. The layout is also great. It sells itself to a higher-class clientele."

He was impressed by her observations but still had a hard time picturing her as a woman who hung out in casinos. Yet here she was, asking to buy into a high-stakes poker tournament. Maybe gambling was a hobby. "So what do you do?"

She tipped her head to the side and smiled. "I'm a principal at a venture capital firm."

He tried not to let his jaw drop in surprise. How many times was he going to be wrong about this woman? "Let me guess. You found a product or service worth millions and are here to take your chances. Maybe personally invest?"

She leaned forward, her expression cool. "I never take chances with my money. I'm here to win."

Now *that* didn't surprise him. He had the feeling whatever this woman went after, she got. But not this time. "I'm sorry you've come all the way out here, Ms....?"

"Pallas Mulroney."

He stopped cold. What kind of name was Palace? Then it clicked. Redheaded Lucky Jack Mulroney, professional gambler. He'd named his four daughters after the queens in a deck of cards. Four beautiful daughters if she was any indication. "Pallas, as in Pallas

Athena, the Queen of Spades and Goddess of wisdom and war, and Mulroney as in one of the daughters of Lucky Jack?"

She nodded, a quizzical look on her face. "My father hasn't gambled in Tahoe for twenty years. You're well informed."

He leaned forward, his curiosity onboard. "I've never met him. But he's something of a legend. Do you really have three sisters named Esther, Argine, and Judith?"

A gentle sigh. "Yes. People rarely make the connection, though. Can we get back to why you're sorry I came all the way out here? Are all the slots taken?"

"I'm not sure the tournament is going to be held. So I'm not taking on any new players."

A tiny frown marred her forehead. "Then why are those people playing out there in the roped-off section?"

He really hated disappointing her. "Because I haven't made any announcements yet."

"Do you mind telling me why the possible cancellation?"

It might be curiosity on her part, or it could be something entirely different. He didn't really know this woman from Eve and sure as hell didn't have a reason to trust her. "Yes, I do."

****

Pallas considered the handsome man across from her. Danny Tarantino and his on-again, off-again tournament piqued her interest. More important than that was the connection she felt. This club would be a great place to play poker. "That's fair. I've only been here ten minutes, and you don't know me. It's just that I get a really good feeling about your place. If there's any chance at all I could be one of the players, should you decide to continue in the next couple of days, I'm in."

His gaze measured her, not giving an inch. "Is that why you're pushing this? Because my club makes you feel good?"

She nodded. "Simply put, yes. I need half a million dollars by the end of the month to buy into a business opportunity. I'm a very good poker player, but I wasn't kidding when I said the room has to feel right. Some places are totally out of the question, some acceptable, and some are excellent. Your club falls into the last category."

He shook his head. "I can't believe someone with your obvious brains for finance is making a huge career decision based on gambling and *feelings*."

Anxious to convince him, she scooted forward. "Why not? Everybody gets through life based on feelings, Mr. Tarantino. Even you. For instance, why did you decide to use soothing colors instead of the bright, shiny ones associated with most casinos?" She held up her hand. "Because people feel calmer surrounded by these colors. They might stay longer and spend more money if they're comfortable. You used that theory to your advantage, so why do you find it hard to believe this is where I want to play? I'm just more honest about it."

His shoulders relaxed a little. "That has a certain logic." Then curiosity lit his eyes, and he changed the subject. "Your business opportunity sounds like a big deal. Is it here?"

She was grateful he hadn't dismissed her as a total

nutcase. "No, it's in San Francisco. Three high-profile venture capitalists are starting their own firm. I've garnered a name as someone who can bring in the big players. Those people the gaming industry call whales. They have new money for the most part and get high on risk-taking. Anyway, the partners want a maximum of five partners, and I've been offered one of the two remaining slots."

He lifted an eyebrow. "Mind if I ask why you're gambling instead of going to a bank?"

She twined her fingers in her lap. She had told this relative stranger more about herself, her family, and her dream future in five minutes than most of her friends knew about her. "I've worked too hard to make it this far only to be answerable to some bank for my dream. I want this on my terms."

A slight nod from the casino owner had her thinking he knew exactly what she meant.

"Very commendable, Ms. Mulroney," he said. "But I still can't let you participate. You could lose something much more valuable than your very beautiful shirt."

So that was it. Something going on he couldn't or wouldn't talk about. Whatever the problem, she might be able to wait it out. Besides, she never turned down a challenge. "I can handle it."

Chapter Two

His veiled comment that it could be dangerous didn't even slow the redhead down.

"I seldom lose, Mr. Tarantino, and please, call me Pallas. I tell you what. If you let me sit in for a few hands before you commit to anything, I'd know if I really want to be in your tournament."

"Okay, Pallas. The answer is, and will remain, no."

"But you're a gambler."

Impatience colored his next words. "Not really. I've never understood the urge to gamble, even though I've been around it all my life. I'm a businessman."

She shook her head. "There are almost a dozen casinos in this small town, yet you opened another one. You don't think that was a gamble?"

He sighed in resignation. "Like you, I never take long odds. Unfortunately, all your arguments have convinced me not to wait to cancel. Much as I hate to, I'm returning everyone's money."

She stood and leaned on his desk, her palms resting on its surface. "Did you sign an agreement with each player?"

What now? "Of course."

"May I see it?"

"Why?"

Her finger tapped the desk's surface. "Because I want to prove something."

"If I let you see it, will you stop pestering me?"

She nodded. "Guaranteed. If I'm wrong."

He shook his head, then slipped his center drawer open and pulled out a sheet of paper. "Pretty standard. Covers all the bases."

She took it from him and turned it around to read. "Ah-ha!"

He leaned forward. "Ah-ha, what?"

An oval-shaped nail poked at a paragraph high on the page. "Right here. It says unless it's an act of God or a death, both parties must agree to the termination of the tournament."

He pulled the sheet toward himself, glancing down. *There damn well could've been a death. That player was lucky he got out of that accident alive.*

"I'm sorry," she said, lifting a shoulder. "But you're not going to get the rest of the players to agree, trust me."

He sighed as she slid the agreement toward her and started reading again. She was aggravating but sharp. He liked the way she used her brains instead of her sexuality, although she had plenty of it.

She finished and laid the paper down. "The contract says fifty thousand dollars brought to the table and an extra consideration for a bonus. How much?"

He thought of the player in traction. He'd really hate to see one of those gorgeous legs broken. Not that he'd seen her legs, but he'd glimpsed pretty ankles when she sat down. "Doesn't matter. I told you I'm canceling the tournament."

She cocked her head and started to leave. "Can't say I didn't try."

Minor panic set in. He had nothing else to say to

keep her from leaving. "Uh, if things change and I decide to re-establish the tournament, I'll keep you in mind if you can beat me three out of five hands."

She looked surprised. "I thought you weren't a gambler."

"I said I've never understood the urge. I didn't say I wasn't any good."

Her eyes sparkled. "Game on. Now?"

"Unless you have something better to do, now would be fine."

She picked up her purse. "I'm always ready."

His imagination slipped into high gear as she turned toward the door. This was crazy, but he hadn't done crazy in a long time, and with her it felt right. "We can play in the office or the bar. Your choice," he said as they entered the hall, hoping she would pick his office.

She tipped her head. "Your office, with one caveat."

"What's that?"

"May I pick the deck?"

"Good vibes?"

"Yes."

He rolled his eyes. "Why don't we both pick?"

"Okay. I like your style."

They left the office, and Bru winked at them. Danny's bartender had few filters and was wide open when it came to approving of beautiful women.

At the pit boss's cage, Danny asked for six new decks, but she stilled his arm as he reached for them. She shook her head and pointed to herself. He made a small sweeping motion, allowing her to do the honors.

"Thank you," she said.

He shrugged and crossed his arms, watching her.

She ran pretty, slim fingers over the sides of the wrapped decks, then slipped two out and handed them to him. "Either of these will do."

Glad he'd thought to offer a poker game, Danny walked to the hallway outside his office where he held the decks to his forehead and closed his eyes, moaning and weaving.

She started laughing, and he joined in.

They were still laughing when they walked through the door. Then he grew quiet and stepped back out of the doorway to glance in both directions. A note-sized envelope sat in the middle of his desk. It hadn't been there a few minutes ago.

He pulled back before slamming his fist into the door. If he found the SOB who was trying to ruin him, the guy was history. The new resolve to tighten his security by locking the door to his office had been blown away, his interest totally fixed on Pallas.

She took the few steps to the desk, leaned over, and nudged the corner of the cream-colored envelope. "Expensive."

That it was. High-grade paper with a thin navy border. Just like the first one. He rubbed his neck and tossed down the decks he was holding. "We're going to have to postpone our game. You can wait in the bar for me if you like." He shook his head. "Better yet, cancel. I need to see to some things."

She nodded, a thoughtful expression on her face. "The note's one of those things, I take it? I'd rather hang around if you don't mind."

His irritation simmered. "Ms. Mulroney…"

"As I said, please call me Pallas."

"Let's get something straight, Pallas. Unless you'd like to use our dining or gambling facilities, we have no further business."

He almost smiled. She didn't look at all disappointed at getting thrown out.

"I'm hungry. And when I'm hungry, I like to gamble," she said. "Want to play our three hands while you're waiting for the law?"

He rolled his gaze upward. "As I recall, I said three out of five. I also said forget it."

She swept up the new decks. "I'll only need three. Then I've got to run."

He felt sorry for this woman's clients. She could introduce the Brooklyn Bridge as a hot new venture and get it financed in a heartbeat. He smiled in spite of himself. What the hell? He could think of worse ways to spend the time waiting for a deputy to show. "All right, three games to kill time. We'll make it two out of three."

She brought her chin up in challenge. "You're an optimist if you think it'll take three. What are we playing for?"

A couple of things swam into the smutty part of his consciousness, but he just blinked. "I'll make a call, then talk to some people and meet you at the bar. We'll play for toothpicks."

She shrugged and held up her tiny purse. "At least I'll be able to carry my winnings."

After she left, the light seemed to dim in his office, but it sure smelled great.

He called a friend in the sheriff's department.

"Tony Mancusco."

"Why is it we only talk when one of us has a

bloody nose?"

A chuckle came over the line. "Not true. Sometimes we talk when one of us *gives* a bloody nose. Speaking of which, you sure put someone's out of joint. We got the report back on that rental. Very sloppy job of messing with the brake lines but effective. It's a whole new ball game with bodily harm involved."

Danny spanned his temples with one hand and rubbed. "I should've shut down the tournament when I got the first note."

Tony chided him. "Don't beat yourself up. If every club or hotel owner shut down when they received a threat from a whacko, half the places here would be boarded up. You took a calculated risk. But you said first note. You got another one?"

"Yeah, this time it was left in the center of my desk, and I doubt if it's an apology. Same stationery. I haven't touched it."

"Well, he's got guts; I'll say that. I'll have a deputy dispatched to pick it up. I don't suppose anybody saw who dropped it off?"

"I'm about to check on that. Let me know what's in the second note as soon as you can, okay?"

"Will do."

****

He locked the door and headed for the bar. Pallas was laughing at something Bru had said. Danny quickened his steps. His friend was damned charming, and for some reason it irritated him that Pallas liked the bartender's warped sense of humor.

He nodded at them and headed into the kitchen where he whistled and waved people over. "An item was left in my office within the last few minutes. Did any of you see someone going in or out?"

Head shakes and perplexed looks greeted him. He thanked the staff and left.

An unmarked door next to the storeroom led to his security office. He knocked. When a bolt clicked back and he entered, the first thing he saw was a screen showing the back of his own head as he went through the door. He scanned the other monitors above the workstations in the windowless room, then turned his attention to one of the occupants. "I have a security problem. Run the tape for the last ten minutes from camera three."

The man nodded and punched in some instructions on his keyboard. The picture flickered, then swung down the hallway between the two sides of his club. Danny clocked a three-second period with each pass when his office was not in view. It would have been easy to step through the doorway, toss a note on his desk, and step back out. About a dozen people walked by in the minute or so he and Pallas were gone. He saw a couple of waiters, two of his tournament players, and other people he didn't recognize, but no one to rouse his suspicion. "Cut a copy, and I'll be back to pick it up."

He left and approached Pallas and Bru at the bar. The bartender had once told him, "Act like you're interested in what she's saying, and any woman is yours." Right now, Bru had his head bent slightly in her direction, an intent expression on his face. She talked animatedly, punctuating her story with hundred-watt smiles. "…and that's how I paid my annual fees."

Bru held up his hand for a high-five, then turned his attention to Danny. "Pallas paid her fees at Stanford by playing poker. Looks like you might have a contender on your hands."

Danny sucked in a breath. "Maybe. Did you see anyone go into my office about ten minutes ago?"

The blond glanced in that direction. "Just you and Pallas. It's usually locked when you aren't in there. Why?"

"Tell you later. Want to hand me the toothpick holders?"

Bru shrugged and gave him the look he always got when he wanted to play for toothpicks. The *oh, for crying out loud, it's legal to play for money here* look.

He sat and swiveled toward her. "Reds are twenty, blues are ten, and yellows are five."

She slid her half of the toothpicks in front of her and held up the two decks. "Want to hold them to your forehead again, swami?"

The guffaw from Bru quickly died as a fake cough. Pallas gave him a sideways glance and winked.

Danny shook his head and tapped the deck nearest him. "This one's fine."

Bru slid two glasses forward. "Ginger ale, compliments of the house." He leaned on the bar, grinning, until Danny frowned and nodded toward a waitress waiting at the end of the bar. Bru tossed his bar towel over his shoulder and shoved away. "My public awaits."

Danny pondered the wisdom of sitting here playing poker when his life's dream was being attacked and he didn't know who or why. Then he glanced into those beautiful blue eyes, and the thought that he might blow a chance with her floated to the top of the list. Hell, he could go for broke on this front, too.

****

Pallas prepared her Mona Lisa face and slowed her breathing. Really good players could discern what kind of hand a player had by reading their expression. She was a master at hiding hers and reading others. Her father had taught her to watch players first, cards second. It worked great. "People who play for fun," he'd said, "don't know that even the widening of their pupils can give them away."

He shuffled, then they cut for high card. It had been a while since she had played, and she'd forgotten how much she enjoyed the sound of new cards snicking against each other. She opened with three keepers.

It wasn't surprising that Danny's expression didn't change a whisker when he picked up his hand. Speaking of whiskers, he had a five o'clock shadow by lunchtime, but that wouldn't deter her. Pallas liked tactile experiences when it came to men. A light tapping sound brought her focus back. He'd said something. Great. She pulled herself together and went for the "sorry, I wasn't paying attention" bluff. It usually made her opponents think she was distracted. Only this time she wasn't bluffing. *Concentrate, girl, or you're going to lose.*

"I said, how many?" he asked.

"Two, please."

One card was great and one was trash. She watched him for any signs that would give away what he held. Nothing. He had a natural poker face. He took three and didn't bat an eyelash.

She blew a ladylike puff of air toward a stray curl that had escaped one of her combs and asked sweetly, "Don't you ever blink?"

Danny Tarantino slowly winked. An action which she thought totally unfair and deserved her best shot.

She tossed in a red toothpick. "Twenty to you."

He slid over a red and blue. "Your play."

Odds were in her favor, and she took them, slipping in enough to cover his bet and call. He held out his hand. A pair of puny tens. It had been a while since she had played someone who managed to look so inscrutable when bluffing. She had to give it to him.

"Told ya," she said and presented two pair, scooping up the colorful toothpicks.

There went that eyebrow again. He would make a great James Bond.

The second game was tough. She'd dealt herself absolute junk. Asking for five new cards would be a little obvious, so she smiled with what she hoped was a winner's confidence. "How many?"

He slipped one card to the bar, his expression blank.

She dealt his card and tipped her head. "I'll just keep what I have."

Two raises later he still wasn't buying it and called. This was definitely not going her way; that ploy should have worked. Not that he tried to lord it over her. He was a gentleman at winning as well as losing.

The third hand started out well. She had three good cards again and asked for two. In leaning forward to give her the cards, he bumped her knee. He caught and held her gaze a second longer than necessary. "Sorry."

What was he up to? She honest-to-goodness couldn't tell if he was intentionally trying to distract her. He dealt himself one. She took a sip of her ginger ale and was about to make a glib remark to see if she could get a reaction when Bru glanced at Danny's hand on his way to serve a customer. That comic instant was all she needed. Danny was bluffing.

"Call," she said.

He laid down a hand of pure garbage. "Thought I had you on that one."

She smiled. "You nearly did." Her gaze went to Bru. "Nametag says Bru. Is that just a funky spelling of Brew, you know, as in a drink?"

Danny shook his head. "No. Short for Brubeck. His parents and grandparents were huge jazz fans. He shortened it to Bru when he started tending bar." He tipped his head. "Enough about Bru. You're as good as you said. I'm sorry you won't get a chance to be in my tournament."

As much as she wanted to play here, she reluctantly nodded. Losing the chance to play in the tournament wasn't her only frustration. She could've kicked herself for bragging that she only wanted to play three games. Sitting knee to knee with Danny Tarantino woke some very sexy feelings. It occurred to her then that road might travel two ways, and he was drawn to her.

Wouldn't she have fun finding out?

Chapter Three

"Would you like…?" Danny stopped and blinked. The entrance to the dining room held a sheriff's deputy who blocked out the light. The guy looked like a carved redwood. The sandy-haired giant passively scanned the room until he took in the bar. A big grin split his face, and he let out a whoop, crossing the room in long strides.

"Pallas, you little darlin'," he boomed.

She didn't even make it off her stool before being picked up and swung around like a rag doll. An answering grin lit her face, and she planted a kiss on his cheek. "Pat! How did you know I was here? Is Sassy with you?"

He put her down, still holding one of her hands in his massive paw, his green eyes sparkling. "I'm here on business. Your sister's at home with the girls."

Danny let out a breath. That explained it. The deputy was married to one of her sisters. He'd stood and been ready to help in case the man's overtures were unwelcome, although nothing short of a two-by-four would have had an effect on him. He held out his hand. "I think you're looking for me."

"Danny Tarantino, this is Pat Murphy, my sister Ester's husband," Pallas said, clearly delighted at seeing her brother-in-law.

Danny was confused. "Then who's Sassy?"

"I'm the only one who calls her that," she explained.

"Which is appropriate, if you ask me," the deputy said. "But we'll talk about family later." He turned his full attention to Danny. "You have something for me?"

Pallas smiled brightly. "It's locked in his office. If you don't mind, I'll tag along." She held up her hands. "I promise to stay out of the way."

The deputy shrugged. "In my experience, the Mulroney women tend to keep their word. It's up to you, Mr. Tarantino."

Danny gave her a look. "I don't suppose you'd rather eat lunch. On the house?"

Shiny red hair swished across her shoulders as she shook her head. "No, thanks."

Like he couldn't have predicted *that* answer.

The three of them went into the office where the deputy carefully slid the envelope into an evidence bag. "I'm told you can call later today to find out the contents," Pat said.

Danny nodded. "Thanks. Security cut a copy of the footage showing the traffic outside my office while the note was left. I'll get it."

He returned to find the deputy looking at Pallas sternly. "I won't tell Essie you're here, but you will be havin' dinner with us tonight?"

She laughed. "Yes, and thanks for keeping my secret." After her brother-in-law left, she turned to Danny, a soft look in her eyes. "My sister is one lucky woman."

He tipped his head. Maybe he was wrong about her feelings for her brother-in-law. "Is that so?"

She nodded. "Want to hear the mushy story?"

There wasn't anything more he could do about the second note, and he wasn't ready for her to leave. "Sure."

She curled her shoulders and sighed. "Sassy used to teach beginning skiers at Heavenly Valley. The classes were mostly small children, and she loved being with them. One day a pair of skis was stolen while a student was in the lodge. The little boy was heartbroken, and his parents called the sheriff's department. Sassy saw Deputy Patrick Connor Murphy crunching across the snow and lost her balance on skis for the first time in years."

He was skeptical. "Sounds embarrassing."

She gave him a wry look. "It gets better. He came back at the end of her shift and asked her to dinner. She was afraid of her feelings and turned him down. The next day he registered for her class."

He barked out a laugh. "Wee officer Murphy in a class for beginners? What if he fell on one of the children?"

She grinned. "Sassy's thoughts exactly. But he was a bona fide novice, so she couldn't say no. She says he skied like a cartoon bear on barrel staves."

He laughed at the imagery. "True love."

Her blue gaze warned him. "That's part of it. He didn't get any better at skiing during the first lesson, but he was very gentle with the children. He managed to throw himself out of the way when he started to fall in their direction. After he came back the next day, ready to do it all over, Sassy relented and went out with him."

She shot him a look of triumph. "And it's turned out to be a wonderful marriage."

He thought of his own parents' great marriage. He

should be so lucky. "I have to say the visuals are amazing."

She sighed. "The best part is they have three beautiful little girls, stubborn redheads all. Every one of them is the apple of her daddy's eye. I haven't seen the baby yet. I'll do that later today."

"Your family lives here in Tahoe?"

She shook her head. "I wish they did. Mom and Dad live in Laughlin, and my other two sisters live in San Diego."

The disappointment was sharper than he would have thought. "And you live in San Francisco?"

"Yes." She smiled. "Here to win my future, so to speak. That's why finding your club and the tournament was so great. Now I have to start looking all over."

"How about dinner tomorrow night?"

Her face lit. "That would be great, but how about lunch instead? I have to find another place to play, and depending on my luck, I may not be available at dinner time."

She was certainly focused, he thought, conceding that he'd also put all he had into financing his club. He held out his hand. "Want to wait while I tell the players? One of them might know of another tournament."

"Sounds like a good idea."

He pulled out his cell and tapped in a number. "Is the private dining room available?" He listened, then ended the call and escorted her out of his office, stopping to lock it.

"I'll keep Bru company," she said as they parted in the hallway.

In the gaming area, Danny interrupted the nine

players and asked them to come with him. His request was met with curious looks, but everyone complied.

After they sat, he held up a copy of the agreement. "According to the contract you signed with the management of Over the Moon, the tournament can be canceled by either party due to death or an act of God. You've all heard about the car accident. The police now believe it was intentional, the result of a threat. As of now, I'm canceling the tournament and refunding your entry fees."

Questions sprang up all over the room.

"What do you mean threat?"

"Why didn't you say so before?"

"Can't we reschedule?"

"What if they catch the guy in the next day or so?"

"Are you sure the threat and the accident weren't a coincidence?"

He held up his hands. "I've received what I'm assuming is a second threat. It's in the hands of the sheriff's department. I'm taking no chances."

That silenced further protests.

"Can I say a few words?"

He nodded at Ty, an older player he'd known for years. "Sure."

The man rubbed the corner of his mouth. "I been dry for a couple years now, and it's been a long haul working my way back to the big pots. I don't want to see this chance ruined by no nutcase. I'd like to see a show of hands from those who want to stay in."

"I vote yes."

Danny shook his head as he turned toward a slightly over-the-top blonde. "Okay, Lou. That makes two. Sorry. Not enough."

Lou scrunched her nose at him and lifted a shoulder. "It'd be a shame for Over the Moon to get a bad rep before you're even established."

Leave it to Lou to get straight to the heart of things. He huffed a breath. "I know. But it would be a bigger shame if another player was hurt."

"I vote we stay in, too."

"Thanks, Del," Lou said, flashing a smile at a small man who had always reminded Danny of a bookworm with a bow tie.

He shook his head again. "That's still not enough. Sorry, but I won't take the risk."

When no one else spoke, he stood. "The tournament is officially cancelled. I have your numbers if it's determined we're safe to start up again. I'll have the cashier issue checks to each of you for your entry fees." He glanced around the table. "All that being said, does anyone know of another no-limits tournament starting up in the next couple of days?"

A player named Elliott Kerr leaned forward. "I'm staying at Suttons. There's one starting there tomorrow. They may have some openings."

Several of the players nodded, then they all stood and filed out of the room, most heading for the bar.

He followed them and held up his hands in resignation as he approached Pallas. "Sorry it didn't work out for you here." He grinned. "Especially since the *vibes* were so good."

Her chin dipped. "I'm sorry, too. I'll let you know if I can still make lunch."

He wanted to make a comforting gesture, something to let her know he understood having to overcome obstacles in the pursuit of a dream, but

29

refrained. "If it's any help, there's a no-limits tournament starting at Suttons tomorrow."

She smiled. "I heard about it from your dad. Guess I'll check it out."

He walked her back through the club and watched her leave.

Bru waved his fingers toward himself as Danny entered the bar and sat down. "Okay, is she seeing someone else? If not, are you going to ask her out? If the answer to the second question is no, I'm calling in a mental health counselor for you, then asking her out myself."

Danny took his time answering while Bru filled an order. He tended bar solo except for a couple of hours during the dinner rush. "She said yes when I asked her to lunch tomorrow, and I didn't see any ring."

Bru bared his teeth and hissed. "Damn, she is one beautiful lady. And smart, too. Just the way I like 'em."

A cough of disbelief escaped Danny. "You wish. When was the last time you dated a woman with an IQ higher than room temperature?"

His friend feigned indignation. "How about Michelle? She was into computers."

"She tested keyboards by typing, 'The quick brown fox jumped over the lazy dog.' "

Bru took no offense. "Is she at least going to be in the tournament so I can see her coming and going?"

Danny slid off the barstool. "There isn't going to be a tournament. Even if there were, being in it was only part of Ms. Mulroney's agenda. Come into the office when Mandy relieves you. I'd like to get your take on what the hell's going on."

****

Pallas thought about her busy morning as she drove back to Suttons. She'd gone from an argument with Charles to meeting Rick, then Danny Tarantino. Something had happened to force the owner of Over the Moon to cancel his tournament. And it had to do with the envelope that had appeared on his desk in their absence. She sighed. If she was smart, she'd forget about him and his mystery and concentrate on winning the partnership money.

That aside, she hadn't expected anyone to recognize her as one of Jack Mulroney's daughters, either. Maybe finding out who orchestrated her father's ban, and why, wouldn't be so hard after all.

She believed in pushing a lucky streak, so she decided to play more blackjack before going to Sassy's for dinner.

All that changed as she crossed the lobby and saw her own luggage sitting in the alcove by the front desk.

She stalked to the hotel reception desk where a smiling young man greeted her.

"Excuse me," she said, trying to hold her temper. "Those are my bags over there. I reserved a room for a week and checked in last evening. Why are my things down here?"

A flush of red crept past the man's collar. "Let me check for you. Name, please?"

"Pallas Mulroney. I'm in room 617."

He smiled hesitantly. "I handled that myself. A Mr. Wyatt said you had a family emergency and had to cancel the rest of your stay." The clerk slid an envelope across the counter. "He left this and said he'd be at lunch in the main dining room if you came back before one."

She took a deep breath. "You can toss that and reinstate me. Mr. Wyatt had no authority to cancel my reservation."

The young employee's color was bright red now. "I've already accepted another reservation for that room."

She smiled sweetly. "Then unacccept it."

He nodded, Adam's apple bobbing. "I'll need your credit card again."

She produced her card and handed it to him. "Please note that I'm the only one who can end my stay here, then have my bags returned to my room. Will my key card still work?"

"Yes, ma'am. I haven't reprogrammed it yet."

She retrieved her credit card and walked past the dining room entrance, not trusting that she could be civil to Charles.

Rick Tarantino was dealing again and had an opening at his table. She sat and grinned at him, pulling a short stack of chips out of her purse. "Back, again."

He winked. "Good luck."

Sure enough, she made a couple of hundred dollars before Rick's turn was up. The new dealer was a thin young woman with a disinterested look. Pallas scooped up her winnings and left.

She was headed for the elevators when Rick's voice stopped her.

"Did you get a slot at Over the Moon?"

She turned. "He had to cancel, darn it."

He looked genuinely surprised. "That was going to be Danny's big draw. Why did he cancel?"

She shrugged. "Sorry, I don't know. You need to ask him."

Rick nodded. "You still looking for a game?"

"Will be tomorrow. Right now I have things to do and family to visit."

"Is your family in the gaming business?"

She laughed. "Only peripherally."

The next thing she knew, Charles' hand gripped her elbow. "Pallas, we have something to discuss."

She pulled away, cutting him a no-nonsense look. "No, Charles, we don't."

The dealer stood firm, disallowing Charles' attempt to wedge himself between them.

Charles sighed and stepped around Pallas to stand shoulder to shoulder with Rick, facing her. "I've rented a small plane to fly us home and taken the liberty of having your room canceled and your things packed. We can talk about this whole mistaken business in the taxi on the way to the airport."

She didn't acknowledge him and spoke directly to the dealer. "Rick, this is Charles Wyatt. He's a co-worker, and we traveled here together. It looks as if he's leaving. I'm not."

That wonderful eyebrow expression the Tarantino men shared appeared on Rick's face. "Glad to hear you're staying. Pallas, was it?"

She grinned. "Right. We haven't been formally introduced, have we? I'm Pallas Mulroney."

That earned her a second look of surprise, and although Rick didn't ask the question, she knew he recognized the name Mulroney. He shook her hand. "Nice to meet you, Pallas. Be seeing you?"

"You can bet on it."

When Rick left, she faced Charles. If they hadn't been in public, she would have let fly her temper. As it was, she spoke through clenched teeth. "I repeat, I'm staying. You can do what you want, except interfere in my life again. Understood?"

At least he had the good grace to look abashed. Too bad that rarely translated into him backing off. He lifted his chin. "This hotel's hosting a conference, and they're overbooked. We have no choice but to leave."

Her fingers itched to reach out and pinch him, hard. "I do, Charles. This is my vacation, my time, and my money, all to do with as I please. If you can't deal with that, then I'll say it again. Go home."

Chapter Four

Pallas loved the sights and sounds of a close-knit neighborhood on a late spring day. The small community of South Zephyr Cove sported bright-colored flowers and kids at play. Two of her nieces jumped hopscotch squares with friends on the driveway in front of her sister's house. She stopped and waved at the girls. When they recognized her, they came running. She held her finger to her lips, then got out and hugged them.

"Is your mom inside?"

"Yes," they chorused. "Are you surprising her?"

She nodded and walked quietly up the steps, the girls close behind her. She knocked, and when Sassy opened the door, Pallas asked, "Can I interest you in a henna rinse?"

A squeal of delight greeted her, then the door opened wide, and Sassy grabbed her in a hug. "This is so great. I was hoping you'd make it for Chloe's baptism. It's been months since I've seen any of you."

Pallas held her sister at arm's length. "Here for the baptism and some other stuff. I swear you don't look a day older than me, darn it. You and mom got the good genes."

Sassy looked down at herself and blushed. "Liar. But I love hearing it. What else are you doing here, and how long can you stay?"

Pallas shrugged. "I'm at Suttons. Going to blow through my inheritance or make it big."

Sassy's eyes went wide. "Tell all." Her glance moved to her daughters. "Stay outside and play, girls. You can talk to your aunt during dinner." She poked a finger at Pallas. "You *are* staying for dinner."

Pallas turned to her nieces. "If you let your mom and me visit for a while, I'll drag out the presents before dinner."

Two freckled faces perked up as the girls clapped. "Okay!"

Pallas sat cross-legged on her sister's couch. She had changed to comfortable jeans and a T-shirt. "Here's the big one. I'm going to enter a poker tournament to win the half million dollars I need for a partnership offer of a lifetime."

Sassy stared, then let out a puff of air. "My inheritance is sitting in a savings account earning a couple percent interest. Tell me you're at least terrified."

She thought about it and held out her palms. "See? Clammy. I really want this. I've had the inheritance for less than a year and the offer for the partnership less than six weeks. I refuse to even think about losing it all."

Her sister peered at her closely. "All right. Move past those finance types that suck all the life out of you. On to the fun stuff. When was the last time you dated? My God, woman, you're twenty-six."

Is this how Sassy sees me? As some dried fig of a spinster?

She squinted at her older sister. "Slow down. Don't retire me to a houseful of cats yet." She stuck her nose in the air. "For your information, I met a hunky man this morning, and I'm having lunch with him tomorrow."

Sassy grinned. "Atta girl. What's he like?"

She lifted a shoulder, remembering how her knee-to-knee poker game made her stomach gallop. "His name is Danny Tarantino. He owns a dinner and gaming club called Over the Moon. I met him when I went to enter the poker tournament he was hosting."

Her sister's mouth dropped open. "Danny Tarantino? Are you freaking kidding me? He is so hot. Half the eligible women in Tahoe would love to park their shoes under his bed."

Pallas bobbed her head in agreement. "It's not just the sexy part, although that's undeniable. I felt really comfortable, too, you know? I blabbed on and on about my dream plans and the partnership. That isn't like me. I kept wanting not to like him so much."

Sassy put her hand to her mouth.

Warmth flooded her cheeks. "Maybe I *should* date more. But I absolutely can't afford to get sidetracked." She sighed. "Too bad. He's definitely worth sneaking out for."

With four daughters in the house, Jack Mulroney had set up strict curfew hours according to age. As the youngest, Pallas had pretty much ignored the rules, sneaking out and, more often than not, getting caught.

Sassy tapped her sister softly on the knee. "Are you nuts? That feeling you described could be—"

Pallas interrupted her. "Too long going without." Her belly jittered. "A week with a sexy man should set me to rights." *Who am I trying to convince?* Danny broke through her calm like no other man had. Ever.

She looked into Sassy's sparkling eyes. No, she definitely wouldn't tell her sister *that*. Sassy would go out and rent a chapel.

Sassy leaned forward. "Okay, say that's true; it's only lust. Why else are you here?"

"What do you mean else?"

"I mean, I can see there's something besides the gambling and the hot date."

Pallas knew where this was going. The Mulroney sisters shared a strong tie and couldn't hide much from each other. Her gaze wandered. "I sort of thought as long as I was here…"

Sassy put her hands on her hips. "As long as you were here, you'd pry into that twenty-year-old business about Dad's ban."

"You know Dad wouldn't have cheated," Pallas challenged. "I can't get over the fact that some people believe he did."

"So what's going to happen if you do find something out? Are you going to take a half-page ad in the newspaper proclaiming his innocence? What good would that do?"

Pallas gave her sister a dead level look. "Other than finally shutting off this giant nagging question pinging around in my brain? I don't know, but I have to try."

****

Anger beat out frustration as Danny dialed, then listened to the ringing. He gripped the cell phone so hard he could feel the plastic edges making furrows in his palm.

"Jimmy G."

"Jimmy. Danny Tarantino."

"Danny! How's my newest competition?"

"Got a problem."

"Yeah? I hope it's Bru or that four-star chef of yours. You can send either or both my way."

He smiled in spite of the situation. "Not likely. This concerns your start-up a couple of years ago. Did you receive any threats?"

Jimmy didn't hesitate. "Nothing, why?"

"Because I have."

"Sorry to hear it. Anything I can help with?"

Danny relaxed his hand. Jimmy might be a competitor, but he was real and honest. "Not right now, but thanks for the offer."

"Sure."

A few calls to other owners and Danny sat back. There weren't that many small clubs at Tahoe, and his was being singled out. Great. He pounded his desk lightly with the side of his fist and had made up his mind to bounce a plan off Bru when the phone rang. "Danny Tarantino."

"What's with the cancellation of your tournament?"

He smiled at his dad's voice in spite of his own black mood. "How the hell did you find out about something I did only about an hour ago?"

"I ran into Ms. Mulroney at Suttons. She knew the what but thought I should get the why from you."

It occurred to Danny he'd have to caution the other players about spreading the story of the notes. Pallas could only surmise, but they knew firsthand. "Some antigambling freak is making trouble. Unfortunately, I didn't take the first warning seriously. Thought it was from a crackpot. Then I found out the car crash involving a player last night wasn't an accident. I also received a second note."

"Another threat?"

"I don't know, but I assume so. The police have it."

Rick was silent for a moment. "Could it be one of your neighbors?"

He had already considered that. Large, luxury homes flanked Over the Moon, and the owners had sued when he started construction. Lawsuits that had seriously drained his resources. "I don't know. They've been mostly quiet since they lost in court, but I can't rule anyone out."

"I'll call in a few favors. See what I can find out."

"Thanks. How's Mom?"

His dad's voice was warm. "Gorgeous, as usual. And speaking of that, what did you think of Pallas?"

"You're on a first name basis?" Danny teased.

Rick laughed. "I'm fifty-four, not comatose."

He felt a frisson of nerves between his shoulder blades and smiled. "Yeah, she's pretty amazing. We're having lunch tomorrow."

His dad paused. "Listen, you know about her father's ban from gambling here?"

"Yes. I understand it was for a year, but Lucky Jack made it permanent. It's been about twenty years, hasn't it?"

"About that. There's quite a story behind it. Remind me to tell you the next time you're at the house."

"Okay. I'll be out Wednesday. Might even get in some practice."

"Bud's been on the range almost every day." Rick paused. "I'm sure it helps him think about something besides Elaine's illness."

Danny's thoughts shifted from his own troubles to those of his friend, Bud. "Maybe if they get her stabilized, he'll be able to get a handle on the bills."

"He's been a good neighbor. Stop by and see him when you come on Wednesday if you have the time. Can you stay for lunch?"

"I'll make a point of it," Danny agreed. "Later."

As he hung up, someone knocked at his door. "Come in." To his surprise, Lou, Del, Ty, and Elliott walked in.

Lou twisted a strand of her blonde hair. "We had a second meeting and decided we like the dynamics of the original group. The four of us are going to another club to practice and give it to the end of the week. If this threat thing gets settled, great, we'll be back. If not, then we gave it our best shot."

Danny's stomach sank. "I appreciate your support, but whoever's doing this is not messing around. I don't want to see another player hurt. A poker tournament isn't worth it."

Del nodded. "As of now, we're disassociating ourselves from Over the Moon. That's why we're going to find another place to play. Sorry, Danny, but you don't have a choice. We just wanted you to know."

Danny took a big breath. He'd known Lou, Del, and Ty for years and didn't doubt their sincerity. He didn't know a thing about the other player. His gaze settled on Elliott Kerr. "What changed your mind?"

The tall man stood in front of a torchiere lamp, an unflattering light shining through his thin hair. He seemed surprised by the question. "I lost almost everything in the stock market on short calls." He shifted his gaze to somewhere over Danny's shoulder.

"I think I can win it back."

It was a pretty bad lie. A guy who'd "lost almost everything" but was still able to come up with the fifty-thousand-dollar buy-in for a poker tournament? Not likely. He surveyed the faces. "Again, I really appreciate the gesture, but that car accident could have been fatal."

Lou grinned. "We thought about that and decided any one of us could get hit by a bus, too. Anyway, you have any suggestions where we could play? And that pretty redhead can join us if she wants."

Danny's skin went damp at the thought of Pallas sitting in with this merry band. "Why would you think she'd be interested?"

Lou twirled her hair faster. "Oh. We heard you telling her you were sorry it was a no-go at the bar and thought, but I can see…" She trailed off. "Never mind."

"Thanks," he said. "And in the interest of helping out, I think I can recommend a place for you to play. Let me make a call, then I'll meet you in the bar."

The four turned to leave when Lou said over her shoulder, "I'd be happy to watch out for your lady friend."

He smiled. "She isn't my lady friend yet. But I'm working on it."

After they left, Danny tapped the number for Jimmy G's into his cell phone.

"Jimmy G."

"Danny, again. Can I take you up on your offer of help?"

"Shoot."

"Four of the die-hard original tournament players want to continue practicing. They want to hold out a few more days to see if the guy targeting me is caught. Are you interested in hosting them?"

A gravelly laugh ensued. "As long as they're paying customers, they're welcome. Unless he's stupid, no amateur's gonna mess with me."

Danny's thoughts ran in the same vein. Jimmy wasn't bragging; he wasn't someone a person interfered with lightly. As long as the players were determined to continue, it was the safest place for them. He also agreed his tormentor was an amateur. A pro wouldn't have left warning notes. Unfortunately, he was a dangerous amateur.

"Thanks, I owe you."

Jimmy laughed again. "We gotta stick together. Besides, my customers are rowdy, down-to-earth types. Most of yours have shiny shoes. I can afford to help."

He couldn't argue with that. "Still, I owe you."

He ended the call and left his office, walking over to the bar. Bru was flirting with Lou, oblivious to Del's hovering. Del was a bookkeeper and a good poker player, but the reason he bought into the tournament was painfully obvious—the pretty blonde.

The other players occupied a nearby table. Ty got up and met him, his trembling hand clasping a glass of ice water.

"Any news?" the older man asked.

Danny nodded. "If you're interested, Jimmy G has space for you to practice."

A smile creased the weather-beaten face. "Couldn't have picked better myself."

****

Danny set aside the weekly receipts when a single knock on his door announced Bru. He glanced at his watch. "Come on in. Mandy's early."

Bru nodded. "She really likes the action at the bar."

Danny shook his head. "What brings her in is you, pal."

Bru frowned. "Mandy's too level-headed to care about a no-strings guy like me." He sat and propped his long legs under Danny's desk.

"Whatever, but you heard it here first. The reason I wanted to talk to you is to bring you up to date on the notes."

The bartender frowned. "Notes, plural?"

"Yeah, I got another one at lunch time. Someone tossed it on my desk while Pallas and I were at the pit boss cage."

"So that's why the deputy showed and you cancelled the tournament. Do you know what it said?"

"Not yet. And I want as few people as possible to find out about them."

Bru nodded his spiky blond head. "That makes sense. What story are you giving people who ask what happened?"

"I was straight with the players because they had binding contracts," Danny said. "Everyone else will be told it was an oversight in the gaming commission paperwork and we'll eventually reschedule."

Bru pulled on his earlobe. "What'd you tell Pallas?"

He might have explained his situation to her, but dammit, she was still a relative stranger, no matter the amazing physical pull. "She saw the note when we went back into my office. She was also here when her brother-in-law, the deputy, came to pick it up as evidence. Not being a stupid woman, she probably figured a connection."

"Right." Bru shook his head. "Think the threats could've come from one of your neighbors?"

Danny tapped the stack of receipts, his satisfaction at the way they were totaling gone. "Dad and I went over that possibility when he called to ask about the cancellation this afternoon. Didn't seem likely."

Bru straightened in his chair. "How'd your dad find out so fast? Is word spreading at the big casinos?"

"No. Pallas told him."

The bartender's voice went up a register. "Your dad knows Pallas?"

Uneasiness slid into Danny's words. "She played at his table this morning. He sent her over here to ask about the vacant tournament slot. Why?"

"It's just weird that she knows he's Rick Tarantino, and that doesn't bother her."

He leaned forward. "You lost me. Why would my dad mean anything to Pallas?"

Bru's expression showed an internal battle. He spoke softly. "Because your dad was partly responsible for getting Jack Mulroney banned."

Chapter Five

Disbelief swept through Danny, and his heart pounded. Rick Tarantino was the fairest, most honest man he knew. If he'd caught Jack Mulroney cheating, it must have been true. Maybe that's what he wanted to talk about on Wednesday. Danny refocused on his friend. "News to me. I didn't realize it was general knowledge."

Bru nodded. "Sorry, man. I really thought you knew. I'm not sure it's a big item around town. I found out years ago when I worked a party that got snowed in. We sat around talking about local legends."

He forced his shoulders to relax. "Nothing to be sorry about. I was maybe nine at the time. Don't think my dad would come home and share something like that."

"You think Pallas doesn't know either?"

"If she does, she hasn't shown any animosity. Her father chose to make the ban permanent. Could be it's not an issue for her." He huffed. "At least I hope that's the case."

Bru tipped his head. "Change of subject. How come some of the tournament players were still hanging out after you pulled the plug?"

He looked over Bru's shoulder to make sure the door was closed. "I was overruled. A few of them discussed the situation and decided to continue practicing to see if something breaks on the notes. If the guy's caught, they'll return and finish what they started. They're going to practice at Jimmy G's."

The bartender grinned. "Good for them. Hey, does that mean Pallas is going to be in?"

"No, and no."

"What's the second no for?"

"Your next question, if it has anything do with hitting on her."

A mischievous spark lit Bru's eyes. "I'm wounded. Are you telling me she's off limits?"

Danny regarded his friend. He'd never asked Bru to back off paying attention to any woman. Was Pallas worth that? That was a big, fat affirmative. "Yes."

He got up and walked to open the door. "Keep your eye out for trouble, okay?"

The tall blond unfolded his frame and grinned. "That was a pretty definite yes. On the other matter, I'll get word out on the bartender grapevine. See if your note writer likes to brag."

"Thanks."

****

Pallas drove back to Suttons, barely aware of her beautiful surroundings. She'd only half listened to the banter at dinner and apologized for being poor company. Sassy and Pat discussed Danny at length, the general consensus being he was okay. Good enough for her to date. She'd held her peace and rolled her eyes at being treated like she was sixteen. As soon as her nieces left the table, she let her sister and brother-in-law have it, denying she needed their vetting of a man she...liked. They both grinned and told her she protested a little too much. None of which prevented her sister from following her out to the car, demanding all the details after the upcoming lunch date.

By the time she got back to her room, she had decided to return to Over the Moon for some recreational gambling. She talked herself into thinking she might dig up some information on her dad's ban. Truth be told, though, all that chatting about Danny had given her an itch to see him. An itch she had no reason not to scratch.

Pallas pulled out the way-too-expensive dresses she'd originally bought to wear to client functions. Her reason for bringing them to Tahoe had been vague. Charles had mentioned going out for dinner "if she was available," so she'd packed them. The winner for tonight was a teal-colored lamé with a funnel collar, draped bodice, and flared short skirt. It had a scandalously bare back and showed off her legs to good advantage. An all-purpose, ivory silk shawl topped it off.

She'd just toweled off from a shower when her room phone rang. "Hello."

"Pallas, this is Charles."

Disappointment flared, and her stomach tightened. The blame for his view of their relationship rested with her she supposed. He'd taken her under his wing at Stanford and paved the way for her interview at their current company, in addition to the partnership offer. Charles had been a convenient escort to client functions, and she never minded or thought about it.

Now he stubbornly saw them as a couple.

"Are you still in Tahoe?" she asked.

"Yes. However, I had to pay for a small suite in order to stay here. That's all they had."

Big deal, you can afford it, sprang to her lips, but she didn't say it out loud. And she certainly wasn't going to apologize for his extra expense. "I see."

He cleared his throat. "I owe you an apology. I'm willing to let your plan run its course, no matter the consequences."

In other words, he hadn't figured out a way to bully her into going back to San Francisco. She sighed. "My plan and its consequences are none of your business, Charles. I'm sorry I ever shared my intention with you."

"I get that. And I made a mistake in checking you out of the hotel."

She saw him run his finger up the bridge of his nose in her mind's eye, a precursor to whining.

"I did it because I care about our relationship."

"So you said. I'm busy, Charles. If you cared about our friendship, you'd leave like I asked."

"One drink. Downstairs, please?"

She looked at the dress hanging on the back of her closet door. Dammit, she was on vacation. "No, thank you. I've made other plans."

A cool, hurt tone entered his voice. "Would it be too inconvenient to meet for breakfast?"

She considered her answer. The partnership wasn't a done deal yet, and Charles couldn't have picked a worse time to push a relationship she didn't want. But, and this was a big one, she couldn't afford to force an abrupt end to their friendship. She clamped her jaw. "Fine. Pick me up at eight."

She hung up and stiffened her spine. The time was coming when she would logically and reasonably make Charles understand he was wasting his time. Not just in

Tahoe, but with her, period.

Having decided that, she dressed, slipped on pale-gold, high-heeled sandals, and grabbed a matching purse.

****

Danny was gratified to see that any word about his problems hadn't affected the dinner crowd. He moved from table to table, greeting diners and accepting compliments on the menu.

When he entered the gaming room intent on congratulating the winners and consoling the losers, he stopped. Even with her back to him, he knew Pallas Mulroney the instant he saw her. She sat at a blackjack table with that red hair tumbling around her slender shoulders. He crossed the room and leaned down, enjoying the exotic fragrance that had enveloped him that morning. "How's Sassy?"

She tapped the three and seven in front of her. The dealer dealt her a Jack and pushed the chips over. Turning toward him, the redhead smiled, eyes shining. "Hello. Sassy's great."

"How come we're getting the pleasure of your company again so soon?"

She scooped up a sizeable pile of chips. "I decided to see how lucky the house is, but I've reached my limit for the day. All work and no play makes Jane a dull girl. Can I buy you a drink?"

His plan to call some buddies in the security business vanished. In its place was a determination to make this alive feeling last as long as he could. "If I can take off my jacket and cover you."

She pulled up the shawl that had slipped. "Is that a compliment?"

"Yes."

"You like the dress?"

"I like the wearer of the dress."

She smiled and fanned herself with her small purse, making the chips inside click together. He extended his arm, and she stepped off the stool to walk with him. He'd been right. She had amazing legs. And in heels, her mouth was that much closer.

"Care to have that drink on my private deck?"

"You live here, too?"

"Got the best view on the lake."

"That would be nice, thank you."

He almost laughed out loud at the look on Bru's face when they entered the dining room. His friend's eyebrows climbed toward his hairline, and his mouth dropped open slightly. Danny had learned long ago Bru failed miserably at hiding his feelings and talked him into staying away from gambling. Mandy's reaction, on the other hand, was not to them, but to Bru. The pretty brunette sighed and turned back to her customer.

Pallas tipped her head. "I'd say that other bartender has a crush on Bru."

He nodded. "You *are* good. Got it in one glance. It's obvious to almost everyone but him. Either that or he's in deep denial."

Bru started pouring a ginger ale for him before they reached the bar, then he winked at Pallas. "What'll it be? It's on me."

She looked over his shoulder at all the colorful bottles on display. "Oh. I was going to buy, but surprise me. Make it light."

He flipped a bottle in the air, caught it, and slid a short stream of a golden liquid into a glass. "I invented a signature drink for the club. Want to try it?"

"What's in it?"

"Not telling my trade secret, but it's garnished with a fresh strawberry. Is that okay?"

"Strawberry's fine, thanks." She accepted the glass Bru offered and took a sip. "Mmmm. A slight kick but very smooth. I predict a big demand."

"That decides it." Bru grinned. "We had the name down to two choices, Moonbeam or Moon Goddess. Since you approve and you're named after a goddess, Moon Goddess it is."

Danny motioned toward Pallas with his eyes and a slight tip of his head. Bru just couldn't help himself when it came to beautiful women. "Glad you made the decision final," he said, emphasizing each word. "Almost as important as the conversation we had in my office this afternoon."

Bru blinked. "Oh, *that* conversation." He slid a comical glance down the bar. "Looks like Mandy could use my help. You two enjoy."

Danny nodded and slipped his hand under Pallas's wrap to guide her toward his quarters. The dress was cut to her waist in the back. A definite rush hit as the play of her muscles under silky skin moved against his palm. Suddenly, his collar and cuffs were warmer and more restrictive than they had been a few minutes ago.

The lakeside part of his club was U-shaped. The dining room and his quarters faced the water, but the dining room didn't jut out as far, giving him a beautiful view and privacy. His side also had a small dock. They paused while he unlocked the door behind the bar, then went down a short hallway to open another door. He flipped a switch to bathe his living room in ambient light.

Every time he came in here, his pulse slowed. He'd taken a lot of pains to make it comfortable and relaxing.

"This is very inviting," she said, looking around. "I like the warm colors accented with black." She ran her hand around the rim of a black clay vase. "Beautiful."

Her approval meant a lot to him. "Thank you."

"Did you pull all this together?"

"Yes."

"Impressive. I like it a lot."

He smiled. "My mother claims I get it from her. Would you like to see the deck?"

She nodded, and he led her toward a pair of glass doors.

"It'll be chilly. You need something besides that wrap?"

She shook her head. "I'll be fine."

Sturdy railing surrounded the large deck, opening on one side to steps leading to the dock. Outside lights blinked on automatically as they walked through.

Pallas leaned against the railing and took another sip of her drink. "Moon Goddess." She sighed. "I envy Bru's free spirit. His sense of adventure. Yours, too."

A strand of hair blew across her cheek. He itched to slide it back around her ear with his finger. He laughed. "You don't think playing poker is adventurous?"

She looked at him seriously. "Not if you pay attention."

"I imagine you do."

She nodded and held out her hand, palm up. "Is all this yours?"

A very direct question. He tipped his head. "I have

some friends and family who've invested, but yeah, it's mine. At least on paper."

"You worked very hard for it, didn't you?"

"I did."

He stepped closer, hoping she wouldn't back away. She didn't, her gaze seeming to read his intention. He tipped his head and kissed her lightly. Her mouth was soft and warm and welcoming. He took the drink from her hand, placing both their glasses on the rail behind them.

She ran her hands up the front of his jacket and leaned toward him.

His chest grew tight as he splayed one hand on the small of her back and the other at her neck, nestling her firmly against him. The liqueur base for the Moon Goddess was the first thing he tasted, then she parted her lips, and he tasted her. She hummed a sigh and ran her fingers into his hair.

When they finally parted, she looked at him, desire banked in her eyes. "I can safely say that was one of the nicest kisses I've ever received."

Since she'd given as good as she got, he could safely say it had knocked him on his butt. "Right up there."

"Yep, right up there," Pallas replied.

Chapter Six

She wanted to hit her forehead with the heel of her hand. Her attitude going in was to have a hot "there, that'll do you for a while" thing. But one damn kiss and she knew she was on dangerous ground. This was going-to-the-movies, top-of-the-line turn-on stuff, and she didn't know if she could handle the consequences of what he—make that they—were about to start. *Run, do not walk, to the nearest exit.*

She casually picked up her glass. He looked like a model for a tuxedo ad, and all she could think of was how he would look out of it. "Great way to get warm," she said lamely.

Dark blue eyes contemplated her. "I agree."

The inky sky suddenly lit up, the white full moon reflecting on the water. The effect was stunning. Pallas took Danny's hand and walked out onto the dock. "That's amazing. It just came from behind the clouds, and this whole end of the lake is shining."

"That's why this is called Over the Moon. Want to hear the mushy story?"

She laughed, glad for the change of subject. "Depends. Is it as good as Sassy and Pat's?"

"Yep."

"Okay, let's hear it."

"My dad dealt part time in a smaller casino when he was starting out. He broke one of their rules when he asked a young woman at his table for a date. She was Mary O'Brien, a beautiful girl celebrating her twenty-first birthday with friends. My grandparents owned a sizeable cattle ranch and didn't like her seeing a dealer. Dad persisted, though, taking her out when he could afford it. He was cash poor, so one night he borrowed a friend's boat and paddled her out onto the lake. It was a rare calm surface, like tonight. The reflection shone so clear it looked like the shore was over the moon. Mother described the scene to Grandmother, and my grandparents bought this piece of land as a wedding gift when my parents married."

She smiled. "Another great story."

He nodded. "They're very happy, and it's worked out well. Dad helped my grandfather at the ranch and kept his hand in at dealing for years. My grandparents recently retired, and my older brother Dugan took over running the place. He loves it and will inherit it someday. Dad gets to deal all he wants now, and I got the land Over the Moon is on."

He stepped close. "This is kind of habit forming," he said, a scant inch from her mouth.

She silently agreed. Her itch for Danny Tarantino seeped out of the neat box she had relegated it to and was scaring the wits out of her. She knew his very private bedroom sat only a couple dozen feet away, and any encouragement on her part would land them there. His handsome, successful persona also made her wonder if his bedroom door was revolving.

Poof. All the bravado she'd exhibited at Sassy's this afternoon was gone. She was so not prepared for this. But after wearing the dress of pure seduction, agreeing to come to his quarters, and enjoying his kisses, she would look like a tease if she broke away now.

He kissed her temple while running the flat of his hand over her back. His warm fingers traced circles in one area then another. How could his fingers be warm when she had goose bumps? And was it the cold causing them or something else?

"Danny?"

"Hmmm?"

"Can we stand inside? It's a little cold out here."

He held her from him. "Stand, sit, there are all kinds of options."

She had been afraid of that. She laid her hand on the side of his face. "One of those options has to be stopping before I act on impulse."

He looked at her curiously. "And if we both have the same impulse?"

She took a breath and let it out slowly. "That's just it, we do, but this is not why I'm here." She waved her hand, encompassing his club. "You have your dream. I'm still half a million dollars away from mine, and I can't afford to lose sight of that." She searched his eyes. "Understand?"

****

He understood completely, but that didn't make this any easier. In a period of time so short it unnerved him, she'd managed to keep him off balance and wanting more without promising anything. "I do. I've also gone without to get what I want. I'm willing to wait until you're ready."

Surprise lit her features. "I'm glad you get it, because I'm not a hundred percent sure I do." She laced her fingers with his, leading them back up the steps.

Once inside, she seemed to relax.

"Want to stay a while?" he asked. "The view's pretty spectacular."

"I'd like that." She wandered around his living room while she sipped her drink. "These block prints are beautiful. I've been to Japan and spent time in an antique prints gallery. The plain, black frames really enhance them."

"Thanks," he said, hoping she'd come sit by him. "Are you warming up?"

She nodded. "Between being inside and the Moon Goddess, I'm downright hot." She immediately waved away her words, looking flustered. "What I mean is yes, I'm warm." Her nervous gaze stayed slightly right of his shoulder.

"I won't bite."

She looked directly at him. "Promise?"

"Promise." Although given the go-ahead, he would walk right through that promise.

Clouds moved across the moon again, and the room was thrown into low artificial light. "Thank you," she said and came to sit and watch the lake with him. "This is nice."

It would be nicer if she was in his arms. He would bargain with the devil at this point to have her skin against his and the consequences be damned, but that was more than she was willing to give, and he'd foolishly said he would wait. So he sat and enjoyed the moment as they finished their drinks, watching the moon slide in and out from behind the clouds.

Bru gave them a look of speculation as they walked back into the bar.

She set down her empty glass. "Lovely finish."

The blond beamed. "Want another?"

"No, thanks. I have to be getting back. I've got to look for a new game tomorrow."

"Our game too risky for you?"

Pallas turned toward the voice. "I beg your pardon?"

Elliott Kerr's expression was mild and slightly unfocused. "Some of us are over at Jimmy G's waiting for the cops to catch the bad guy. Room for one more."

Danny shook his head at Kerr over her shoulder, but the man was concentrating on Pallas.

Ty leaned around Kerr and smiled. "True. There's always room for another die-hard, Miss...?"

"Pallas Mulroney."

Danny saw the older man pale significantly. "Are you all right, Ty?"

Ty nodded and addressed Pallas. "You related to Lucky Jack?"

Her expression softened. "Yes. Do you know my father?"

Ty sipped some water, the tremble in his hand back. "Everybody's heard of Jack." Then he turned to face the bar.

Kerr looked at Pallas. "Going to join us or what?"

She nodded. "Interesting question. Did you inform Mr. Tarantino of your plans?"

Now Kerr focused on Danny. "Sure. He found us the place to play."

Danny rolled his eyes as Pallas pulled her wrap tight and faced him, disillusionment in the set of her mouth.

"Were you planning to tell me?"

It would be ludicrous to say he didn't want her

exposed to danger, but it was okay for the others. "No."

Pallas tipped her head to Elliott Kerr. "Thanks for the invitation. However, at this point I'm not sure I even want to be in Mr. Tarantino's establishment." She leveled stormy blue eyes at Danny. "I was being humored. Good enough for that," she nodded toward his quarters. "But not good enough for your tournament."

Adrenaline drugged his system, but he couldn't act on it. He wasn't really about to lose this amazing woman over a stupid poker tournament. *I can make her understand, I can make her understand*, he chanted inside his head. He reached for her elbow, intending to guide her back to his living room. All he needed was five minutes.

He stepped away from the bar.

She didn't.

"Can we discuss this in private?" he asked, moving back to her side.

She didn't look at him. Either she had a slow fuse, not likely from what he'd seen so far, or she didn't care whether they worked it out. An option he didn't want to consider.

She finally met his gaze. "Do you agree to be open-minded and truthful?"

That was a tough one. He already knew rationality did not extend to his actions where she was concerned. Where were his damned negotiating skills? When he was a security specialist, he'd talked people out of jumping off roofs, others into handing over guns. They were easy compared to this. He decided to consent in hopes of getting her to see this his way. "Agreed."

She allowed him to lead her back to his quarters.

Once inside, she fiddled with the fringe on her wrap but didn't sit. "I don't think this is going to work."

Danny reached for her hand, sliding the ivory silk through her fingers. "Those players came to me this afternoon after you left. They wanted to keep the tournament alive. I told them it was a bad idea and dangerous as well. I've known some of them for a long time. They think I'm getting a raw deal and don't like it. We agreed there was to be no connection between their games at Jimmy G's and Over the Moon."

She frowned. "But you did arrange for them to play there?"

"Yes. Look, you only know part of the story. That note tossed on my desk this morning was the second of two threats. I ignored the first one, and a player's brake line was cut. He ended up in the hospital with a compound leg fracture, but it could have been worse. Whoever's got it out for me is serious. The other players know all about it, and I figured if I couldn't talk them out of it, I might as well find the safest place I could."

She nodded.

Good. Things were going his way.

"And you decided on your own I wasn't to be informed," she said.

Here was the sticky part. He played with the ends of her fingers, his stomach flopping around. "One, it may take more than a few days to catch this guy, and you're only here for a week. Two, if I knowingly put you at risk and anything happened, I would take it personally."

Her expression calmed. "I don't know how to respond to that."

The ground grew firmer under his feet. "By telling me you won't get involved with them."

She stepped back. "You don't know me well enough, so I'll tell you. I can take care of myself."

"Uh, that's not entirely the reason." He watched her carefully for tells indicating she was going to blow him off. "I'd just be more comfortable if you weren't associated in any way with this whole mess."

She gave off heat that matched his own. The sexual tension from both of them complicated his argument.

"I'm not here to make you comfortable," she blurted.

He responded with a look anyone breathing could interpret, then slowly grinned. "I'm painfully aware of that."

She blushed at his inference. "Sorry." Then she fisted her hands on her hips. "I can see you're going to be as stubborn about this as me. Unfortunately, it's your game. So what's the answer?"

"Not one you're going to like. I make a few calls and find you another tournament."

The redhead squinted at him. "You're right. I don't like it. But it seems I have no choice. I still need the potential to win half a million, a fifty-thousand-dollar or less buy-in, and the vibes have to be there."

He rolled his eyes. "Right. Vibes."

She tipped her head. "You are so rude. Besides, if I'm in another tournament, we can't spend much time together while I'm in Tahoe."

He put his hands lightly on her waist. "We'll make do. I've also been thinking about visiting San Francisco."

"Liar."

"Not so. I've been thinking about it since this morning."

Her smile turned serious. "You have an answer for everything and apparently no qualms about withholding information. That bothers me, but I accept your offer."

Relieved that she didn't just blow him off, he huffed a breath. "I…"

A noise building outside was followed by Bru knocking on Danny's door and shouting, "You better get out here!"

Chapter Seven

Danny pulled away. *What now?* "Be right back."

Pallas straightened her dress. "I'm coming, too."

He shrugged and slipped her hand in his. They opened the door to the dining area to see half the diners had abandoned their meals, and the other half were getting to their feet. Raised voices led them outside. In the parking lot, pandemonium reigned.

He pushed his way forward as customers rushed toward their cars, multiple alarms sounding on the east side of the lot. Several men had surrounded the parking attendant, yelling and gesturing. He dropped Pallas's hand and hurried over. "What's going on?"

A florid-faced man turned. "What the hell kind of place is this? The finish on my car is ruined."

Another voice joined in. "Mine, too."

"You'll hear from my lawyer."

Danny took the parking attendant by the shoulder, steering him toward the club. "Call the sheriff." Then he nodded at the first man. "Show me."

The man led him to a vintage, dark-green Jaguar XKE in mint condition except for the front quarter panel. At first Danny thought the wavy paint was a trick of the light, then he realized the surface had been splashed with some kind of acid. He let loose an expletive and stepped back to the center of the lot. Most of the alarms had been turned off, but he half shouted for emphasis. "Please don't touch your cars. The sheriff's department has been called."

Bru appeared beside him and whispered, "Pallas said she'd catch you tomorrow. She suggested free drinks and dinner might help smooth feathers. Smart girl." He edged away. "Gotta check my ride."

Danny approached couples and small groups of people. "I'm sorry for the trouble. We're hoping there are only a few isolated occurrences. Please return to the dining room. Dinner and drinks are on the house tonight for those with damaged cars. Let's make room so the deputies can do their work."

His next headache approached in slow strides, face flushed in anger. Jonathan Chase was his neighbor and never gave an inch, especially to him. "This racket is against noise ordinances, Tarantino. I knew this would happen when your kind was permitted to operate in a decent neighborhood."

The crowd in the lot had thinned, and the first sheriff's department silver cruiser eased into the driveway. He stepped away from Chase, afraid he would get up close and personal if provoked further. He spoke in passing. "You have my apologies."

"That's not good enough." Chase grabbed his arm, his bony fingers digging in. "I've recorded this whole fiasco, and I'm taking you back to court."

It was the proverbial straw for Danny. He wrenched his arm away and turned to face the older man. He couldn't understand the look of fury. Chase's reaction was totally out of proportion to the noise that had lasted three or four minutes. "I can't stop to discuss this now. If you want to waste your money over the results of a prank, go ahead."

A deputy Danny knew walked up, pad and pencil in hand. "What's the problem?"

Chase looked down his nose at the officer. "He's *negligent.* That's the problem." He turned, stiff-backed, and moved slowly away.

Danny pinched the bridge of his nose. "Hey, Carl. I've got an ugly situation that might be connected to a case already under investigation."

Bru interrupted. "You better see this, man."

His head was starting to throb. "Can it wait?"

"Don't think so. Bring the uniform."

He veered off to follow Bru and hoped as they got near his classic car they weren't being dragged there because of a ruined paint job. When they got close, Bru pointed to an envelope tucked under his windshield wiper. "It looks like the first one you got."

Two notes in one day plus the car vandalism. Danny was more than fed up. Especially since he'd already canceled the poker tournament.

He filled the deputy in on the likelihood of the note's source and asked that Tony Mancusco call him in the morning.

The deputy nodded. "As soon as I finish here, I'll want to talk to you for a minute. You going to be around?"

He rubbed under his eyes. "Sure. Have one of my employees show you to my office."

The deputy knocked on the door an hour later. Time Danny had spent soothing customers and contacting his insurance company. The unlucky owners of the four damaged cars were told their cars would be impounded and tested before being released for repair. That was fun. "Something here you might want to see," the deputy said, crossing the space to the desk and opening his hand.

A half dozen BB pellets were in it.

"What do these have to do with what happened in my lot?"

The deputy looked like he was enjoying himself. "It shakes out like this. Someone hid at the corner of the lot and waited for your parking attendant to take a break. As soon as he left, the perpetrator sprayed the four most expensive cars with an acid of some kind, then used an air gun to shoot these pellets at as many cars as he could, setting off the alarms. We found them all over that part of the lot."

Danny rubbed his forehead. This had to be related to more than just the gambling. Who had he pissed off enough to target him like this? He sighed, releasing a pent-up breath. "At least no one was hurt."

The deputy continued. "Something weird about this whole thing. Your parking attendant says he was almost to the door that exits to the lot when the alarms started going off. He ran outside and swears no one was there. I walked the area and don't see how anyone could have gotten past him."

Great. An invisible tormentor. "I'll look around in the morning when it's light. Maybe the perp had a boat, or maybe he did the damage, then hid in the trunk of one of the cars until there was enough confusion to cover his reappearance."

The officer shrugged. "Mancusco should be out in person tomorrow. Good night."

"Good night and thanks."

Danny locked his office and took a tablet and pencil to his quarters. He sat and thought for a while, jotting down a few names with scribbled reasons behind them, but none had the kind of hostility it would take to attack him like this.

Of course, it could be totally random. A guy on a righteous crusade to save the world from evil gambling, who'd chosen him because his club was small and relatively isolated. That alternative was the most depressing. Where could he start looking for an unknown zealot?

He chucked the list onto his nightstand, put on a T-shirt and sweatpants, and wandered barefoot over to the window. The moon had coursed to a different position in the sky but still slipped in and out of the clouds to light up the lake.

His thoughts shifted to Pallas. Maybe all the Tarantino men were lucky. His father and brother had certainly married wonderful women, and both claimed they knew from the first meeting it was right for them. He smiled. Wouldn't that be something?

Cold reality brought him up short. A smart, beautiful woman like Pallas was not likely to abandon the chance of a lucrative partnership in San Francisco to hang around a guy up to his eyebrows in hock. *And trouble*, his conscience reminded him. *Up to my eyebrows in trouble.*

Chapter Eight

Pallas lay in bed, wide-awake. She rolled to her side and slid her hand over the smooth, empty sheet next to her. In the dark, her imagination found Danny's taut muscles and flat belly. She stopped her fingers in their fantasy exploration. *You could've had this for real, dummy. What were you thinking?*

Eight a.m. and Charles would arrive way too early.

She was lying on the bed, fully dressed with a cold, herbal eye mask when someone knocked at her door. She peeked at the bedside clock. Charles had always been punctual. After her restless night and the conversation she planned to have with him this morning, a post-breakfast, pre-lunch nap would definitely be in order. That is if she could find a high-stakes game first.

She peered through the little viewer in the door and saw Danny Tarantino on the other side. Her spirits went into high gear until she realized her circumstances. And he looked as bad as she felt. Apparently, he'd gotten about as much sleep as she had. The dark stubble she only imagined yesterday shadowed his jaw, and his eyes were heavy-lidded. She opened the door, holding the mask behind her. "Hello."

He held out a white pastry sack. "Croissant?"

"You came all the way over here to bring me that?"

He grinned. "I had other motives."

The view from her hotel window wasn't nearly as spectacular as the one from his deck, but they could sit for a minute. She smiled. "Which were?"

"Invite me in?"

"Oh, of course."

He stepped into the small room, and she felt there was no place safe for her to go. He exuded a maleness that expanded in small spaces.

He pulled a slip of paper from his pocket. "Here are two games. There's a pro-am at Rainey's with an amateur opening and one slot left in a tournament that's been moved up to start here at Suttons' new rooms tomorrow. Either one has the potential for the money you need. Check for vibes and let me know if you want either by lunchtime, and we can make the arrangements. You smell great."

She was with him right up to the compliment. The subject changed in a disconcerting but charming way, as did the mood of the conversation. "Thank you."

He stepped closer, then cupped her chin. "See you at eleven?"

"That's a little early for lunch."

"We'll think of something to do."

A crisp knock sounded on her door, breaking up their cozy conversation. No doubt a good thing.

"Excuse me," Pallas said.

As she figured, Charles stood on the other side. His glance went from his watch to astonishment as he saw Danny over her shoulder. "Who is this?"

Well, this is interesting. She opened the door. "Come in, Charles."

He looked at each of them, taking in their bleary eyes, then his gaze strayed to her rumpled bed and lastly to the sack in Danny's hand. Charles had too much breeding to voice his baser thoughts out loud. "You agreed to breakfast this morning..." He glanced at his watch again. "At eight o'clock."

She recognized the expression on Charles' face. It was reserved for waiters who had given poor service or cab drivers who had not gone the way he thought they should. She considered crawling back into bed and starting the day over in a couple of hours. "Yes, I did, Charles. I met Mr. Tarantino yesterday, however, and he didn't know that."

Danny held out his hand. "Danny Tarantino."

Charles shook it with little enthusiasm. "Charles Wyatt."

Danny grinned, seeming to enjoy the situation. For which she could have gladly pummeled him.

"Say, I got this little gambling and supper joint. It's got a pretty great cook. You wanna join Pallas and me for lunch?"

She was dumbfounded. Where had the Italian gangster accent come from?

Charles shrank back, a look of strained politeness on his face. "Lunch? No, thank you. Pallas and I must be going. Nice to make your acquaintance."

"Same here."

She didn't need this, although she bit back a laugh. "I'll meet you in the restaurant, Charles. Five minutes."

To his credit, Charles straightened his shoulders. "I don't mind staying, really."

She shook her head. "Order me some coffee, french toast, and bacon, please."

The men gave each other one last perusal, then Charles left.

Danny held up the sack. "Guess I should've called first."

She shrugged, not feeling as though she had to explain. "Guess so."

He pulled her close, making her belly do flip-flops, then kissed the tip of her nose. "See you at lunch."

She envisioned another sleepless night with a wound-up libido and reluctantly eased away. She turned and hurried toward the bed when her direction dawned on her. She looked over her shoulder, slipped the mask under her pillow, and reached for her purse on the nightstand. "Can't forget this."

He raised an eyebrow that said how cute it was he'd flustered her, then swung an arm toward the door. "Ready?"

They'd almost made it to the restaurant, and she was mentally kicking herself for not enjoying more of his company when she remembered last night's events. She put her hand on his arm and stopped. "What happened at your place after I left?"

He frowned. "Someone sprayed acid on four expensive cars, then fired BBs at another half dozen to activate the alarms."

"Didn't the attendant see anyone?"

"That's the odd thing. From the location of the damaged cars, there's no place the guy could have gone. The private property on that side has a hedge. It's not solid, but the owner has guard dogs. They're perimeter-trained and start barking loudly at anything that comes near. A customer had a flat tire in that area a week ago, and the dogs went nuts."

"What are you going to do?"

"Meet with a friend on the force who's working the

case, and call in a former associate." A muscle worked in his jaw. "Guess I didn't cancel the tournament quickly enough."

Anger pushed through her at the situation he faced. She rubbed her fingers together. "Is there anything I can do?"

He squeezed her shoulders and huffed out a breath. "Thanks for asking, but no. I'll work it out." He smiled. "Don't be late for lunch."

She wanted to hug him, soothe away some of his frustration. But she watched him walk away, then turned toward the restaurant, steeling herself for her talk with Charles.

He stood and pulled out her chair, wasting no time. "Was Mr. Tarantino the reason you went out last night?"

"I didn't have a date with him, no."

He persisted. "But you did spend the evening with him."

She clamped her teeth. Here's where the being careful part came in. "Some of it, yes."

He waited for the waitress to bring more coffee, then continued. "He doesn't really seem to be our sort."

She hated the way Charles categorized everyone. "By your definition, very few people are. Even me." She smoothed the edge of her napkin. "Actually, he's is a very successful businessman who knows his customers and the local demographics intimately. He was kidding you with that accent."

He reddened, shaking his head. "It's not important." He ran a finger along the side of his plate. "I spent a lot of time last night thinking about the path you're taking here."

She took a cleansing breath and unclenched her teeth. "Charles, I've appreciated your help and kindness over the years, but…"

He reached across the table and covered her hand with his. "Please, let me finish. I want you to get this partnership, but I really believe you're going about it the wrong way. Let me help you arrange for some conservative financing."

"I can't afford that."

"You mean the payment, plus interest and fees?" He shrugged. "That would depend on the amount of course, and the terms of the loan. I'm sure with your new partnership, the terms would be very favorable."

She carefully slipped her hand from under his. "I mean I can't afford the personal cost."

He frowned, then his eyes cleared. "Oh. No strings attached. I'm hurt that you'd think so."

Even if she and Danny never got together, and she was surprised at how much that thought bothered her, Charles had to get the message. She waited for their server to leave the food, then looked at him directly. "We both know that's not true. I've told you several times we have no personal relationship other than as friends, and I'm not interested in pursuing one."

He avoided her gaze. "I'm willing to wait."

The headache that had camped behind her eyes became full blown. Two men were "willing to wait," yet she only wanted one to be there when she was ready. "Think about this. What you call our relationship, I always refer to as friendship. You also said whatever I decided would be all right with you as long as it made me happy. Well this"—she indicated the casino and view of the lake—"makes me happy.

Something different might make me happier next week, but it won't be us as a couple." Her voice rose at the end of her response.

He blanched and looked at the tables nearby. "You're only thinking in the moment. However, if that is your true wish, how do you plan to handle our constantly being thrown together as partners?" He laid down his fork purposefully. "Assuming your gambling scheme works."

"Like others do. As professionals."

He leaned back, contemplating her for an uncomfortable half minute. "I wouldn't want a partner who had an estranged relationship with another partner. I'm sure the other members wouldn't either, *if* they found out."

Of all the petty, grasping attempts. He'd finally crossed her line in the sand. "I disagree. I met with each of them separately within the last two weeks. They seem to think I would be bringing good business and a desire to succeed, besides the half million dollars. I don't think personal attacks bordering on harassment and rumor mongering would be welcome." She recognized the look. A dazed expression that told her the other player realized he was losing.

He stood. "I've underestimated your behind-the-scenes skills," he said, then stalked away.

She sighed. Her cooling food no longer appealed. She wasn't foolish enough to think this was the end of it. Charles Wyatt III did not like losing. This was the second time he'd mentioned a connection with the new firm, and that worried her.

The partnership offer was solid, but the old boys' network went back generations in San Francisco, and her solid offer could slip away unless she was prepared. *Generations?*

Pallas smiled as her next move popped into her head.

Leverage.

Chapter Nine

Danny locked his car and started across the lot at Over the Moon. Tension knotted his shoulders. He'd gone to see Pallas, hoping she could restore balance to his whacked-out world. Before he got the chance, however, Charles Wyatt interrupted. Who was he anyway? The guy radiated animosity. Danny looked at his watch. He didn't expect Tony for another hour. He took a deep breath and decided to go for a run. Maybe that would work off some of his frustration.

When he got back, Tony Mancusco sat on his deck, drinking coffee. His friend since junior high, Tony had opted for public service rather than private security after they graduated from the same Police Sciences program. They had worked on a number of cases involving casinos or the stars they featured until Danny gave it up to build his own club. As he approached, the lieutenant waved two pieces of paper at him. "Photocopies of yesterday's notes. Whoever this is sure has it in for you."

Danny sat and read them. The first one took credit for the car accident and reiterated the demand to close the tournament. The second one started as the other two had, with his last name. *Tarantino, I'm not stupid. I know about the players at Jimmy G's. I'm going to start hurting people again, and it's your fault. Walk away from everything and close the club now.*

He swore, letting the pages fall to the glass-topped table.

He shook his head. He'd never experienced the kind of physical anguish these threats presented. His chest tightened, and his knees felt rubbery. "That's it. All for nothing." He shot a thumb over his shoulder. "Everything I ever wanted and it's a Jonah."

Tony faced him, then poked him in the sternum. "What kind of crap is that? You believe in yourself, not luck. You're giving up after two days. That's bald-assed pathetic."

His friend's vehemence snapped him up short. He pushed his hand away, but Tony continued. "You never gave up on anything this quick in your life. So what if it's more personal this time?"

Danny fisted his hands, then crossed his arms. "He already hurt one man. Which proves he means what he says. How the hell he found out about the players at Jimmy's, I don't know, but he does, and that caps it. I have seventeen people employed here. People I *like*. Not to mention customers. Many of whom might never return after last night's fiasco. I have to close down. It's not worth putting anyone else at risk."

The lieutenant shoved his hands in his pockets. "You do that, and we'll never catch him. The longer you can stay open the better chance we have. You know that."

Danny did, but he didn't like it. "You're saying I should choose the club over the people in it."

"Maybe it's not your choice."

They looked toward the french doors.

Bru stood there with an orange juice. "Have you asked the people who work here? I bet enough of them would stay to man a skeleton crew and keep the place going if you gave it until the end of the week."

Tony nodded, tapping the table. "I can arrange three extra surveillance rounds on night shift. Have you got anybody else working this?"

Danny's hope began to rise, but the niggling worry was still there. Especially since the guy was able to pull off that sleight-of-hand and damage his customers' cars right under his nose last night. "I have a call in to Derrick Van Howe, but he's out of town until tomorrow."

"Don't cancel the call," the lieutenant said. "He's sharp. The four of us should be able to come up with a short list."

Danny pulled out a chair for Bru. "I'll lay it out for the rest of the staff. Tell them what's at stake. Maybe you're right about enough of them willing to stay."

Bru grinned. "If nothing else, the bar will be open."

"I'll also let the players know the danger has escalated," Danny said. "They might want to change their decision."

He felt a solid, almost physical, shift in his attitude. Tony and Bru were right. This guy was an amateur, and he was pushing it. If he continued to do so, he'd be caught.

He snapped his fingers, turning to Bru. "Can I use your car tonight?"

The grin slid away. "My car?"

Tony laughed out loud at Bru's expression. "I've seen better color on a corpse."

The bartender looked affronted. "It's a classic. I like to be careful, that's all."

Danny shook his head. "Not to drive. To sit in."

Tony and Bru looked at him, eyebrows up.

He sighed. "I was going to have Van Howe stake out the lot tonight. I'll do it myself, and since I'll be out there for hours, and your car has a large, comfortable back seat…"

Bru's expression changed to skepticism. "No food or drinks allowed."

"I'm aware of the no-no list," Danny said.

It took a sock on the arm from Tony, but Bru agreed.

After Bru went in to prepare for the lunch crowd, Tony and Danny walked the area the deputies had isolated as the spot the shooter had stood the previous night. Tony took out a report and scanned it. "No smoking gun, no cigars, cigarettes, or gum wrappers. Nothing distinctive at all. The guy did his dirty work and levitated out."

Barking drew Danny's attention toward Jonathan Chase's property. "D'you suppose he went through the hedge because the Dobermans already knew him? They're trained to stop at the perimeter and wouldn't bother anyone they recognized."

Tony shrugged. "I can't see Jonathan Chase standing here in the dark taking potshots at your customers' cars."

Danny couldn't either. "He lives alone except for daily maid service."

The lieutenant gave him a sharp glance. "Been checking on your neighbor?"

"Routine, superficial stuff. I ran him when he started hassling me about my building permit. He's got a lot of connections. Had his fingers in every pie in town twenty, thirty years ago. Maybe it's time to dig a little deeper."

Tony looked in the direction of Jonathan Chase's house. "I'll start digging. Let you know what I find."

****

Pallas took a short nap and still had time to check out the games Danny found for her before leaving. She walked into the dining room at precisely eleven.

Bru waved her over to the bar, took her hand, and kissed it. "I've been warned off any attempts at trying my considerable charm on you. This is purely platonic."

She looked at his funky blond hair, clear gray eyes, and devilish grin. Danny disapproved of Bru's attentions? Interesting. "You don't say?" she teased back.

"Don't you have a tray of ice cream piña coladas to prepare for the private party?" Danny asked from behind her.

Bru dipped his head and swirled the air with his hand. "As you command, oh great one."

She couldn't stop the giggle or the stomach flutter. She turned and met Danny's gaze. *Dark hair and gorgeous blue eyes. Now we're talking.*

"Want to go for a walk?" he asked.

"That would be nice."

They went outside and up the driveway, then strolled toward a beautiful home that bordered his club. "Expensive neighbors," she commented. "Does their property start at that low stone wall?"

He stopped, frowning. "Yes."

She shaded her eyes. "Do you mind if I ask why there's a wide greenbelt on this side?"

"My original blueprint included a larger gambling area. The footings in the dock area had already been done when I decided to scale back."

"Too big for your bankbook?"

A muscle ticked in his jaw. "I could afford it when I started. My neighbors, especially Jonathan Chase"—he indicated the property on the other side of the club—"went after me with red-tape, court injunctions, and lawsuits. I won, but it cost me too much. That's why the lopsided positioning. Someday I hope to finish what I started."

She shook in anger and clenched her fists. Besides the extra traffic, Danny had made every effort to fit in. As a matter of fact, she'd driven past yesterday before realizing it. She unclenched her hands and ran her fingers lightly over his jaw, smoothing the knotted muscle. "I'm sorry."

He slid her hand to his mouth, kissing her palm, then slipped her fingers in his. "Thanks."

She warmed down to her toes at his tenderness and momentarily wondered what his stuffy neighbors would say if she kissed him right here. There was always the privacy of his deck, too. She pulled in a breath at the thought of what almost happened last night. Her resolve to make her partnership money hadn't wavered, but she was hedging toward the thought that she could have it all.

Danny's fingers tugged at hers, and they walked back to the club.

"I'm hungry," she said.

"See, I told you."

"Can we eat on the deck?"

He grinned. "I'm way ahead of you."

They'd just closed the door to his quarters when his phone rang. "Hello." A smile split his face. "Derrick.

You're back a day early."

Pallas pointed to the deck, indicating she would give him some privacy. He shook his head.

"Does this mean you can make it tonight?" he asked. "Oh. Then we're still on for tomorrow." He hung up.

Whoever Derrick was, Danny seemed anxious to see him.

"Someone to help find out who's harassing you, I hope," she said.

He nodded. "The note writer's an amateur with a lot of luck so far. Derrick's going to set up a surveillance of the parking lot. He's even sneakier than I am."

"And how sneaky is that?"

He caught her wrists in one hand and held them loosely behind her. "Enough to do something I've wanted since I left your hotel." He cupped her head with the other hand, his mouth closing in. "Still hungry?"

You want it all. Take it. She answered him by standing on her toes and meeting his mouth. After a moment, they became aware of her growling stomach.

He released her and smiled. "I get the point. Let's eat."

She nodded and started for the deck.

He stopped. "Hey, wait a minute. How can you be that hungry? You had breakfast less than three hours ago with what's his name. Charles something."

She faced him. Charles something, indeed. Her growling stomach rumbled on. Charles was probably on his way back to San Francisco to challenge her partnership offer right now.

"Not exactly. We didn't finish."

"Why not?"

She looked longingly at the dishes of food, kept warm by domed covers. "Charles and I go back about eight years. He was my mentor at Stanford, and we work in the same office. My name is up for that partnership at the start-up because of him."

Danny looked puzzled. "He acted a lot more territorial than just a friend or co-worker."

She was surprised at his intensity. "Exactly. That's the reason we didn't finish breakfast."

"You said he got you the partnership opportunity. Could he have it withdrawn?"

She thought for a minute. Chances were about even. "He could try."

Chapter Ten

Danny let the subject drop. She didn't seem to want to discuss it, and her relationship with Charles was none of his business. It gave him a lift to learn, however, that she'd apparently told the guy to back off.

She took the cover off her plate, inhaled, and smiled. "This looks and smells wonderful."

He liked watching her eat. She made little sounds of pleasure for the first few bites, sighed, then relaxed. "I was right, it's very good." Her gaze drifted over his shoulder. "This is much nicer than getting all suited up and sitting in a stuffy downtown office analyzing spreadsheets."

"Worst part of any job," he agreed. "The paperwork."

She nodded. "Best part of my job is negotiating the deal."

He had no doubt that was true. Too bad all that negotiating took place in San Francisco. "What kind of businesses do you finance?"

Her eyes lit. "I go after the newer, hemorrhaging-edge tech wizards. The 'I built it in my garage from old vacuum cleaner parts' guys. There're always the new rich who want to become the old rich and are willing to put money into well-documented ventures."

"Really? In this economy?"

She practically hummed with excitement, leaning

forward with an earnest look. "That's the beauty of it. Take the real estate market. It has cyclical lows and slumps. But during any downturn, the two million and up residences are hotter than ever. Just goes to show even the rich are interested in a bargain."

He couldn't help blinking a couple of times. "I guess I never thought of venture capitalists as bargain hunters."

She grinned. "Maybe that's an oversimplification. But buying shares in an as-yet-unknown commodity with the potential to earn you millions can make even a millionaire's heart pump double time. The old 'it takes money to make money' adage is very true."

His own heart thumped faster just watching her get excited. "So if you become a partner, could you buy in, too?"

She nodded. "The firm gets a healthy percentage the first two years. As the partner who brought in the moneymaker, some of that cut would be mine."

Again, he couldn't help himself. "Would you compete directly with that Charles guy?"

Her blue eyes sparkled. "Not really. Charles is firmly entrenched in the old boys' network. Not as many risk-takers there. They usually want proof upfront the magic is really happening, then they come out as second-string support. Kind of a wait-and-see-but-I-can-still-get-richer group. He does very well."

Danny could see she loved her job as much as he loved what he did. The realization made him happy for her, but stung. Maybe she could be swayed away from the big city. "You could work in Tahoe," he said. "It's a real growth area."

"Thank you." She sighed.

"You're welcome." He was a little confused about why she was thanking him. "Henri does make a mean salmon mousse."

She lifted a shoulder. "The lunch was lovely, but I was thanking you for inserting me into your dream here in Tahoe."

His mouth went dry, and he took a sip of wine. Had she actually said *inserting* to a man drowning in his own lust? Not that she'd done it on purpose, he realized. But what the hell was wrong with at least half the single men in San Francisco? She said something he totally missed. "Sorry?"

"Tempting," she murmured. "Very tempting."

"Glad to hear it." He wondered now if he could coax her into telecommuting from here.

She leaned forward and rubbed her arms. "It's cooling off a little. Got any warm desserts?"

"The old standbys. Cherries Jubilee? Bananas Foster?"

Her eyes widened. She liked sweets? Good to know. Danny grabbed for his napkin as it tried to blow off his lap. The temperature had definitely dropped. A light wind stirred the waves and moved a strand of her hair to nestle in the hollow of her throat. Why had he never been fascinated by hair before?

She yawned. "I don't usually nod off after eating. Especially with such nice company." She brushed at something on her lap, then turned pink. "I had a difficult time sleeping last night. Must be the altitude."

He nodded. "It takes some getting used to." He didn't add that his sleep was affected by the mess created in his parking lot and *her*. "Let's use the club dining room for dessert. I'll call the kitchen from inside."

"Okay." She ducked her head, then clasped her fingers together. "Change of subject?"

He sensed her mood shift. "Sure."

"I thought about your problem on the way back to the hotel last night. I could talk to Pat. He might be interested in some off-duty security work. I know you already said this guy Derrick is going to help…" She banged a slender fist on the table. "It's so unfair."

He tried to keep it light. "Nice of you to ask, but I'd rather not have any more people involved than necessary." He shook his head, staying her next protest. "Though I'm sure your brother-in-law is trustworthy."

He pried open her cold fingers and held her hand. "I spent eight years as a security specialist at Suttons after college. I'm good at this, and Derrick is one of the best. We're learning a little more about this guy every time he acts or leaves another note."

She sat up straight. "Did he leave another note last night? What did it say?"

He sighed. So much for wanting to forget his troubles and spend lunch getting hot and bothered over a gorgeous woman. Correct that, a gorgeous, *inquisitive* woman. "This isn't for public knowledge."

She nodded, eyes shining, fully awake now.

"He knew about the players at Jimmy G's. Said he was going to hurt more people and I should walk away." He couldn't tell her the guy also said it was his fault. He had to salvage something.

She squeezed his hand. "Sounds like he's a coward, too. I'm sorry."

He was beginning to hate the word sorry. He took a deep breath, trying to unknot his stomach.

She stood and led him toward the french doors. "Promise to let me know if I can help?"

"Sure."

"May I use your powder room before dessert?"

He walked to the door leading to his bedroom. "It's right in here."

As she stepped around him, he saw his messy bed and damp towels hanging crookedly in the bathroom. "Uh, maid service comes on Mondays. I didn't make much of an attempt this morning."

Pallas mumbled something and hurried into the room. She came out with fresh lipstick and brushed hair.

It occurred to him he hadn't set another time to see her, and a small wave of panic overtook him. "Henri's special tonight is filet mignon with a hunter's sauce including fresh shiitake mushrooms. How about dinner?"

She shook her head. "That sounds wonderful, but I'm slated to play round one at Suttons this afternoon, then out to Sassy's for a barbeque. I won't get back to the hotel until late."

Registered for a tournament already? He'd half hoped she'd be grateful for his help, but not this woman. She wanted something, and she went after it. Warmth spread in his chest. Why not set himself smack in the middle of her path whenever possible?

He'd forgotten she had other things to do in town besides being available for him. "How about breakfast? We can use the time to discuss dinner tomorrow night."

Geez, is food all I have to offer? Anybody could feed her.

Her eyes regarded him narrowly. "We have a

dinner date tomorrow night?"

He smiled his most winning host smile. "Didn't I tell you? I reserved a table near the band."

"You don't have a band."

"I could hire one if I wanted. Or we could make do with the sound system I have in here."

"Ah," she said wryly. "That's one of those details we're going to discuss. Okay, my room, nine o'clock. Bring two croissants."

He moved close and slipped a hand around her waist. "We could always order breakfast from room service."

Her look turned serious. "I'm about to start the tournament that'll make or break my career, and you have a lunatic to catch." She gave him a warm hug. "Let's revisit your suggestion in a couple of days."

She was right, of course. He fairly ached to make love to her, but there were other, more pressing parts of their lives to attend to. He sighed, kissed her temple, and escorted her out.

Bru waved them over as they started past the bar. "I've got a date tonight, and Mandy is covering my shift. She's decided to hang in there with the rest of us thrill seekers." He tossed a set of keys to Danny. "Take these before I forget. My date's picking me up and taking me home to change."

"TMI," Danny interrupted in a soft tone. "Zip it."

Pallas turned toward him. "Don't tell me on top of everything else your car's not working?"

Bru jumped right back in the deep end. "Nah, his car always works, but mine's got more comfortable seats."

"Apparently, 'zip it,' when spoken by your boss

means nothing," Danny said. "We'll talk." He turned to Pallas. "Let's go."

Bru looked from Danny to Pallas and back. "Oh. Sorry, man."

Danny walked her to the exit.

She sidestepped when he opened the door. "Thrill seekers? Keys to a car with more comfortable seats? Really? What was that about?"

He said nothing, just held the door.

She set her lips in a determined line and crossed her arms. "I can leave and come back when you're in your office. Bru's so easy to crack I won't even break a sweat, so you might as well tell me now."

He sighed. She was irritatingly right. Faced with a beautiful, clever woman, Bru would spill state secrets. He needed to set up a password to use when he wanted his friend to shut the hell up. "Fine. Since Derrick can't cover the lot tonight, I'm watching from the back of Bru's car. It's got a big, comfortable back seat."

Her mouth opened, like he knew it would, and he held up a hand. "I know you want to help, but the answer's no."

She caught and held his gaze. "Why not?"

Because being alone with you in the dark under a warm blanket is a hell of a distraction, and I can't afford to be distracted.

He returned her gaze, trying for stern. "It didn't occur to me that you would enjoy sitting for hours in the back of a cold car, staring into the dark. It could also be dangerous, and we've already discussed how I feel about putting you in that type of situation." He shot her a look of victory. "Besides, you said you weren't available."

She pursed her mouth, an action that made his insides go from mix to puree. "I was going to spend the evening at Sassy's after the tournament this afternoon, but I could leave early and still make it here before dark."

He put a fist against his chest, feigning hurt feelings. "You turned me down for dinner but can rearrange your schedule for this?"

Her eyes lit, and she held out her hands, palms up, moving each up and down slowly, as if weighing. "Steak in. Stake-out."

Chapter Eleven

He burst out laughing. How many women did he know who'd make that choice, let alone be honest about it? Guess she'd find out for herself how boring and cold a stake-out was. "Be here by eight thirty. I have very strict ground rules. If you break even one, I toss you out on your pretty butt. Got it?"

She looked like she was going to object and thought better of it. "That's fair. And you can spend part of that long, cold, boring time explaining why Bru referred to your staff as thrill seekers." She popped a grin and left.

What was the old saying about a curse and a blessing being the same thing? Something like that was happening to him. For all her beauty and savvy and intellect, the other side of the redhead's coin was stubbornness, curiosity, and *stubbornness*.

He returned to the bar where Bru was busily scrubbing at a nonexistent spot. "If she so much as tears a fingernail tonight, your ass is grass, and I'm the lawnmower."

Bru continued wiping.

Danny tapped the bar, and the bartender looked up, a quiver of a smile on his lips. "New rule," he said, giving Bru a measured stare. "Make that a new *serious* rule. When it comes to Pallas, filter everything you say, *before* you say it."

Bru blinked, comprehension dawning. "Last time you laid down a serious rule, it involved the club. You've known her less than two days, and she's in that league?"

Danny nodded. No hesitation, no take-backs, just a knot deep in his gut. What had he gotten himself into?

****

Pallas sat in her rental car for a few minutes, taking deep breaths of the fresh mountain air. She'd never felt this alive. Danny had dressed for lunch in a dark-blue, pigment-dyed shirt that perfectly matched his eyes and snug, well-worn jeans. She'd seen through the glass-topped table that they'd gotten snugger during their conversation. She had barely resisted the urge to fold her napkin into a fan and cool herself.

Then she'd nearly lost it when she walked with shaky knees through his bedroom. The fragrance of his soap and aftershave hung in the air, and it had taken a major effort to keep from dragging him in there and making his bed messier.

Another deep breath and she mentally switched gears. The physical attraction to Danny was very strong, but she was only here for a week and had barely started to work on her goal to win the partnership money, let alone figure out a way to get some information on her father's ban.

In the meantime, she contemplated her schedule. She couldn't change her place in the poker game rotation at the last minute, and Sassy would be disappointed if she didn't show up for dinner. She'd have to leave early without telling her why.

Lunch must have given her a second wind. Pallas held the steering wheel and tapped the sides of her thumbs against it. The players loyal to Danny could still be practicing at Jimmy G's, a small club she'd passed on the way to Over the Moon. She could kill some time watching them and maybe, just maybe, talk to that older man, Ty. His blink pattern increased when he'd denied knowing her father. That meant he was probably lying, and she wanted to know why. He might even know what really caused the ban. It was worth asking a few questions.

She pulled into Jimmy G's parking lot. Hopefully the players were there.

The interior was pure sixties. Lots of dark-red, gold accents and low lighting. Unlike Over the Moon, there wasn't a separate room for smokers, and a hazy pall hung in the air. Especially around the noisy slot machines in one corner. There was a small space to the side for diners, although how they could enjoy food with the smoke and noise was beyond her.

She saw the group sitting at a large table toward the back and smiled. After this many days they should all know exactly what each others' skill levels were and who was likely to come out the winner. *Should*, but gamblers always thought they could make a comeback; hope sprang eternal.

Pallas started across the room but was intercepted by a tall, deeply tanned man dressed all in black.

"Welcome to Jimmy G's. Your first time here?"

Wow. The seventies called. They want Johnny Cash back. She nodded.

The man smiled. "Can I get you a table?"

"No. I'm here to watch the tournament players."

"What tournament players would that be?"

He almost got away with it. But not quite. She

caught his tell, a subtle flick of his right eyelid when he lied.

Her gaze shot to the table of players. Of course. They wouldn't broadcast their presence, and she'd given away the fact that she knew they were here. "I heard someone at Over the Moon say there were people down here practicing for a poker tournament. I thought it would be fun to watch."

He didn't look to be buying a single word. "There are poker games all over town. Why here?"

She smiled sweetly. "Are you saying I can't watch?"

He held up his hands, palms out. "Not at all. I'd be foolish to turn away a beautiful woman. Lends class to the place." He stepped aside and waved her on.

She eyed him in passing. He had challenged her twice, then suddenly folded. Why? She watched as he walked down a short hallway without looking back. Guess she wasn't going to find out.

As she neared the table, she saw only three of the four competitors playing. The man who had mentioned the game to her yesterday wasn't there. A pretty blonde, the only woman in the group, smiled and nodded to her.

"Come to join us?"

"No, thanks," Pallas said. "I thought I'd watch a while."

The blonde shrugged and picked up her cards. Pallas began to think this was a dumb idea. Serious players didn't chat during play, and the man called Ty didn't lift his gaze from his cards. She was about to leave when someone sat next to her.

"Change your mind?" It was the missing player. He must be on a break.

"No. I've committed to a tournament at Suttons starting later today," she said. "Thought I'd see if the local talent was any good. You winning?"

He extended his hand. "Elliott Kerr, and I'm holding my own. How come you're not here practicing with us if you and Tarantino are so tight?"

She took his hand, ignoring the skitter sliding up her spine. "Tight?"

He dropped eye contact. "Nothing personal. I happened to see the two of you on his deck last night. Real cozy."

The skitter intensified. "I guess we thought that was private."

His attention switched to the game. "Whatever. Not really my business."

Then why did you bring it up? She frowned, trying to remember what could be seen from Danny's deck. She failed. Other things had been more interesting.

Elliott stood. "Time to rotate back in. See you around."

"Wait a sec." She touched his arm. "Is it close to Ty's break?"

He looked at the older man. "Not for a while."

She nodded. Ty showed no signs of having heard her. As Elliott sat down, the blonde stood and turned to her.

"Hi. Pallas, right? I'm Lou Stockman. I sure wish you were playing, too. It gets lonely being the only woman in the game."

Pallas glanced at the stack of chips in front of the chair Lou abandoned and smiled. "Hasn't seemed to hurt your game."

Lou grinned and looked around. "Danny's club is

much nicer, don't you think? Jimmy's a sweetheart, but this is kind of gaudy and old Vegas, like Mike's Place."

"Mike's Place?"

"Yeah, a club owned by Mike Partain. He's a good friend of mine."

"Are he and Danny good friends? Is that how you found out about the tournament?"

Lou laughed outright. "The relationship between those two is a lot of things, but friendly isn't one of them. Mike knows he'll never have the class Danny has. And Danny's self-made. Every bit of Mike's start-up came from his uncle."

That was interesting. An old rivalry. Jealousy crept in at the thought that part of the rivalry might include Lou Stockman. But maybe Mike Partain had lost clientele or disliked Danny enough to try and drive him out of business.

She looked at her watch. She could go back to Danny's and tell him about the conversation with Elliott Kerr or wait until tonight. Going back to see Danny won. "Oops, gotta go. Nice to have met you, Lou, and good luck."

Afternoon sun blinded her for a moment when she walked out the door. It took her a second to realize the man striding toward her was Danny.

Chapter Twelve

Her first reaction was pure pleasure, and heat pulsed under her skin.

Until she saw the look on his face.

The smile died on her lips when he reached her.

He grasped her upper arm and propelled her across the lot. He wasn't hurting her, but when she tried to put on the brakes, her light straw sandals were no match for whatever was fueling his anger.

"What are you doing? Let go of me."

He opened the passenger door of a dark blue coupe and took her other arm, pulling her nose to nose with him. "Get in."

The rosy, lovely fog that had enveloped her only seconds ago dissipated. She sat down and crossed her arms.

He slid into the driver's side and stared straight ahead, his jaw clenched. "What the hell possessed you to come over here?"

She didn't quash the edge in her voice. "Why?"

He had a white-knuckle grip on the steering wheel. "Not ten minutes after I tell you the note I received mentions the players practicing here, you show up. Do me a favor. Don't help."

She turned toward him. "What are you talking about? I did not come here to spy on the players. I came here on personal business."

He shifted in her direction. "Personal business? Is that why you said you were there to watch the tournament players?"

She huffed in indignation. "How do you know what I said?" When he didn't answer, she continued. "So that guy...that guy who questioned me is some kind of stooge? He reported my actions?"

His gaze refocused on the windshield. "Jimmy's a friend. He's hosting the players as a favor. When you showed up and mentioned they were tournament players, he thought I should know."

Heat smoldered behind her anger. "I'm sorry if I set off all kinds of alarms, but as I said, my reason for being here was personal. I don't appreciate you dragging me across the parking lot like some kind of demented control freak."

He gaped, frowning. "Control freak?"

She nodded. Still agitated, she rubbed her palms on her slacks. "Look, I like you, a lot. But I just severed an eight-year friendship with Charles because of his overbearing need to manage my life. Now you pop up this afternoon, uninvited, showing the same signs. There's a fine line between wanting someone to be safe and controlling them. You crossed it."

Dark blue eyes regarded her as he shook his head. "I guess I went a little crazy when I thought you were putting yourself in danger, especially on my account. I never intended to push that hard. Sorry."

She sat back, slightly mollified. "I'm sorry, too. I should have found another way to take care of...to handle it."

"Your personal business." He cast a cautious glance at her. "Sounds like it involves one of the players. Could I help? Without interfering?"

"Thanks." She wasn't sure yet that she wanted him to know what she was after. "I'll think about it."

"One more thing. Warn me before you do anything like this again?"

Considering everything else he had on his mind, it wasn't an unreasonable request. "All right."

"Great." He leaned across and brushed a kiss on her cheek. "I'll let you get back to Suttons. When Jimmy called, he said the players have only been here a short time. I need to talk to them anyway."

Pallas had gone from zero to sixty and back again within a few minutes. Her heart still raced, and her skin tingled. In her experience, men didn't usually admit they were wrong one minute, then offer to help the next. Danny Tarantino had a rare generous spirit. She was sure that generosity would extend to his lovemaking, a belief that curled her toes. Just a little.

And back to zero, but she wasn't done yet. "Don't you want to know what I found out?"

He raised an eyebrow. "You were only in there for five minutes. What could you have found out?"

She played with the latch on her purse. There might be a simple answer, but she didn't think so. "That player, Elliott Kerr, said he saw us on your deck last night. I can't see how, but that's what he said."

****

He stared at her. That bit of information was very interesting. He wasn't going to tell her that, however. Despite her having called him on his over-the-top behavior, which he supposed she had every right to do, he still didn't want to encourage her in getting involved. "Maybe we should have our conversations inside from now on."

She looked disappointed and somewhat skeptical but accepted his reply with a shrug. "Okay. We're still on for tonight?"

He couldn't help the eye roll and got a punch in the arm for his trouble. "Rules."

"Hey, I said I'd cooperate, and I will," she said.

He watched her drive away a few minutes later and went into Jimmy G's. Del stood at the bar, paying for a cola. Danny didn't recognize him at first. He wore painfully new jeans, glaring white athletic shoes, and a yellow golf shirt. In all the years Danny had known him, he'd never seen Mike Partain's bookkeeper in anything other than a dark suit, white shirt, and bow tie. He must have stared because Del spoke up.

"Uh, Lou thought I should try something different."

Danny nodded, wondering how far out of his comfort zone a man in love would wander. "You'll get used to it."

The bookkeeper walked away, still carrying himself like a man who'd lost his way to the suit department.

"Did you find her?"

He turned to Jimmy, leaning against the bar. "Yeah. I caught up with her in the parking lot. Thanks again for calling."

"No problem. She really brightened up the place, but I can understand you not wanting her to hang around the players after the threats you received. Your interest personal?"

He regarded his friend. Tall, tanned, and about forty, Jimmy was a perennial bachelor out to have a good time. He didn't think Pallas would go for the diamond-pinky-ring type, but he wasn't taking any chances. "Yeah, it is personal."

A smile creased Jimmy's face, and he winked. "All the more for me."

Danny shook his head. First, he'd asked Bru to back off, now Jimmy. He was beginning to understand Charles Wyatt's desperation.

He took a deep breath and moved his attention to the players, especially Elliott Kerr. He still couldn't figure out what was familiar about the man, and that bothered the heck out of him. Doubly so now that Kerr had claimed to have seen Pallas and him on his deck.

Lou waved him over. "Your friend Pallas came in. Stayed for a couple of minutes, then left. Said she was starting in a tournament at Suttons. Too bad. She seemed sharp. Pretty, too." She laid her cards face down and gave him her full attention. "Maybe you should do something to see to it that she sticks around."

He raised an eyebrow. He didn't know half the people at this table very well and had no intention of letting his feelings for Pallas become general knowledge. He smiled. "She's only here for a week."

"Oh, that's a problem." She shook her head. "By the way, we all heard about the commotion in your parking lot last night. Discussed it amongst ourselves and here's our decision." She swung out her hand to include everyone at the table. "We're all still here."

Danny pulled up a chair and straddled it. "I think you'd better hear the rest of the story."

The rest of the group laid down their cards and waited.

"I received two more threats yesterday demanding

that I close the club, or he'll start hurting people. He specifically mentioned knowing about the four of you practicing here."

Danny held up his hands. "I know we said we were severing ties between you and Over the Moon, but it looks like he's not accepting our compromise. My request? Quit now. We can always pick up in the future." He looked around. "If I'm still in business."

"Sounds like somebody has the inside track," Del said, glancing at the other players. "Even though we all agreed not to broadcast our intention. I say we give Danny a break and cancel our practice before someone else gets hurt." He eyed Lou first then the rest for confirmation. When they nodded, he held out his hand to Danny. "I guess that puts an official end to our rebellion. Let us know when we can start up again?"

He took Del's hand. "Thanks. This is one less thing to worry about."

"You close to catching the guy?"

Danny turned to Elliott Kerr. His tendency in any investigation was to give no information without seeming rude. In Kerr's case, he felt especially reticent about divulging anything. "Not that the police have told me."

Kerr nodded slightly as the rest stood. They all trailed over to the bar except Ty.

"Got a minute?" he asked Danny.

"Sure. Sorry this didn't work out."

The older man blinked, his face etched in regret. "Me, too. Hope they catch the bastard, and soon."

"Couldn't agree with you more."

Ty stuffed his hands deep in his pockets but showed no signs of leaving.

"Was there something else?" Danny asked.

"That Pallas girl snooping around today was asking about me. You know why?"

Danny shook his head. Ty's question was totally unexpected. Pallas had said she had personal business and didn't disagree when he suggested it was with one of the players. But Ty?

"Not a clue. Why don't you ask her what she wants?"

Ty shook his head. "It's too late."

****

Pallas hurried across the lobby to the private playing rooms. She checked in and was seated at a table with seven others. It took about fifteen minutes to sort out the players. She was one of the youngest and surprised at one grandmotherly type whose efforts to bluff consisted of acting like a novice. Pallas wasn't fooled. The older woman had a keen eye and quick hands. The most colorful character was a famous player look-a-like. The man was tall and slender with a drawl. His cowboy hat band sported a rattler's head with ruby eyes. That's where the similarity ended. She'd seen the real deal in action once, and this guy didn't come close.

The four-hour stint on top of last night's poor sleep and her delicious lunch threw her off. She had hoped to be ahead by more than the sixty-eight thousand dollars she'd won by the end of her first round, but it was a good start.

She logged out and got her score card signed off by the observer. Sassy didn't expect her for two hours, and she had offered to pick up dessert on her way. If she hurried, she could still get an hour's nap before leaving.

A piece of hotel stationery had been slipped under

her door. The message from Charles was brief. *I've arranged to fly back to San Francisco at 7:00. If you've changed your mind, call me before 6:00.*

The message light on her phone flashed, and Pallas pressed the number to retrieve it. She'd been right to assume Charles wouldn't just walk away after the abrupt end to their breakfast.

The message said the partners were meeting to discuss her qualifications after some new information had come to light. If she would like to address the issue, please call at one p.m. tomorrow.

She wrote down the number, then sighed and sat on the bed. The amazing thing was, she wasn't sure she wouldn't be okay if the partnership decision went against her.

Had her goals shifted?

Chapter Thirteen

Pallas ventured around to the patio area of Sassy's house in response to voices. Pat hurried over and took her hand. "Sassy's inside. Let me introduce you to some people."

He escorted her to a group seated at a picnic table. "These are some of our neighbors, and that good-looking guy down at the end is a friend of mine, Gavin Andrews. Everyone, this is my sister-in-law, Pallas Mulroney."

She sensed immediately that Gavin was being served up as a possible date and/or dinner companion. Ah, the life of a single Mulroney woman. Pat's heart was good, but she'd heard from her other sisters that he'd snuck in cop and firemen friends at innocent gatherings, so she came semi-prepared. She gave hellos around the table and excused herself to find Sassy.

Several women were busy in the kitchen and pointed down the hall. She entered the colorful room her two oldest nieces shared. Sassy was tying ribbons into their newly braided hair, and baby Chloe lay on one of the beds, gurgling.

Sassy grinned. "Glad you could make it. You and I have private stuff to discuss before we join the others."

Pallas picked up Chloe, breathing in the wonderful baby smell. Happy babies always made her want to bury her face in their tummies and go *pfffft*. So she did.

Her sister finished and shooed the girls out the door. "Go tell Daddy Aunt Pallas and I will be out in a few minutes."

Sassy closed the door after them and sat on the twin bed across from her. "Before I forget, Mom and Dad are coming for Chloe's baptism Saturday. It's a surprise for the girls, but I wanted you to know since you're already coming, right?"

She nodded. "Of course. The tournament will be over, so the timing is good. That's great about Mom and Dad, too. I haven't seen them since they came to San Francisco last November to celebrate their anniversary."

Sassy leaned forward. "Family stuff over, now give. How did the lunch go today? Is he nice?"

She tried for nonchalance. "Yes, he's nice."

Her sister narrowed her eyes and sent out her own *pffft*, zeroing in. "Don't give me the sanitized version, girl. How nice? Any sparks?"

She lifted a shoulder. "Okay, I should be carrying my own tank of cold water and a hose."

Sassy's gaze bored into her. "One hose?"

"Okay, two hoses. One for him, too. But I had a change of heart last night about going for the lust-fling thing."

Sassy fairly squealed. "What happened?"

She pointed to the drowsy baby and shushed her sister. "I did a little recreational gambling at Over the Moon and got invited to the owner's quarters for a drink."

"And?" Sassy whispered.

"And I put the brakes on before it went too far."

Her sister sucked in a breath. "Don't tell me. You

remembered Mom's old saw about men who won't buy the cow when the milk is free. Did he get mad?"

She hung her head. "Not really. I explained I was here to win the partnership money and didn't want to get distracted."

Sassy snorted. "I'll bet he liked being thought of as a distraction."

"Actually, he understood. He's already made good on his future. He was disappointed but said he'd wait."

"What? You asked him to wait? That's like asking an avalanche to wait until you're emotionally ready to deal with it."

"Nope. That was his choice."

"I'm liking the way he sounds," Sassy pronounced. "Most men would chalk it up as your loss and be back in the game before the door hit you in the butt."

"He didn't get the chance." She sighed. "Someone trashed several of his customers' cars last night. Didn't Pat tell you?"

Sassy gasped. "Be serious. He never brings his work home. Thinks it would upset me and the girls too much. Real world overload."

"I think that's sweet."

"Yeah, but living in the no-tell zone, I miss out on a lot of interesting stuff. Wouldn't trashing cars be loud?"

She shook her head. "They threw acid on some cars and ruined the paint jobs."

Sassy pulled her head back, staring. "Acid? Is he in danger? Are you?"

Danny certainly thought so, but she wouldn't worry Sassy. "I feel perfectly safe when I'm with him," she hedged. And that was the truth.

Her sister's shoulders relaxed, then she got a sly look. "Any heavy necking?"

She tilted her head. "What are you, some kind of voyeur?"

Sassy's mouth turned down. "I have to get my jollies somehow. Between Pat's schedule and the three girls, we can't find five minutes alone anymore."

She sighed. Her own practically non-existent love life was pretty sad, too. "I could stand in his arms all day, except I get rubber-band knees. He showed up at my hotel room this morning with croissants, but I had other plans. I had to wait until lunch for another fix."

Sassy clapped hands over her ears. "Geez, I'm sorry I asked. Do you think anyone would get suspicious if I dragged Pat into the house for about a half hour?"

Pallas gently laid down Chloe and moved her sister's hands. "Hey, you wanted to know. And yes, your guests would get suspicious. Speaking of which, is that Gavin person by any chance here so I won't get lonely?"

"It was Pat's idea," Sassy confirmed. "The big goof likes the guy and thinks everyone should be in a happy relationship like ours."

"Here's the deal." Pallas patted her sister's hand. "I don't want to hurt your feelings or Pat's or Gavin's, but I have to leave in about two hours and get back to Over the Moon."

Sassy shot her fist in the air and pulled it back sharply. "Yesss. Do the Mulroney sisters proud."

"Um, what do you think is going to happen?"

"Accelerated necking?"

Pallas grinned at her sister's enthusiasm. "That's

not the exact purpose of this evening, but I might get lucky." Had that been in her mind all along? Her grin widened at the idea. She held up a hand when she saw Sassy poised for another question. "I can't tell you why I'm going there."

"Can you tell me tomorrow?"

She shook her head. "Exactly how long has it been between adult conversations for you these days?"

"Very funny."

****

Danny stood on his deck with night vision binoculars, scanning for places from which Kerr could have seen him and Pallas. A straight shot from the corner of Jonathan Chase's deck overhang provided a clear view he'd never noticed before. At almost sixty yards away, it would have to have been intentional. There was no tie between Chase and Elliott Kerr that he knew of, but he'd ask Tony to look into it.

He lowered the glasses to see if there were any other vantage points. Unless the man had been in a motorless boat without running lights, there were no other possibilities. Then how in the hell had Kerr seen them? Had he just been guessing?

"Find any ninjas?"

He started and turned to Bru, standing in the doorway. "What are you doing back? I thought you had a date."

Bru shrugged and looked at the decking. "She wanted a top-notch bartender for her sister's wedding reception. When I told her I didn't do weddings, she split. I had to take a cab back."

He laughed. "Serves you right. Thought you were going to get a hot night and your date uses you, for a change. Bet Mandy wouldn't have done you dirty."

Bru's forehead furrowed as his gaze slipped sideways. "Mandy already knows how to tend bar."

He snapped his fingers. "This does have an upside. I can tell Pallas you're going to watch the parking lot with me."

The blond crooked an eyebrow and grinned. "The only reason you want me is you're afraid of being alone in the dark with her."

He hated it when Bru was right. He didn't trust himself where she was concerned. Especially since a cold, dark, back seat wasn't nearly enough room to satisfy his interest in her. "Okay."

"Okay, what?"

"You're right. So are you going to help me or not?"

Bru smiled. "Can't. I already promised Mandy as I came through I'd work the stockroom and back her up. You're on your own."

He scowled. "I'll remember this conversation the next time you want a favor."

The bartender spread his fingers and slapped his chest. "Hey, it's not my job to save you from yourself. Where's all that macho Italian self-control?"

A knock at the door interrupted them.

"Get that on your way out, would you?" Danny asked. "It's probably Pallas."

"Sure, but I came by to remind you about the rules for my car. That back seat is in pristine condition, and that's how I want it when you're done."

He shook his head. "I'll remember. But if you treated women the way you treat that car, they'd be lined up around the block."

Bru made a parting shot over his shoulder. "If I

ever find one that beautiful and dependable, I will."

His anticipation rose as Bru headed for the door. In spite of what he'd said, he was looking forward to spending several hours in close quarters with Pallas. He'd already stowed a blanket, flashlight, cell phone, and although expressly forbidden by Bru's list, a thermos of hot coffee laced with chocolate liqueur.

He heard her voice and questioned for the dozenth time since he'd met her, why now? Why, when his whole future depended on his resolving what was behind the threatening notes, had this almost perfect woman shown up? *Better now than never*, a voice in his head censured as he walked inside to greet her. He had to agree.

She swung a brown paper bag in one hand.

"I'm afraid food isn't allowed in Bru's car," he said.

Bru made a U-turn and stood behind her.

She stared at him blankly, then followed his gaze and laughed. "Oh, this isn't food. I brought a change of clothes. I thought it might fool someone watching into thinking it was food. Guess it worked."

She opened the sack and held it out for Bru's inspection.

The bartender peeked inside, gave her a look that said she was strange, and left.

Danny checked his watch. "You can change in the bedroom."

She stayed where she was.

"I promise not to watch." He bobbled his eyebrows.

She shook her head and rolled her eyes. "That's not it. Aren't we going to put some of that black stuff on our faces?"

He bit back a laugh. "Uh, that isn't necessary. Bru's car sits in the shadows. None of the lot lights will reach us."

He could see she had looked forward to her idea of a woman on a covert mission. "You did bring black clothes?" he asked as seriously as he could.

She smiled. "Yes."

"Better get ready, then. I want to be out there by 20:45."

She saluted. "Yes, sir."

Five minutes later she emerged in a long, black, turtleneck sweater and black leggings that disappeared into lightweight ankle boots. The thought of those long slender legs wrapped around his waist came so hard and fast it rocked him.

"What now?" she asked.

I kiss you senseless, and you let me make love to you right here on the floor because I convince you how damned needy I am when it comes to you.

He picked up a navy windbreaker he'd retrieved from the club's lost and found and tossed it to her. "Put this on so it looks like we're going for a walk."

He wore a tan canvas field coat over his black shirt. After she'd slipped the windbreaker on, he took her hand and stepped toward his door. "The valet ducks in for a sandwich right about now. We'll wait until he goes into the kitchen, then go out to the car." He wondered how she thought they were going to cut across the thirty feet behind the bar and out the door with camo grease on their faces.

The walk to the back of the lot was uneventful. He unlocked the driver's door and held the seat forward as she climbed in.

When he'd gotten in and settled, she turned to him. "What kind of land yacht is this? I have smaller closets."

He grinned in the darkness and quoted his friend's litany. "This is the finest Detroit Iron built in 1959. Original paint job, tucked nylon interior, and mileage."

She ran her hand over the seat. "Very comfortable. And you don't see many turquoise cars these days."

He continued. "Bru found it two years ago in the garage of a woman he was dating. It had belonged to her grandfather, and she thought it was too ugly for anyone to buy. Imagine her surprise when he wanted it."

She looked out the back window. "It probably came off the assembly line thirty years before she was born. The fins alone are bigger than the door panels on my car."

He chuckled and brought the binoculars out of his coat pocket to have a look around. "Bru takes his one obsession very seriously."

She tipped her head. "Who was he referring to when he said thrill seekers?"

Chapter Fourteen

Danny thought she'd forgotten about that slip, but he was learning she was not the forgetful type. "I'm keeping the club open despite the warnings in hopes the guy might make a mistake. The staff has been told about the risks, and most of them have agreed to work until the end of this week. Bru's dubbed them the thrill seekers."

Pallas contemplated him. "They're very loyal, but I'm not surprised. You seem to instill that."

He didn't know what to say. He'd been startled that all but two of his staff had decided to stay. "Uh, they're good people."

She nodded. "So what do you want me to do?"

His thoughts edged toward a certain fantasy that had been forming. "Do?"

She nodded. "I came to help, remember?"

This could be a problem. He gazed around the murky interior of the Buick. He hadn't expected her to actually want to help. The rolled-up blanket caught his eye. "Uh, there's a thermos in that blanket. You could pour us some coffee."

"You invited me here to pour coffee." It was a flat statement.

He was going under, so he might as well fight. "Actually, you invited yourself. I had intended to do this alone."

She was silent for a moment, then sighed. "That's true. You did say it would be cold, dark, and boring. I really was hoping to help, though." She stifled a yawn. "Maybe I should go back to my hotel. I only made a tiny dent in the money I need—too tired to concentrate."

The valet stepped out the back door of the club and lit a cigarette.

"Sorry to hear that," he said. "Too late to leave, though. I don't want to give us away. Why don't you curl up under the blanket and take a nap? I'll wake you if anything exciting happens."

She pulled the blanket onto her lap and carefully unrolled the contents. "How long did you plan to stay out here?"

"A couple of hours, anyway, why?"

"Maybe we could take turns. I'll sleep for an hour while you watch. Then your turn. Neither of us got much sleep last night."

"Neither of us..." He laughed but heard the yearning in her voice. The thought of her curled beside him was tempting, and he could certainly let her have the binoculars while he pretended to sleep. "Okay, but first we go over the ground rules I mentioned this afternoon. I meant what I said about tossing you out if you broke one. Agreed?"

"Agreed. This is great. I can hardly wait to tell..."

He grasped her arms and brought her face close to his. "Tell no one. That's the first rule. Even if nothing happens, things have a way of getting around, and I can't afford to let whoever is doing this know I'm personally laying for him. This isn't a game."

Her pupils were big in the half light, but she didn't

jerk away. "Of course it isn't. I've never done anything like this before. I…well, I wasn't thinking."

He rubbed her arms. He was tired, and she brought his emotions, good and bad, boiling to the surface like quicksilver. "Let's start over. The first rule is tell no one. Even if you think they're the safest person in the world."

She shook her head as he talked. "You can throw my butt out now if you want."

He laughed again, the tension easing out. Then the full moon slipped from behind some clouds, and he saw her beautiful, earnest face.

For the first time since he could remember, he wanted something more than he wanted his own place. He pulled her to him and kissed her deeply. His only thought was how to maneuver her closer. She responded in kind, pushing at his jacket and making needy noises in his mouth.

Something very wet soaked his lap. What the hell? He jerked back.

She jerked away, too, until she saw he was dragging at the edges of the blanket. A dark spot moved outward from the thermos. She grabbed it and set it upright. The lid had come loose. "Oh, you're in trouble now," she said.

He hung his head and huffed out a breath. "Only if the coffee made it past my lap. I'm afraid to look."

She started laughing. "You'll never fool Bru."

He rolled down the window and tossed out the blanket. "He'll be off shift in a couple of hours. Even if he hangs around, I can hold my jacket in front of me. You be my wingman and distract him."

She laughed even harder, gulping in air.

"Okay, okay," he said. "It sucks to be me. Back to what we came out here for."

Pallas nodded, her eyes shining with tears. "What's rule number two?"

He leaned in and kissed her lightly. "If I leave to investigate anything, do not follow. Stay right where you are until I come get you."

"What if you need help?"

It was his turn to sigh. "That's rule number three. If you break rule number two, do not, under any circumstances, consider helping. I don't care how bad it looks. Understand?"

"Absolutely." She suppressed another yawn. "How many more rules are there?"

"Those cover it. Don't tell, follow, or help."

She brought her legs under her and rested her head against the back of the seat. "If I can't tell, follow, or help, wake me in an hour so I can *look*."

"Sarcasm is not a flattering trait."

She closed her eyes. "Shhh. You're telling."

He shook his head. He would have shown any other woman the door had they meddled to the extent this one had, even once. Yet both times, he was sure she meant no harm in her efforts to help. And both times he had reacted the same when she repented.

He was either getting soft, or...

Never mind the either.

****

She bunched her hands. Her fingers fairly itched to touch him again. He'd kissed her, and she'd responded like a rabbit in heat. Her control, or what passed as control, had succumbed in an instant. Sassy would laugh her rear off. *If* she could tell her about it. Guess

119

that was one good thing about the rules.

She drifted off for a while, waking to a gentle nudge.

He held out the binoculars. "You still want to take a turn? It's been an hour."

She attempted to focus on the small black instrument, then stretched her arms in front of her. "Sure. Where do I watch?"

He pointed all around them. "Pretty much anywhere you can see. Concentrate on the area that separates the parking lot from Jonathan Chase's property. It's on the other side of the hedge and is guarded by Dobermans. If trouble comes, it'll probably come from that direction."

The muscle tightening in his jaw caused an instant dislike for Jonathan Chase to take root within her.

"Do you know how to focus binoculars?" Danny asked.

She brought them to her eyes. "It's the knob in the center, right? Wow!"

"What is it? What do you see?"

"Oh, nothing. Sorry. The clarity surprised me, that's all."

He smiled. "What did you expect?"

She lifted a shoulder. "I thought they were, you know, regular binoculars. Everything's much sharper."

He leaned back and closed his eyes. "They're night vision equipped. Remember the rules."

"Emblazoned on my brain. Your lap dry yet?"

"Wanna check it?"

"You're a sad man, Tarantino."

He arched an eyebrow without opening his eyes. "Just pay attention."

She eagerly scanned the lot. Slowing as the hedges came into view. After three or four passes, the glamour waned. But he was right; she'd invited herself and insisted on helping. So she'd give it her best shot. Especially since he'd been so patient with her.

A movement behind the hedges made her suck in her breath as glowing eyes shone in the spiky blackness of the hedge. It creeped her out until she figured it was one of the guard dogs.

A half hour into her turn, she took a break and watched Danny for a few minutes. She thought he might pretend to sleep, but his breathing was deep and regular. The feeling of proprietary closeness toward him surprised her. She sighed. It was no longer a question of a vacation indulgence, she realized, but of a possible commitment to a relationship.

She wouldn't lose sight of the buy-in to the partnership, but the attraction she and Danny had for each other was becoming important, fast. The next few days would tell on both counts.

He shifted in his sleep, turning to face her. In order to overcome the temptation to lean in and kiss him, she took up the binoculars.

The last part of her shift was boring, and at eleven o'clock she softly touched his shoulder. "Danny."

There was enough light from the cloud-smeared moon for her to see him smile and reach for her, his eyes still closed.

"No, you don't. We're here on business, remember?"

He opened his eyes and let his arms drop. "Must've been dreaming." Rotating his head to stretch his neck, he sighed. "Which means I fell asleep. Guess I needed it, thanks. Anything interesting happen?"

"Not really. I saw what I assume was one of the guard dogs on the other side of the hedge. Creepy glowing eyes."

Her observation was punctuated by two car alarms starting nearby. She stared in the direction of the sounds but saw no one. She reached to push the seat forward.

Danny took her arm. "Stay here."

He pushed out of the car, and she grabbed the binoculars to watch helplessly as he faded into the darkness.

Chapter Fifteen

It couldn't have been longer than a minute, but Pallas's fingers tightened on the binoculars to the point of pain.

The parking valet must have called for help. He and two white-coated kitchen staff charged onto the scene. As they reached the area where Danny had gone, he emerged supporting an older man. Danny spoke to the employees, and they took over, helping the man toward the club.

She eased her grip on the binoculars as Danny spoke briefly to a woman who came out to deactivate her car's alarm. As he approached Bru's car, she forced herself to take full breaths.

He opened the door and stuck in his head. "Let's call it a night."

She nodded and scooped up the items he'd brought in the blanket.

He held it out and rolled them up before leaning in to kiss her cheek. "You waited."

"Rules," she said, not telling him how hard it had been. She scooted out. "What happened?"

He shook his head. "A customer came out to get a wrap for his wife and stumbled, dropping his keys. When he tried to catch himself, he bounced off his car and the one next to it, which belonged to his sister. He set off both alarms."

She squeezed his fingers. "We should have known it wouldn't be that easy. Want me to run interference for you? It's a lot brighter inside."

He shifted to hold his jacket in front of him and indicated the blanket. "Going to put this stuff in my car in case Bru's still here."

She nodded. "Guess I'll head back to the hotel."

"Are we still on for breakfast?"

She brightened. "Nine sharp."

On her way back to the hotel, she tried to sort the feelings whirling through her. No doubt about it, Danny Tarantino was the most exciting, interesting, sexy man she had ever met. And it wasn't just due to his current situation. He approached life the way she did, giving it everything he had. He was his own driving force, and it was wicked hot.

Unfortunately, he lived 200 miles away from everything she'd established for herself. What had happened to pop in, get the money and the truth about her dad, and pop out? Especially since Danny had never indicated anything remotely resembling permanence. She rubbed the furrow on her forehead and concentrated on her drive.

****

Danny woke with a positive slant on things. He'd not received a note or had anything bad happen yesterday. Even Bru's car had escaped stain-free. Best of all, he was going to have breakfast with Pallas. Dinner, too, if she could make it.

Although, if she showed up in another little slip of a dress—he shook his head. The smartest thing was to have dinner in the dining room, contrary to the picture he'd already presented of them eating in his quarters.

Less pressure. Yep, things were definitely looking up.

He showered and dressed, then picked up the phone. His mother answered on the second ring.

"Hello."

"Hi, it's Danny."

"Danny, who?"

He grinned. "I talked to you Sunday, Mom."

"Saturday, but who's counting?"

"Apparently, you," he teased. "I called to ask if it's okay to bring a friend with me tomorrow."

"Is it that pretty redhead your father has been talking about?"

"Yes. Her name's Pallas Mulroney."

"You've only known her two days, and she's Irish. This is a girl I've got to meet. Of course. Invite her."

He laughed. "I can hear the cogs in your brain turning from here. You harass me on a regular basis about the absence of women in my life. This one happens to be special. And I'm sure she can take care of herself when it comes to interrogations."

"Special?"

"As you pointed out, it's only been two days, so I'm committing to nothing. Can't you be happy Dugan and Susan are ready to make you a grandmother?"

His mother sighed. "The more the merrier?"

"One step at a time, Mom. We'll be there about eleven. And don't fuss."

"It's what I do best. Bye."

He hung up and went to find his pastry chef to get her recommendation for Tahoe's best bakery.

Packing some croissants, he still arrived at Suttons fifteen minutes early.

She answered her door in a short silk kimono. The

turquoise, red, and gold colors looked killer on her. And the light dusting of freckles that disappeared down her collar fascinated him. It apparently didn't fluster her to be caught early, either.

She smiled. "Come in. I'll be a few more minutes." She pointed to a tray with coffee fixings. "Go ahead and make the coffee, if you wouldn't mind. There are some spreads for the croissants in that sack. I like mine sweet." With that, she went into the bathroom.

He started the coffee, then looked around for coasters. His gaze fell on the notepad by the phone. He picked it up, glancing at a telephone number and three words, *partners, 1:00,* and *fight*. A prickle tightened his scalp. Looked like it referred to the partnership Pallas was trying to buy into.

He wondered briefly why the fight and what she would do if she lost. Damn. She wanted that partnership, and he was too strapped for resources to help.

"Interesting reading?"

He hadn't heard her come out and was a little embarrassed at having been caught. "I was looking for coasters for the coffee cups." He held out the slip of paper. "Trouble with the partnership offer?"

She smiled wryly and nodded. "My qualifications are in question."

"That Charles guy have anything to do with it?"

Her answer held no condemnation. "Most likely."

He tamped down the urge to find the rat and break his nose. On second thought, having been cut loose by Pallas, the guy was probably miserable enough. "Wish I could help."

She shrugged. "Actually, I've worked out a very

effective approach to any objections they might have. If it falls through, I can always stay where I am now. The money's good. Thanks for the moral support, though."

Stay here, did she really say stay here? His blood zinged in his veins. Until he figured out she meant stay at her current firm in San Francisco. He crashed. "But you'd rather have the partnership."

She smiled. "Yes, I think I would."

Another frisson of hope. She said *think*. That meant her decision was not set in concrete. He had to stop thinking so literal. It would drive him crazy.

He watched her walk to the table. She wore a cream silk tunic over straw-colored slacks. The tunic was cinched at the waist with a gold belt. Clear, blue-green stones set in gold hung at her ears and repeated in a matching bracelet. She looked beautiful.

She slipped the note into her purse and sat down. "How about you? Everything okay at Over the Moon?"

"As of half an hour ago."

She tilted her head, looking at him through dark lashes. "Good. If it stays that way and you're free, I'd like you to come with me to my niece's baptism this Saturday. It starts at two. My folks are coming, and we're going to dinner afterward."

Danny considered the implications. They had separately arranged to meet each other's parents after only a short acquaintance. He already wanted to be around her, felt comfortable with her, and God knew he wanted to sleep with her. Something elemental was happening, but he didn't want to name it just yet.

"I'd like that," he said. "Now it's my turn. I'm taking a couple of hours to go out to my folks for lunch tomorrow. Will your stint at the tournament start late enough for you to come, too?"

A smile lit her face. "I play from two to six today and tomorrow. As long as I'm back on time, I'd love to."

Her immediate acceptance brought him a ridiculous measure of satisfaction. "Pick you up at ten thirty, then," he said.

Danny couldn't remember ever having breakfast with a date, and whether it was his frame of mind or the company, he felt more relaxed than he had in days.

Too soon, he looked at his watch. "I have to meet Derrick this morning and my friend on the force this afternoon. Did you decide if you could make it tonight? I need to be in the dining room during dinner, but I'll bribe you with a Moon Goddess if you'll hang out with me on my deck later."

He knew from the smile in her eyes she'd be there.

Chapter Sixteen

Danny's sense of well-being carried over to his meeting with Derrick Van Howe. Derrick and he had worked security together for a few years, and he'd stood up for him once in a questionable bust. The big man had not forgotten the gesture.

"I like your place," Derrick said. "I bought a house not too far from here last year, but haven't gotten to spend much time in it. Going to fix that, soon. I sold my surveillance group."

Derrick looked like a body builder, or a Navy SEAL with his blond hair in a military cut, but he'd parlayed a small investigation service into an international group with offices in New York, Los Angeles, London, and Hong Kong.

Danny laughed. "So that leaves you with your body guard, electronics, and casino security training groups. What're you going to do with all your free time?"

Derrick nodded. "Right now, help out a friend."

"Thanks." Danny outlined his problem, including the contents of the notes. "There are only coincidences to support it, but my gut feeling is that somehow my esteemed neighbor, Jonathan Chase, is behind this. He tried every legal avenue to get my project canceled and doesn't miss an opportunity to wedge in more complaints. Now that I'm here, someone doesn't want me to stay, and he's the most obvious."

"What are the coincidences?"

"The parking lot fiasco took place at the edge of his property, and the perp seemed to vanish from there. Also, I was entertaining on my deck a few nights ago, and unless we were observed somehow from the water, the only way anyone could have seen us is through binoculars from the deck on his house. And yet my date was told we'd been seen. I need to know if there's a connection between the guy who saw us, Elliott Kerr, and Jonathan Chase. Tony's looking into it, too, but you can always get a little dirtier."

Van Howe didn't deny it. "What have you got on Kerr?"

He pulled a piece of paper from his desk. "He and three others decided to hang in there after the car accident even though I told them it was dangerous. They played at Jimmy G's until I received the second and third notes. I have no idea where he is now, but he's the only lead I've got." He slid the paper across to Derrick. "Here's a copy of the contract he filled out."

As Derrick scanned the contract, Danny cleared his throat. "I can only afford you for a couple of days."

A smile that included his green eyes appeared on the man's face as he looked up. "No charge. I just helped a Costa Rican gambling consortium get out from under the pressure of their Japanese competition. Their generous payment has given me a couple of free days, and you happen to be next on my list."

Danny knew better than to argue. He stuck out his hand. "Thanks, I owe you."

Van Howe shook his hand and stood. "I've got a plan to work in the lot tonight. Talk with you tomorrow morning."

****

His meeting with Tony Mancusco went along the same lines. He gave his views on Kerr, then asked, "Anything new?"

Tony nodded. "About what we expected. The handwriting on the notes and the paper manufacturer appear to be the same on all three. One oddity, though. Whoever used the stationery for the threats had carefully cut it across the top. We're betting there was a monogram there."

Danny sipped his coffee. "I noticed that on the first note. Our guy must have access to some custom stuff. Maybe he's using it to flaunt a connection he has, although I really don't think he's that clever. I think it's just handy."

Mancusco nodded. "Yep." He shifted in his chair. "Jonathan Chase has a lot of friends in this town. We'll do some discreet digging about any ties to Kerr, but officially we'll have to pretty much nail the damn lid on before we can make any formal accusations."

This was a pet peeve of Danny's, and one of the reasons he hadn't gone into law enforcement. "People with the big bucks and friends have to be handled with kid gloves, right?"

It was a sore point with Tony, too, and Danny knew he fought it from the trenches.

Tony sighed. "We both know influential people are treated differently. Chase was part of a very exclusive group in this town for years. People that still have a say about who do and don't get their buttons pushed by us." He winked. "Besides, Bru told me a blind man could feel the heat coming off you when you're around Ms. Mulroney. The fact that someone said you were cozy doesn't take much imagination."

He shrugged. "That may be, and I'll talk to Bru about sharing his observations, but Kerr told Pallas he *saw* us together on my deck. That's pretty specific."

Tony stood. "I know this is driving you nuts, but don't wade in over your head. I hate getting bad news. Especially about friends."

Danny made no promises, and he knew Tony didn't expect any. "Derrick is working this for the next two days. If nothing breaks, or someone else gets hurt, all bets are off."

The lieutenant shook his head. "Had to say it."

"You know I'm careful."

"Yeah."

****

Pallas scribbled notes to herself as she finished the Cobb salad from room service. She'd done extensive research on the people offering the partnership when the subject had first come up and documented some interesting facts. That being said, it didn't mean she wasn't nervous.

At one o'clock sharp she called the number left for her yesterday. "Hello. This is Pallas Mulroney."

Phil Brennan's assistant responded. "Mr. Brennan is expecting your call."

Pallas let out a held breath. Good. Phil Brennan had put the partnership concept together. She thought he was a fair man.

"Ms. Mulroney. Thank you for your promptness." The voice sounded slightly hollow. She was on speakerphone.

"You're welcome. Your message indicated concerns about my qualifications. I thought that had all been covered in the pre-offer interviews."

"True, all the formal questions were answered satisfactorily. However, some new information has come to light that we would like to discuss."

She played with the edges of the notes in her lap. "What kind of information? And may I ask who else is on this call?"

"The clarification we're looking for is of a personal sort. Here with me are the other partners and Mr. Wyatt."

Charles hadn't wasted any time. She rolled and unrolled the edges of her notes with her free hand. Even though she didn't think her resources for the partnership money was any of their business, one good thing would be realized. They would know exactly the type of person they were bringing in. If the call was successful. "Thank you. What are your questions?"

"It's been brought to our attention that you intend to raise the money for the partnership offer by gambling."

"That's correct. I'm playing in a sanctioned poker tournament here in Lake Tahoe this week."

"Have you considered the impact on our reputation if word got out our firm is being funded by gambling profits?"

She hesitated. Her answer could keep her afloat or sink her. "I have. And it's my considered opinion that if handled right, it could enhance our position."

An undercurrent of low voices, then Phil Brennan. "How so?"

"By its very nature, venture capital investing is a gamble. My plan all along has been to bring in large amounts of money. That money, for the most part, will have been earned by men and women taking a gamble on a product or service they made available to the world. I believe that type of investor might actually get a kick out of it."

"Uh, thank you for your views," he said. "I'm going to put you on hold for a moment."

Followed by nothing. She'd give a lot to be a fly on the wall during their discussion.

After a few anxious minutes, she heard the click of reconnection. "We're back. Ms. Mulroney, although we don't have one hundred percent agreement, the majority of us accept your unorthodox method."

"Thank you very much."

She heard a smile in his voice. "I'm curious. Did you think this call would go your way?"

She let her voice reflect her happiness. "Personally, I never saw a problem. Everyone gambles. Your own forefathers gambled by investing in railroads, gold mines, and commerce over a hundred and eighty years ago."

A number of chuckles and one harsh whisper ensued. She thought she also heard, "don't be a pompous ass."

"I see you've done your homework," Brennan said. "We wish you the best of luck and will welcome you into the firm should you decide to accept the offer. Most of us do, because we like your style and wouldn't want to go up against you in negotiations for clients."

Pallas grinned, and her free fist shot up. "Thank you. Is there anything else?"

The smile in his voice continued. "On a personal level I congratulate you on your research skills. If your poker playing skills are half as good, I'd like a few tips.

I can also tell you we intend to work you very hard at Brennan, Stone, Compton, Wyatt, and Mulroney."

She let a laugh escape. "Thanks again and good-bye."

"Good-bye."

She replaced the receiver, did a touchdown dance, then flopped back on the bed. It was all going her way. Life was good.

Soon after the euphoria, a wave of doubt rolled in. The reason life seemed so good right now was also due to Danny Tarantino. It occurred to her that when she considered her career, thoughts of him slipped in, but when she thought about Danny, there was room for nothing else. She sighed. She believed when her inner voice talked, she should listen. And her inner voice had been chattering about Danny almost non-stop.

She pulled her herbal mask out of the little refrigerator. If she was going to be in top form for the afternoon's games, she needed to relax.

The four hours of play went very well. She won a hundred eleven thousand dollars. Added to her winnings from yesterday, her grand total put her on schedule for the money she needed for the partnership. It looked to be a close match between herself and another young player. Two of the original players dropped out, leaving five. She figured the look-alike guy would be next.

It was a day for victories, and she had one more to gain.

Back in her room, she knew the dress to wear tonight. A quick shower and she slipped into a copper-colored sheath with a triangle-shaped cut-out, the peak starting just below her collar bones. It had sheer sleeves and thin velvet piping at the cuffs. She finished with dressy black patent leather heels and matching evening bag, twirled once in front of the mirror, and left.

Chapter Seventeen

Danny gravitated toward the gambling side of the club and glanced at the entrance every few minutes. He'd already given instructions for the details of their dinner, including assigning his best server to the area where he and Pallas would be sitting.

He'd seen Derrick earlier and felt confident the parking lot was secure. The only other ripple was a minor logistical problem at the bar. Mandy was sick, and Bru had called a friend for backup, but the guy was pretty inexperienced.

His first indication that someone special had arrived was the look on a dealer's face. He had his back to the door and had been called over to answer a question. As he responded, the dealer's gaze wandered, and his mouth went slack.

He turned and stopped short of whistling out loud—Pallas.

He went over and took her hand. "You look amazing."

"Thank you. You're looking pretty great yourself."

As they turned to walk into the dining room, she slipped her hand to rest on the inside of his upper arm. "I know I'm not mistaken. You looked disappointed when I came in. Why?"

"It showed?"

She laughed. "Like a flashing marquee."

Why did this woman make him feel like a kid with his hand in the cookie jar? "I was regretting changing the location of our dinner."

"I'll take that as another compliment."

He took a key ring from his pocket and steered them toward his office. "I have to make a quick wire transfer."

She followed him into the room and examined a watercolor hanging behind his desk while he used his cell phone to make the transaction. He ended the call and studied her profile, wishing he could kiss the soft part of her neck below her ear and any place else she would let him.

She glanced over. "Mary O'Brien. Your mother painted this?"

He looked at the whirling colors depicting a roulette wheel, craps spread, cards, and blackjack table all spinning together like *Alice Down the Rabbit Hole,* a story he'd never gotten tired of when he was little. "Yes. As a gift when I opened the club."

"She's very talented."

"I think so, too. She's self-taught." He stepped toward Pallas and took her hand. "Since I've condemned myself to sitting across from you in the dining room, may I have a kiss now?"

"I'd like that."

He leaned in and kissed the spot on her neck below her ear. Lifting his mouth fractionally, he said, "Thank you. Tell me again why we're waiting."

"Because you have to be in the dining room," she said softly. "And because I came hungry."

"Right." He sighed and looked at his watch. "Food."

She leaned back and smiled. "I have news worth celebrating, too."

Instinctively he knew she'd prevailed in the partnership call. "San Francisco is only four hours away by car and less than an hour by plane," he pronounced.

"How did you know that was the news?"

Good question, he mused. They were leapfrogging into each other's thoughts and finishing each other's sentences. That had never happened to him.

He ran a finger around her ear and down her neck, not wanting to break the closeness. "I've figured out over the last couple of days you usually get what you go after, and the partnership is important to you."

"So are you."

He stilled for a moment. His gut reaction was immediate and positive. He pulled back to stare into her eyes. "Does it scare the hell out of you, too?"

She nodded. "I guess we don't get to pick the time and place in our lives for what we're feeling. It sure complicates things, though."

"A major understatement." He grinned. "I suggest we let things take their natural course."

She stared at him, unblinking.

He put his arms around her and hugged, then put his cheek against her head. "I don't have an answer, but anything worth having is worth working through. Are you with me?"

Her answer was to lean back, gently place her hands on either side of his face, and kiss him tenderly. "Danny?"

"Mmmmm?"

"Let's make dinner a small celebration, then continue to your quarters."

He ached for wanting her, and with that came a certainty of all his feelings. They would somehow come to an arrangement about their conflicting life dreams. Later. They had to. He kissed her temple. "Okay."

The dining room was bustling when they entered. She waved to Bru as Danny guided her to the table. Their server brought over menus.

He wanted everything about this dinner to please her. "Would you like a drink?"

"Maybe a Moon Goddess to start, then a small glass of wine with dinner." She moved her gaze to the table top. "I want to remember details."

Since it would be juvenile to jump up and do the Snoopy Dance, he smiled and reached for her hand.

Bru brought the drinks over. Danny's usual ginger ale and a Moon Goddess for Pallas. "You guys are such a cute couple. Enjoy." He winked and left.

Pallas looked at Danny's glass. "Ginger ale?"

"Yep."

"How come you don't indulge?"

"I do. But I figured out a long time ago it doesn't pay to drink around patrons. Besides, I like remembering details, too." He raised his glass. "*Slainte.*"

She looked delighted by the Irish toast and raised her glass for a healthy sip.

The transformation was terrifying. Her eyes widened in shock, and her skin paled to parchment. She sucked in a gasp and set her glass down hard before clutching her temples. "I seem to be having a bad reaction…"

He stood and reached for her as she slid to the floor.

Chapter Eighteen

Danny shouted, "Call 911," over his shoulder and went to his knees beside her.

A female hand gently but firmly pulled at his shoulder. "My name is Elise Tomlinson. I'm a registered nurse practitioner. Let me help."

It took all the power he had to leave Pallas's side, and he only moved because her eyes fluttered open.

The woman studied her watch as she took Pallas's pulse. "Can you sit up?"

Pallas squeezed her eyes shut. "My embarrassment is exceeded only by this horrendous headache." She tugged at her short skirt, then raised herself to a sitting position against her chair.

His heart thudded. He'd never been so scared in his life. "Pallas, honey, can you hear me?"

She nodded and opened her eyes. "Did I have a stroke or something?"

The nurse took her hands. "Your pulse is a little high. Can you tell me your name?"

"Pallas Mulroney."

"That's a pretty name. Pallas, can you push my hands together?"

He watched as Pallas focused on the woman, then pushed at the hands she held about a foot apart.

"Good," the woman said. "Let's help you stand."

Pallas reached for him, and he pulled her up,

supporting her weight. He spoke to the nurse. "Is it okay if I take her to my quarters in the back?"

The woman looked at the ring of staring patrons. "I'm sure she'd appreciate it."

Bru stepped around him. "EMTs are on their way."

"What?" Pallas said. "No. I'm feeling much better." She looked down. "I've lost a shoe."

Danny bent and took off her other shoe. "Do this for me, please. I need to know you're okay." He looked at the nurse. "It's worth a bottle of *Dom Pérignon* for a few more minutes of your time."

She smiled. "Not necessary. Your friend looks like she's recovering, but I'll stand by until the EMTs get here."

As they headed for his quarters, Danny jerked his head at Bru. "Set aside our drinks and everything used to make them. Show the EMTs back when they arrive."

Bru nodded and veered off to the bar.

They entered his quarters, and he helped her to his couch. He noticed she was still a little shaky. "Anything I can get you? A drink of water, cold washcloth, a blanket?"

She shook her head. "No, thanks, on all counts. I really do feel better."

"That's good news," a woman's voice said from the doorway. "But we'll take a look as long as we're here."

He stood and moved around behind the couch, making room for two uniformed medical technicians. He reached down and took her hand. "Your color's back, but cooperate, okay?"

She took a deep breath. "Okay."

He spoke to the woman in the lead. "You got here

fast. Thanks."

She grinned. "Thank the drunk we patched up in the parking lot of the bar down the road. The call came in when we were right by your driveway." She acknowledged the nurse. "Hi, Elise. What's the good news?"

"Hi, Sheila. This is Ms. Mulroney. She passed the hand strength and recognition of her surroundings test. She's also looking much better than a few minutes ago, but you should probably check her out anyway." She nodded at Danny. "I'll get back to my dinner."

"It's no doubt cold," he said. "Have your server bring you new plates and drinks of your choice. On the house."

She grinned. "My husband's going to like a free birthday dinner. Best to your girlfriend."

The EMT sat on the edge of the coffee table across from Pallas and took out a pencil and clipboard. Her short navy jacket sported a nametag that read S. O'Hearn. "Can you say and spell your name and give me your address?"

"Pallas Mulroney. P-a-l-l-a-s-m-u-l-r-o-n-e-y. I'm visiting from San Francisco and staying at Suttons."

"Okay, Irish. Dispatch said you passed out in the dining room. Do you remember what happened before that?"

"I didn't really pass out. I slid sideways off my chair. I'd taken a sip of a Moon Goddess when I got a sudden blinding headache, and the room started to spin."

The woman looked to him for clarification. "Moon Goddess?"

He nodded. "The club's signature drink. I asked the

bartender to set her glass and the ingredients aside."

The EMT refocused on Pallas. "How many drinks did you have before that?"

Pallas looked tired and a little annoyed. "None."

S. O'Hearn swept a light across her eyes, then wrote something on the form she was filling out. Next, she took Pallas's pulse. "Your heart rate is a little high, but not erratic."

Pallas blushed. "What I feel is foolish. Nothing like this has ever happened to me. I'm very healthy as a rule."

The EMT nodded as she fitted a blood pressure cuff around Pallas's arm and pumped the bulb. "That takes care of my next question. How about medications? Have you had any change in your regular medicines that may have reacted violently with alcohol ingestion? Any heart or blood thinner medicines? Any allergies? How about a history of migraines?"

"No, to all," Pallas said.

"Hmmm. Your blood pressure is lower than average. Is that normal for you?"

"I honestly don't know."

"Do you do recreational drugs?"

"No."

The technician spoke to him. "I heard you say her color was coming back. Did she pale significantly during the episode?"

"Yes," Danny said. "The difference was startling."

The woman made a few more notes, then helped her partner put away the equipment he had pulled out before addressing Pallas again. "You seem to be coming around nicely. I don't think there's a need to transport you, unless, that is, you want to?"

Pallas shook her head. "You've all been very kind, but this little adventure has sucked out every last ounce of energy. I just want to go back to the hotel and sleep."

"Then I recommend you see a doctor tomorrow if you can, or get yourself down to emergency right away if you have a repeat episode."

Danny held onto Pallas's hand. "Could this have been caused deliberately?"

The EMT showed no surprise at his question. "Yes. There are a number of drugs that would bring about this kind of an immediate reaction, and from which a healthy person would recover quickly. Unfortunately, most of them dissipate in the system and aren't traceable unless you know what to look for."

She gave him a quizzical look. "If you suspect your friend's drink was tampered with, you need to report it to the authorities and have the contents analyzed."

"I intend to."

The county employees left, and Bru came in. He looked pale and kept pulling a bar towel through his fingers.

Pallas patted the seat beside her. "Sit down. You look worse than me."

Danny sat facing them. He pinned his gaze on Bru. "Did you lock away the ingredients and what was left in Pallas's glass?"

The bartender nodded.

Pallas held up her hands. "You really think this was intentional?"

Danny rubbed his fingers up and down his forehead. "With everything that's been going on here, I wouldn't be surprised."

Bru slid his hands along his pants. "So do you

think this was aimed at you or Pallas specifically? Or whoever they could get to and they just got lucky it was someone close to you?"

The thought made his stomach drop. He turned to Bru. "Think carefully. What happened out there?"

Bru shrugged. "I've gone over it in my head a dozen times. I saw you go to your table and fixed your drinks. Then Greg got a request for a Rainforest Buzz. He didn't know how to make one, so I went down to show him. I wasn't gone for more than forty-five seconds, tops."

Danny edged closer. "Do you remember anyone leaning near our drinks? Anyone at all?"

Bru closed his eyes and pinched the bridge of his nose. "It was so crowded. There were a dozen customers at that end of the bar. It was a blur of noise and people." He blinked. "Wait a minute. A few of the tournament players were hanging out there. Lou asked me if there was any news on catching the guy who'd been threatening you. But Lou wouldn't…"

"No," Danny said. "Lou wouldn't. Which of the other players were there?"

"Del, for sure, and Ty. Maybe one or two others. Everyone was talking about the crazy goings on. That's all I can remember," Bru said, shaking his head. "Sorry, man."

Pallas patted Bru's arm. "Hey, it's not your fault. I'm almost good as new. Only tired. Whatever zapped me went away pretty quick."

Danny ran a hand through his hair, then shot to his feet. He'd exposed his patrons and especially Pallas to danger. "I've been stupid to let down my guard because I didn't get a threatening note yesterday."

"Not true," Bru said. "The cops and Van Howe are both working this with you. I'm the stupid one. I should have been paying more attention."

Pallas held up her hands. "Guys, guys. The next time I'm in the dining room, I'll have to wear a disguise. This whole thing has hurt my independent woman image."

Both men stared at her.

"Well, it has." She turned to Bru. "How did you explain my dramatic exit?"

Bru actually blushed.

"Uh, oh," she said. "I'm not sure I want to hear this."

"Bru?" demanded Danny.

The bartender straightened defensively. "It caught me off guard, you know. The only thing I could think of was when my sister was pregnant. She fainted a couple of times."

She aimed an indignant gaze at Danny, and he tried unsuccessfully to keep his lips from turning upward.

"What?" he asked.

Bru's answer had broken the tension, but she looked appalled. "Nice try," she said. "It's not funny."

"Too late for that," Bru choked out. He levered himself off the couch and away from her reach quickly. "I'm sure Greg's overwhelmed. Gotta go. Get better."

Danny cleared his throat. "I'm taking her back to her hotel. Come into my office when things slow down out there."

Bru nodded. "Sure."

She stood slowly. "See. No residual effects. I can drive myself back."

He moved to her side. "I'm driving you. End of

discussion. But not until you get something in your stomach. Humor me and sit down while I bring in a couple of plates from the kitchen?"

She nodded. "All that dizziness on an empty stomach. Not a good match. Okay, I'll eat."

He watched her for signs of recurring distress while they ate. He couldn't help it. When she'd slumped to the floor in the dining room, he'd never felt so powerless. At what exact moment had the club become less important than her? *Be careful what you wish for,* his dad used to say. *You just might get it.* Danny figured he was way beyond that.

"You're staring again."

"I know. Sorry."

She laughed. "I promise to give you plenty of warning before I pitch over next time."

He knew she was kidding, but it unnerved him anyway. "Let me call my mother. Her GP's receptionist is a good friend of hers. I bet they could squeeze you in tomorrow morning."

He saw the refusal coming before she shook her head.

"No, thanks."

"But the EMT said…"

She returned his stare. "She used the word recommend as I recall. You're not going to bug me about this, are you?"

"Is there a chance I might change your mind?"

"None."

"Can we discuss this stubborn streak of yours?"

Her look turned wry. "Next you'll be telling me I also have a temper because my hair is red."

"No comment." He could see she was tired.

Smudges deepened under her eyes, and she'd yawned twice in the last five minutes.

"Got your other shoe. Time to get you to bed," he said, bending over to pick them up and dangle them.

Finely shaped eyebrows arched at his pronouncement.

He leaned over his small dining table. "Don't go there. I've never taken advantage of a helpless woman, but that waif look you're giving off is tempting."

She gave a ladylike snort. "You only think you want me well-rested."

He drove to Sutton's slowly, watching as Pallas laid her head back, relaxed. At one point he nearly panicked because of her shallow breathing. He pulled over, his own breath caught and held until he saw she was deep asleep. Finally, they arrived, and he escorted her to her room.

"I'll have your rental driven back tonight and the keys left at the front desk. Let me know if you want to cancel lunch at my folks. I'll understand."

She poked him in the chest. "Give me the number in your quarters, and if I have a restless night, I'll call you every time I wake up."

He grinned. That was more like it. "Okay, okay, I was only trying to be sensitive to your ordeal."

She pulled him to her for a lingering kiss. "Put that in your sensitive pipe and smoke it."

He wrapped her in his arms. "Maybe I was too hasty in canceling the interesting part of our evening."

She dropped her head to his shoulder. "Oops, that used up all my energy. Sorry." She raised her face to kiss his chin. "Tomorrow at ten thirty, then."

"All right, tomorrow."

149

Chapter Nineteen

He ticked off the list in his head on the way back to the club. The notes, the tournament, the tampered brake line, the damaged cars, Pallas's drink, his inability to get a handle on whoever was tormenting him. He hit the dash with the side of his fist. A connecting thread ran through it, but he'd be damned if he could figure out what it was. His gut told him there was a lot more history involved, but he had no starting place.

And then there was Pallas.

He smiled and nodded to the patrons who tried to wave him over as he skirted the tables in the dining room. He unlocked the door to his office to find Derrick sitting in the chair across from his desk. He looked stupidly at the keys in his hand. "Guess I need to upgrade my locks. This type is only supposed to keep out mortals."

"Pathetic" was the one word reply from the security specialist.

Danny pulled off his loosened tie and sat down. "Anything break?"

Derrick grinned. "Got the plate numbers on every car that came into your lot. Unless your hitter can beam himself in and out at will, we should be able to narrow down the field by early tomorrow afternoon. By the way, sorry to hear about your lady friend. Bru pointed her out to me. That is one fine redhead. She feeling better?"

"Yeah, thanks. We aren't sure the drink spiking wasn't meant to be random. I'm having the contents analyzed, but from all appearances, the reaction was temporary and geared to scare the hell out of me. Which is what it did. Tell me about your theory."

The big blond flipped open a small palm unit. "Nobody left in a hurry tonight except for a few staff and regulars. No customer's car was a repeat of Monday night's. The cops wrote down the plates of all the cars in the lot when they were here investigating the ones sprayed with acid. Tony gave me a copy of the list. When we run the lists for owners, we can eliminate ninety-nine percent of the drivers."

"Anyone walk in from the road?"

Derrick shook his head. "Nor by boat or parachute."

Danny rubbed the back of his neck. "I want to see the lists so I can scrub them for past associations that didn't end friendly."

"You're thinking this is personal."

"About as personal as it gets." He glanced at his watch. "As of about an hour and a half ago."

****

"You look pissed."

He nodded at Tony Mancusco, squinting over his friend's shoulder at the sun sparkling on the lake. "I don't care if you are a cop. Who let you in? And yeah, I'm pissed, mostly at myself. And how come you're out here so early?"

His friend took another sip of coffee. "Bru. Because the coffee on your deck is much better than that at the cop house and because I have an extremely efficient partner. She read last night's call-ins and knew I'd want to talk to you, so she intercepted my commute, and here I am."

Danny liked Tony's partner, a savvy woman named Barbara who was married to another cop. "Can you speed up the analysis of the drink samples I turned over to the deputy last night?"

Tony shook his head. "The queue for the lab is huge." He shrugged. "I can call in a giant favor, but it'll cost you."

Danny nodded once. "Agreed." His former stint as a casino security chief brought him into contact with some of the top names that played Tahoe hotels. The big favors came in the form of tickets when somebody's idol was booked into town.

"Let you know as soon as I hear anything. How's Derrick doing?"

"He's running a list of plates he took of visitors coming and going over the last twenty-four hours. Which includes, of course, the time in which Pallas was drugged."

Tony looked at him deadpan. "You've only known her for what, three days? In those three days your misery meter has gone off three times. You sure it was something in her drink?"

Danny figured his friend would get around to wondering if Pallas might be involved in the threats. The thought had also occurred to him, but he just couldn't believe she'd want to see him ruined. The dark part of his brain awoke. *Unless you count the money she needs for her partnership. How badly did she want that?*

"Positive."

His friend showed his surprise. "You already checked her out."

"Two days ago," Danny said. "Everything from San Francisco through her stay at Suttons."

Chapter Twenty

Pallas gave herself one last primp, then dialed her sister's number. Sassy picked up on the third ring.

"Hi, it's Pallas. Can I come for a visit?"

"Sure. Guess I can give up my fainting couch and put away the bonbons for a real live connection to the outside world."

"Wow, somebody needs a time-out."

Sassy sighed. "Life in the fast lane. Could you bring some designer decaf? I'm still nursing. Oh, and pastries for grown-ups? You know, without sprinkles or purple icing."

"You got it. I'll be there shortly."

She stopped at the front desk and got directions for a small pastry shop named *Tous du Ciel*. Her college French confirmed it was aptly named All About Heaven when she entered and inhaled. Their decaf even tasted real. A half hour later she pulled up to Sassy's house.

She knocked a couple of times and let herself in. "Sassy?"

"Back here."

She followed her sister's voice and walked into a very small bedroom where Sassy was adjusting her nursing bra. When she saw the pale green bags, her eyes rolled back. *"Tous du Ciel.* You're my new favorite sister. Make yourself at home in the kitchen. I'll be there in a minute."

She had finished setting out plates and forks when Sassy tiptoed in. "She's out for a couple of hours, and the girls are at school. Thank God you're a Mulroney. The big, strong, silent type I married never has any good gossip."

Pallas eyed her sister. "What makes you think I'm here to impart gossip?"

Sassy's gaze drifted to the larger of the paper sacks. "First, tell me what's in there."

"Beignets and almond-glazed croissants."

Sassy reached for the sack and ripped it down the middle, sighing. "They ought to sell these with those tiny tape measures. You know, before and after."

"Enough about you. Danny's picking me up at the hotel to have lunch with his folks at their place. I need a shot of Mulroney woman sense."

"Go," Sassy said around a mouthful of beignet, swiping at the powdered sugar that had drifted down the front of her shirt.

Pallas took a sip of coffee, gasping. She hadn't expected it to stay so hot. "Here's the deal. If I continue to win at my current rate, I'll have enough to buy the partnership." She took another, more careful sip. "The thing is, I'm becoming very fond of Danny Tarantino."

"Fond."

"Okay, bad word choice. When he walks into a room, every sex nerve I have starts pulsing. He is gorgeous, intelligent, hard-working, loves his mother, and is kind to small animals. Here's my question. Am I crazy to be thinking about throwing away the partnership, which is the biggest thing to come my way since acceptance at Stanford, or are my hormones right?"

Sassy reached for another pastry. "Let's see. Go after the perfect man or wear sensible shoes? If you only had one choice, my vote goes to Danny Tarantino, but—and this is as big a but as mine's going to be after I finish these pastries—why can't you have both?"

Pallas reached into the sack. "I'm still processing. What do sensible shoes have to do with it?"

Sassy nodded vigorously. "Say you buy the partnership. In your zeal to get ahead and try to forget him, you work fourteen-hour days, the time passes, you become rich, own cats, and pretty soon you're fifty, and the only people you have to leave any money to are your nieces, but you can't remember their names. You're also still hanging out with men like Charles and are now wearing sensible shoes." She threw out her arms, flinging powdered sugar. "I say go for broke."

Pallas felt her forehead furrowing. "Uh, that's quite a leap."

Sassy finished her second pastry and reached for Pallas's hand. "All kidding aside, if you think these feelings for him are real, do something about them. I still wake up in a cold sweat, remembering how I turned down Pat the first time he asked me out." She grinned. "Sex nerves, huh? Done anything about it yet?"

Pallas pulled back her hand and licked her fingers. "None of your sisterly business. But Danny and I might work something out."

Sassy rolled her eyes. "That sounds like a corporate merger. Give in to your urges, for cripe's sake."

"You're pretty free with my urges."

Her sister plunked another beignet onto Pallas's plate and grinned. "Yeah, well, you know what I mean.

And I meant it when I said you could have both. That's a goal worth shooting for. Besides, if the two of you get serious, we could have lots of girl talks." She leaned back and swallowed a yawn. "Anything else I can help with?"

She shook her head. "I was concentrating on having one or the other. Now I have to start all over." Her gaze lit on the window to the sunny backyard. "How are things in the Murphy household?"

"You mean besides the upcoming christening, the girls getting out of school next week, and I can't fit into half my clothes? Wonderful."

Pallas laughed. "On that note, I'll leave. Good thing we're going horseback riding before lunch. I need to burn a few calories." She stood and backed toward the door. "Before I forget, I invited Danny to the christening."

"Great," Sassy said. "But you're not going anywhere without the rest of those pastries. I can't be trusted. Besides, why'd you buy so many?"

Pallas winked. "I happen to know Pat has a sweet tooth, and I thought by putting two temptations in his path, you might work off a few calories yourself."

The corner of her sister's mouth turned up. "You already know the answer to your question, don't you?"

"Thanks for being my sounding board."

****

The mid-morning traffic was light on the way back to Suttons. Did she already have the answer as Sassy had surmised? A week ago, buying into any future but the one she'd worked so hard for would have been unthinkable. Had she wanted the partnership so badly because there was no one special in her life? She had a chance at both, but if she could only have one, the scales were tipping in Danny's favor.

She made it back to the hotel in time to brush her teeth and put on some lip gloss before he knocked on the door. She opened it and gave an appreciative glance. Jeans were made to be worn by this man. So were cowboy boots and work shirts. If she'd thought he looked sexy in a tux, his ranch clothes...

Pallas realized she was staring. "Come in."

She grabbed her jacket and purse to get out of the room before she turned shameless.

Danny, however, was not in a big hurry. "Slow down. What's the rush?" He studied her face, then wrapped her in his arms. "How are you feeling? I worried about you last night."

"Fine." She snuggled against him. "I took a couple of aspirin and slept great."

"You have lots of energy?"

She tilted her head back and saw his look of blatant need. "I do."

He brought his mouth to within a whisper of hers. "Hold that thought." Then he kissed her, and it was weak-knee time again. She slipped her hands into his back pockets to bring him closer. He ended the kiss. "Tell me again whose idea it was to have lunch under the watchful eye of my mother."

"You started it."

He kissed the tip of her nose, and the wistful glance he gave her bed was comedic. "Care to end up at my place tonight? Dinner at seven thirty?"

She picked up her jacket. "Dinner is my treat, casual dress, your deck, and it's a deal."

He did that wonderful thing with his eyebrow

again. "Done, but why the casual dress? Please tell me it's because they're quicker to…"

She put her free hand over his mouth and grinned. "Save it. It's going to be hard enough getting through this lunch without constantly thinking about dinner, and after."

Danny put his hand over hers and laced their fingers together. "You know, my mother's going to love you."

Chapter Twenty-One

The ranch house outside Minden was worlds away from the club, not just a fifteen-hundred-foot drop in elevation from deep mountain lake to low mountain valley. It had the same effect on him as his quarters—instant relaxation. At least it usually did, but the beautiful redhead sitting next to him pegged his stress meter. The physical one, anyway. He refocused on the house. Memories of growing up with his brother and parents and grandparents were strong and happy.

They got out of the car and crossed a gray and blue flagstone patio to the side entrance. Danny couldn't remember the last time he'd used the front door. This way led into the great room that included a spacious kitchen, dining, and seating area.

His parents were both in the kitchen. His mother had her back to them and was whisking something in a bowl she held. He put his fingers to his lips to shush his dad, then snuck up behind her. He peered in the bowl and swiped his finger quickly inside the rim.

Her frown locked on him as she turned, then she broke into a big smile and held up her cheek for a kiss. He obliged, then put his arm around her shoulders.

His dad ambled over to inspect the contents of the bowl. "How come I have to wait?"

His mother gave him a saucy look. "Because I feed you all the time. Now mind your manners. Our guest will think your fingers have been in all the ingredients for lunch."

She stretched some plastic wrap over the bowl, then wiped her hands on a towel tucked into her apron before crossing the room to greet Pallas. She took Pallas's extended hand into both of hers. "So you're the lovely girl my men have been talking about. It's nice to meet you."

Danny watched the two women, willing them to like each other. They were both slender and fair with pretty blue eyes, but Pallas was a few inches taller than his mother. His thoughts wandered for a moment, wondering if the gene for hair color was stronger for red hair or dark. No matter. Any child Pallas bore would be beautiful.

He brought himself up short, hoping his thoughts didn't show. He glanced at his father, who was watching him, grinning. Danny frowned and switched his attention back to Pallas.

She smiled. "It's nice to meet you, too, Mrs. Tarantino. If you cook as well as you paint, I'm in for a treat."

Mary Tarantino beamed with pleasure. "Call me Mary, please. You must've seen the painting in Danny's office. I'm glad you like it." She turned to him. "Why don't you show Pallas around, then go for a ride? Lunch will be ready in about an hour."

"Did you find your game?" Rick asked her.

Pallas smiled again. "Yes. Not the one I wanted, but it's proving profitable."

"If you play poker like you play blackjack, I'm not surprised." He turned to Danny. "Going to get in any practice today?"

He shrugged. "I'll show her the range. If she's interested, I'll give her a quick lesson. I can shoot a few rounds if there's time after that."

They walked outside, and he steered them toward a large shed. She had been playing in her tournament for two days, and he hadn't asked how she was doing. It sounded like she was winning. He should congratulate her but couldn't bring himself to put any heart in it. If she was successful this week, she'd leave, take up her busy partnership, and he'd probably never see her again. He tried not to think about it as he nodded toward a door. "This is the tack shed."

She put her hand on his arm, stopping. "What was that about practice and a range? Are you talking golf or guns?"

She was fast becoming his fiercest passion, and he wanted her to like his other interests as well. "Neither. I compete in archery."

He studied her expression for signs of dislike or disinterest, but she was only looking at him quizzically, with her lips slightly parted. He took the opportunity for a quick kiss.

She chucked him under the chin. "I thought you weren't competitive."

He ran his finger softly around her lips. "I enjoy the solitary aspect, and it's a great tension release." He leaned closer. "Although there are other, more preferable ways to release tension."

She turned pink and batted at his hand. "Your parents are probably watching and wondering at our rude behavior right under their noses."

He shook his head. "Nope. I think they'd approve. They're very affectionate. Dad's probably sneaking a kiss as we speak. Especially if Mom's hands are full. He used to get Dugan and me to help him. He'd send us into the kitchen with a knotted shoelace or other diversion, then come up behind Mom and grab her around the waist. As soon as she'd squeal, that was our signal to run and hide. Dad would come looking for us in about five minutes."

Pallas looked at him wide-eyed. "Sneaking up on women runs in the family?"

He started backing her toward the shed. "It not only runs in the family. It's expected."

"In that case," she said, glancing at the door, "I'll just wait out here."

He laughed. "No dice. Come in so you can pick out your tack."

She followed him inside and took a deep breath. "Nice."

He also appreciated the scent of well-oiled leather. He pointed to an older, hand-tooled saddle. "That's Mom's. Or you can borrow Susan's. She's due any day now, so it hasn't been used in a while. Neither of them will mind."

"Who's Susan?"

It surprised him that he hadn't shared his sister-in-law's name. He had to stop and remember Pallas had been part of his life for such a short time. "Susan is my brother Dugan's wife. They live here, too. Dugan does most of the day-to-day work of running the place. They're at the obstetrician's but will be back in time for lunch."

"Is this their first baby?"

"Yes. I think Mother's even more excited than they are. She'd like a roomful of grandchildren. The fact that she only has two sons isn't important."

Pallas nodded. "My mother's the same way, but so far Sassy's the only daughter who's accommodated her."

He started taking tack off the wall to keep his hands busy. She looked so damn sexy in those jeans and black boots. Come to think of it, he'd never seen her when he didn't want her. He was hopeless. "We're lucky to have the kind of parents we do. Want to go down to the stables and see your horse?"

She looked a little nervous. "I haven't ridden since college. Do you have one that's short and slightly lame?"

He was taken aback. "I get the lame part, but why short?"

"Closer to the ground."

He laughed out loud.

She lifted a shoulder. "It's like riding a bicycle, right?"

He hadn't laughed like this in days. It felt good. "We'll take it nice and slow." He wiggled his eyebrows. "But you'll have to repay my kindness."

"There are all kinds of reparation."

The room got warm. He pointed out the door with his free hand. "The stables are down that path between the trees. We'll bridle the horses, then bring them back to saddle up."

****

Pallas loved everything about the Tarantino ranch. Not the least of which was Danny's nearness. San Francisco was a distant, crowded, and right now, not-altogether-pleasant memory. It depressed her to think a week from today she would be pushing equity shares for a risky, but potentially profitable, venture.

She stole a glance at Danny as they walked down the path. *This is great, but don't get used to it,* her inner voice said. *Besides, you may be more attracted to him than any man in your sketchy dating history but not be sexually compatible.*

She sputtered a laugh. If she and Danny Tarantino weren't compatible, human chemistry didn't exist.

"What's so funny?"

She thought fast. "Remembering a theory in my college physics class."

He gave her a look of disbelief. "A physics theory? In relation to what?"

"The speed of a galloping horse in relation to how high I would bounce if I fell off."

He choked out a laugh but stopped walking. "If it bothers you that much, we can skip the ride."

"No, no. I'm just being silly."

"Okay, if you're sure." He reached for her hand, pulling her toward a row of well-kept stalls. "Here we are."

The overhang provided shade, and the day was warm. She could smell the hay and overturned earth somewhere nearby. Danny led her to a stall with a weathered wooden nameplate. It read *Cherry.* Inside was a beautiful bay mare. The horse rushed over to nuzzle him and whinny softly.

He scratched the mare between her ears and kissed the slope of her nose. "Hi, girl. Wanna go riding with a friend?" He turned to Pallas, slipping her a cube of sugar. "Give her this, and she's yours."

She held out the sugar on the flat of her hand. The horse slurped it up, and Pallas could swear her eyes rolled back. "Does she like cherries, too?"

He chuckled. "No. When she was a filly, her coat shone almost red in the sun. I named her Cherry."

He slipped the bridle on the mare and walked her out before handing the lead to Pallas. A few stalls away, a big black horse poked its head around the door and snorted loudly. He was magnificent and a little scary. Danny walked right up to him. The horse bobbed his head in greeting and took the sugar he offered.

Pallas huffed out a breath and swallowed. "Is he the one you're riding?"

Danny turned, his eyes shining. "Yes. An extravagance of mine. His name is Black Irish." He rubbed the horse's cheek briskly. "How did you know Black was male?"

She grinned. "Look at him. He couldn't be anything else."

Danny slipped a bridle on the black horse and led him to her. "Go ahead." He held out the reins. "Pet him. I won't let him hurt you."

She wanted to please Danny, so she patted Black. The horse bobbed his head and blinked. He was even more striking up close.

Danny grinned. "He likes you. Ready to go back to the tack room?"

She nodded and observed as they walked that horse and owner had a lot in common. Both were dark and handsome, had restless energy, underlying strength, and intelligent eyes.

She chose Mary's tack, and Danny saddled Cherry first so she could sit on her and get used to the horse while he finished with Black. He adjusted her stirrups and asked if she was comfortable with the reins. She nodded.

As Danny swung the heavy saddle onto his horse, she watched in admiration at the play of muscles in his shoulders and arms. Arms that she loved being held in. Weak sunshine glinted off his dark hair. Pallas had noticed both of his parents had the same rich shade but sprinkled with white.

That and they were a close-knit family, a nice thing to know about a man you cared for. That's what it all boiled down to. How much she cared about Danny Tarantino.

Somewhere along the line the idea that she could give up her future in San Francisco and establish herself in Tahoe had gained momentum. A life-changing decision based on no pronouncements from him but several self-realizations about her feelings. She knew they liked each other a lot, but he hadn't made nor pushed her to make a commitment. So where did that leave her? Not analyzing it to death, that's where. She'd enjoy his company while she had it and let things happen. One of which was tonight. Heat pooled inside her at the thought of making love to him.

He snapped his fingers. "Earth to Pallas. Are you with me?"

Warmth flooded her cheeks at being caught daydreaming. "Yes, I'm just appreciating the peace and quiet. It's a nice change from what I'm used to."

Cherry shuffled her feet and fell into step beside Black.

"It's a pretty big place," Danny said. "I thought we'd head for the range first."

They followed a dirt road that wound behind the stables, then dropped to border a large field with cattle in it. She couldn't get over the stunning backdrop provided by the Sierra Nevadas. San Francisco was a beautiful city, but it was a different kind of beauty.

She refocused quickly as Black broke into a trot and Cherry followed suit. After about five minutes, they slowed to a walk and entered a small gravel parking lot that fronted a long, narrow meadow ending with large mounds covered in dark blue tarps. Nearby was a metal shed on concrete footing.

Pallas felt a little wobbly after dismounting. She put her reins in Danny's extended hand. "Thanks."

"You okay?"

"Fine. Is this the archery range?"

He nodded, removing a bulky leather carrying case from Black. "It's not much, but it serves the purpose."

He leaned the bag against the building and unlocked the door before stepping inside to retrieve a large paper target.

She watched as he then pulled a slick bow from the bag.

Danny held it out. "Want to look it over while I set up the target?"

She reached for it. "Sure."

"I'll be back in a few minutes," he said and took off down the field.

She examined the bow. The center part was a compound of some kind. Pulley wheels at either end engaged the string. She held it up and tried to draw back the string, but it would barely budge. All in all it certainly wasn't what she'd expected.

He came back at a trot. "Want to give it a try? It'll be too long, but I can adjust the draw."

She handed it to him. "I would. It's beautiful."

"Come on, then."

They went to the shed where he produced some tools and made some changes to the tension. The side wall of the shed had a rack with arrows in it.

She studied the colorful feathering. "Are the colors customized?"

He glanced up. "Yes. The green, white, and red striped ones are mine. I have them made in the colors of the Italian flag."

"Clever. Ireland's flag is similar, except the last stripe is orange."

"So my mother tells me," he said, grinning. He handed her the bow, taking a leather loop full of his arrows from a shelf.

He stood behind her and patiently showed her where to hold her hands and the knack for keeping the bow level. She had a hard time concentrating with his warm breath on her cheek but made the effort. She shot a couple of arrows at the target, but they fell pitifully short. After her third try, she handed back the bow.

"Now show me how it's really done."

"You sure you're interested?"

She glanced at her watch. "Of course. We don't need to leave for another half hour."

His first shot bordered the center and next ring. The second and third were dead center and second ring.

She clapped. "That's incredible. You really are good."

He laid the bow on a nearby stump. He stepped toward her, and she could see the intent in his eyes.

"Thanks," he said. "What do I earn?"

She went into his arms. "Do you bring all your women out here to impress them?"

He kissed her. "I've only brought one woman out here."

She pulled his head down for another kiss, slid her thigh up his, and leaned in. Her action elicited a low-pitched groan.

His hand moved across her breast, and she quivered as she tried to press closer, past thinking about consequences.

His mouth moved close to her ear. "Pallas, honey. Are you sure you want this now?"

She froze. *Crap.* What the hell was she starting? In the middle of a gravel and dirt parking lot on his parents' ranch. She stepped back and saw undisguised need on his face, yet he'd asked if she was sure.

She shook her head. "I'm sorry. The waiting…the stress of the last few days. It seemed like a good idea…"

He blew out a huff of air, sliding his hands up and down her arms. "It's an excellent idea. And it's going to happen, but not now."

She nodded. "Bad timing." *Crazy woman pawing at him. No wonder he's backing off.*

He lifted her chin gently. "After last night, really bad timing. Otherwise, with your permission, I'd pull that clean blanket off Black and have my way with you, but someone's coming."

Chapter Twenty-Two

Pallas sprang back, pulling her jean jacket closed and pushing at her hair. She looked at Danny. He wasn't so lucky at hiding his arousal.

"It's our neighbor, Bud," he said, then tipped his head down the field. "We compete in the same category. I'll get a new target for him." He stepped inside the shed and took out a fresh target, holding it strategically.

She almost giggled until she saw the expression on the man who got out of the truck that pulled in. He wasn't especially happy to find them, or at least her, at the range. His smile looked forced.

She wasn't overjoyed at seeing him either.

The neighbor nodded at her but spoke to Danny. "New competition?"

"This is Pallas Mulroney. A good friend who's visiting Tahoe," Danny answered. "I was showing her the range. Pallas, this is our neighbor, Bud McKee."

Now that he was closer, she could see red-veined eyes and white compressed lips that the man was making to appear in control.

Bud stuck out his hand. "Nice to meet you."

She gave him a firm hand shake. "Same here."

The older rancher looked at Danny's bow lying on the stump. "If I'm interrupting, I can come back later."

Danny shrugged and held up the target. "Now's

fine. I only put in three. Do you want me to replace the target while I'm retrieving my arrows?"

"Not necessary," the older man said. "I'll take care of it."

"I heard Elaine wasn't responding to the new treatment as well as they'd hoped," Danny said. "I'm sorry."

Bud stiffened. "We're managing. Can I drop by the club later this afternoon? I need to talk to you in private."

Danny looked surprised. "Sure. Any time after three."

Relief crossed the other man's face. "That'll work. See you then." He nodded at Pallas. "Enjoy your stay."

"Thank you," she said as he walked back to his truck and pulled out a bag similar to Danny's.

Pallas handed Danny his bow and watched while he repacked it and put the case on Black.

****

Danny glanced at Bud. He could swear his friend was pretending to adjust his bow so he wouldn't have to talk. Things with Elaine must be worse than he thought.

Pallas laid her hand gently on his arm. "Your friend is hurting. I'm sorry."

She really was. Danny could see it in her eyes as she watched Bud consciously keep his back to them.

Danny wanted her to understand where Bud was coming from. "His wife is dying of cancer. They both worked hard to make their place turn a profit. Three years ago, they got an offer for some land they weren't using, and the price was huge. They even invested in Over the Moon. Elaine was diagnosed last December. They didn't have good insurance coverage, and the medical bills have wiped them out."

His jaw clenched. "My legal hassles drained any financial margin I might've used to help. Life sucks sometimes."

Pallas slipped her arms around him and laid her head on his shoulder.

That made him sadder. Even with his situation, he had so much, and his friend was losing everything. He hugged Pallas tightly, then they saddled up and left.

He held Black in check so the ride to the compound went slowly. All too soon Pallas would be subjected to his family's curiosity.

She looked more relaxed when they got out of sight of the range. She took a deep breath, staring straight ahead. "I guess we can be thankful Bud's interruption wasn't five minutes later."

The thought hadn't even occurred to him. "I could've explained you as an encounter with a wood nymph," he teased.

She blushed. "A very embarrassed wood nymph."

He shook his head. "My fault. You deserve better than a scratchy blanket on rough ground. I didn't have any protection, either, and that's plain stupid."

She shrugged, still not looking at him. "I wasn't exactly fending you off."

"I'll make it up to you," was all he could think to say. He felt like a first-class jerk, and it took the entire ride back to the compound for him to ease his, uh, stimulated condition.

They dismounted at the tack shed, and he put away the saddles. "Want to help stall the horses and rub them down?"

Her enthusiasm shone. "I've never done that. I'd

like to."

He grinned. Surprised she didn't get squeamish or think it would stink. "We should still have time to walk around my mother's gardens before we go in for the grilling."

She looked startled, then scrunched her nose. "I already know Rick, and it can't be any worse than trying to impress San Francisco's elite." She connected with his gaze. "It really matters if they like me."

He took the bridles and quickly secured them to a large hook, then pulled her into his arms. "They do count, that's why they'll understand how much you mean to me."

He loved the way she stared at him with those beautiful eyes when he gave her a compliment. He gave in for what, the fourth time today, and kissed her.

They walked the horses back and gave them a light rubdown before they went to the gardens.

"This is gorgeous," Pallas said. "There's so much color for this early in the season."

He nodded, reaching for her hand. He didn't care if anyone saw them from the house. "Mom's always been able to coax flowers and vegetables out most times of the year. Dad gave her a big greenhouse for Christmas last year for her starts."

She squeezed his hand. "Let's go in. I don't want to keep your family waiting. Besides, I'm starved."

****

Never be ashamed of your people or beginnings, her father had taught his girls. *Anybody you envy would most likely want to be in your shoes.*

She had always tried to follow his advice, but when they walked into the kitchen, and she saw Susan

Tarantino, it was hard. Susan was a petite, green-eyed natural blonde who looked like she might be carrying a few rolled up athletic socks under her maternity smock.

Mary came over and put her arm around Pallas but spoke to her son. "Shoo yourself into the den with your brother and Dad."

He winked at them and left.

Mary hugged Pallas. "Here she is, Susan. Didn't I tell you she was pretty?"

Susan walked over and held out her hand, smiling. "Hi, nice to meet you. Dugan and I have been looking forward to lunch ever since Rick mentioned Danny was bringing someone." She pulled her hand back and rubbed her belly, grimacing. "They're certainly active at this point. Think I'll go sit down for a minute if you'll excuse me."

"Sure," Pallas said. "My oldest sister just had her third daughter. Do you know the sex yet?"

Susan grinned. "Mary says a boy for sure, but we don't care as long as the baby is healthy."

Pallas instantly liked her for that. It wasn't going to be so bad after all.

Mary had gone back to her pots steaming on the stove.

"Can I help?" Pallas asked. "My best dish the last couple of years has been the Chinese deli down the street from my apartment, but I can follow directions with the best of them."

"You'll learn I never turn down a free hand," Mary said. "There're soap and towels by the sink in the pantry."

Pallas took off her jacket and cleaned up, then Mary showed her how to prepare garlic-roasted red potatoes for browning. They set the table, then Mary headed back into the kitchen as she talked to Pallas over her shoulder. "One more trip for the gravy boat. Would you go down the hall and get the boys? It's the last door on your right."

Pallas approached the open doorway in time to hear an unfamiliar voice. "Does she know Lucky Jack was banned for cheating?"

Chapter Twenty-Three

Pallas stood rooted to the spot, hurt washing over her. The skin on her arms turned cold, and she rubbed them, but heat suffused her face. At six years old she had understood least of all when the neighborhood children had parroted their parents' unkind words about her wonderful father.

The man's voice had to be Danny's brother, Dugan. He sounded curious, though, not mean. Why wasn't Danny saying anything?

Before she could go in, pretending she hadn't heard them, Dugan spoke again. "Does she know the part you played in it, Dad?" Her heart thumped. Rick had helped frame her father? Because it had to have been a setup. She pressed her heated face with the back of her hand. How could she have been so wrong about these people? Was she blinded by her love for Danny? *Oh God, she really did love him.*

The realization hit hard, but it was something she would deal with when she was alone.

She walked in before Rick had a chance to answer. She could bluff with the best of them and was brought up better than to cause a scene without finding out the facts. "Maybe we could discuss that after lunch."

All three men jumped as if their chairs were electrically charged. Danny came toward her, his gaze searching her face. "Yes, we need to talk about this."

He turned toward his brother. "This is Pallas Mulroney. You're going to be seeing as much of her as you do me in the future."

Dugan Tarantino was a shorter, slightly broader version of Danny, but the warmth of his smile was the same, even if he seemed a little unsure of its reception. "Welcome."

Danny's introduction took the edge off what she'd heard but didn't end her distress. "Thank you."

Danny took her hand, his face displaying empathy. "Did Mom send you to pry us out?"

She nodded. Her glance swept the three of them. "As I said, maybe after lunch we can meet here and swap stories about my father. Right now, Mary has worked hard and expects us."

The three men gave singular nods. "Dugan doesn't know very much and Danny almost nothing, but I'll fill you in on what I know," Rick said.

The fact that Danny hadn't been holding anything back eased her hurt another notch.

They walked into the dining room, Danny still holding her hand. He let go to pull out her chair and whispered in her ear, "You're terrific."

She smiled, trying to focus on enjoying her lunch. Mary Tarantino had outdone herself according to everyone there, but Pallas dwelled on the conversation to come and barely tasted anything. After dessert, she checked her watch. There were still thirty minutes before she and Danny had to leave for Suttons. She had no clue how she'd be able to concentrate on playing this afternoon.

As soon as Danny's mother stood, everyone grabbed some dishes and headed for the kitchen. Rick took Mary aside and spoke quietly. She turned to Pallas. "Susan and I have cleanup under control. Why don't you take some time to visit with the guys?"

Susan gave an odd look in their direction but remained placid.

Pallas was grateful for the understanding. "Thank you."

Back in the den, Danny seated her in a large overstuffed chair, then sat on the arm protectively.

Dugan held out a small cheroot. "Do you mind?"

She shook her head. The room was definitely male oriented and already smelled of leather and boots and mild cigar smoke, just like her dad's den in Laughlin.

Rick leaned forward and clasped his hands between his knees, a frown marring his brow. "Twenty years ago, I was the new man at Suttons, the small casino I started at having been bought out and razed. I was about Dugan's age at the time."

She looked at Danny's older brother and tried to imagine Rick at his age with a wife and two young boys depending on him.

Rick continued. "I'm not offering that as an excuse, just setting the scene. It all happened so fast I still have trouble believing it wasn't sleight of hand."

"It had to have been something like that," she said. "My father has never cheated in his life."

"Did he ever tell you what happened?" asked Rick.

She shook her head. "I was very young at the time, and even though the ban was only for a year, I think he was so humiliated, or angry, he made it permanent."

Rick nodded. "I wondered about that. I also wondered at the time why the casino owners so readily agreed to take such meager evidence and turn it into such a big deal. I'm sorry I didn't have enough brass to stand up and ask questions. After a while it blew over, but I've never felt right about it."

Pallas sensed his reluctance to reveal the part he'd played in the whole mess. She gave him an encouraging smile. "What exactly happened?"

"First, let me ask if your father still wears his trademark camelhair sports coat?"

She blinked. *What an odd question.* "Yes. How does that figure into this?"

Rick shrugged. "It wouldn't have been hard for somebody to plant a few cards in the pocket twenty years ago. To be conveniently discovered later by an impartial young blackjack dealer. People tend to hang their jackets on the backs of their chairs. Jack was having an incredible string of luck, the place was packed, and it's not impossible, in all the jostling of the crowd that had gathered to watch, that the cards I found in his pocket were as much a surprise to him as they were to me."

Her throat went scratchy, and a burning gathered behind her eyelids. "You do think it was a setup. But why?"

"That's the million-dollar question," Rick said. "Don't know that you'll find answers, though. Most of the people involved have moved on or are retired. Ty Addison might've been able to help, but he crawled in a bottle, and it's likely cooked his memory."

"That may not be the case," Danny said. "He's been making a comeback on the poker circuit in Vegas and here. His brain can't be too fried. He got the fifty-thousand-dollar entry fee for my tournament together."

Rick raised an eyebrow. "That's interesting. He

was the one who gave Jack away to one of the spotters, claiming he'd seen Jack palm a card, then drop it in his coat pocket. Pretty astonishing if you knew Ty and your father were good friends at the time. Drunk as he could be and still stagger around upright that afternoon. Afterward, rumor was, he paid off all his markers and got drunk permanently."

She dropped her gaze, anger at the injustice making her stomach hurt. Somebody with power and money had wanted Jack Mulroney out of town badly enough to frame him twenty years ago. She might never find out why, but it was a consolation there was doubt he cheated.

Part of her anger was replaced by sadness. "Didn't anyone vouch for my father?"

Rick's gaze found the carpet. "Your father's friends talked of protesting the ban and boycotting the casinos involved, but I heard it never caught on. Just a ripple in the lives of men and women who were probably grateful it hadn't happened to them."

She took a deep breath, feeling awkward. "Thanks for being honest with me. I'm sure it couldn't have been easy."

"That's very generous of you. Next time you see your dad, tell him I'm sorry for the way things worked out."

"I will."

Danny stood and pulled her up. "We have a few minutes before we have to leave. Let's take a walk."

They went through the kitchen where Pallas stopped to talk to Danny's mother and sister-in-law. "Thank you for having me to lunch, Mary. And Susan, take care of yourself and your new little one."

Mary came over and hugged her. "Anyone who can make Danny as happy as I've seen him today is always welcome."

As soon as they drove past the first curve of trees, Danny stopped and took her in his arms. "You going to be okay?"

She closed her eyes. The churning in her stomach had eased somewhat thanks to him. "Somebody trashed my father's reputation and got away with it. I still want to know why." She paused. "Could you ask Ty to lunch on Saturday? I'll bring Dad."

He pulled back to give her a curious look. "I can't promise anything, but I'll ask. Are you sure your father would want all this brought up again?"

She wasn't sure at all. He did know how crazy it made her, though. She sighed. "No, but I'm hoping he might have distanced himself over the years to the extent that he's at least curious about it."

Chapter Twenty-Four

Danny tapped a staccato on his steering wheel as he drove back to the club. He'd dropped Pallas off for her tournament and had a full afternoon planned before they met for dinner.

The connection through their fathers amazed him. He'd known from Bru that his dad was involved, but he also agreed it definitely looked like Jack Mulroney had been boxed in, tied up, and delivered. No mention of police being called, and if they'd had hard proof, Mulroney would have been banned from every casino in Nevada, not just Tahoe.

When Pallas walked into the den, he'd panicked at her stiff posture and pale face. She'd looked like she wanted to be anywhere else, yet she stuck it out.

At that moment, he'd made an internal decision about their relationship. Call it commitment or maybe love, if that was possible, but it had happened. He pushed the revelation to the back of his mind and concentrated on what they had learned.

If it meant tracking down and solving the twenty-year-old mystery personally, he would do whatever it took to make her happy.

He was wondering exactly where he would start when he unlocked his office and walked in. Derrick was sitting there, feet up on the desk, his blond buzz-cut and green eyes covered by a cowboy hat. Danny knew he wasn't asleep. "Maybe I should install a cot."

Derrick tipped the hat back with his index finger and grinned. "That would be accommodating, but I don't think we're going to be on this one much longer."

The best news Danny'd had all day. "How come?"

Size thirteen ostrich-skin cowboy boots hit the floor, and Derrick reached into his jacket to bring out some pages folded lengthwise. "Because the critical list is short. I think you'll find an interesting name among those we weren't able to clear."

The list was a printout with a line through most of the entries. Some had a check or question mark or margin note. Six were in red, but one might as well have been in neon. *Jonathan R. Chase.*

Danny slapped the list with the back of his hand. The model, color, everything was correct. He looked at Derrick. "What the hell was Chase's car doing in my lot? It can't be more than a three- or four-minute walk from his front door. Besides, he hates this place."

"Good question. But it was here. Could be he, or more likely somebody he hired, thought he could bypass the recon in the parking lot by driving in in plain sight. Would've worked, too, if we hadn't taken down all the plate numbers."

He paced the floor behind his desk. "That makes more sense than Chase himself being here. Bru tended bar until the drink was served to Pallas, and he certainly would've mentioned seeing him."

Derrick nodded. "That's why I'm guessing it was somebody he hired."

"He hired a flunky who had to borrow a car?"

"It's unlikely, but the guy may have intended on coming in another way and spotted us." Danny's friend took off his hat and ran his hand over his hair. "Arriving in a cab from the house next door would be too easy to trace, or he may have used Chase's car because his own was conspicuous. Remember those two guys we caught because they were seen driving a DeLorean?"

Muscles tensed in his jaw, and he made an effort to unclench his teeth. "I'm going to have to think this out. What about the other plates in red?"

"Rental cars all paid for by the same corporation. Probably a bunch of conventioneers out for a good time, but the corporate ownership takes some twists and turns, so I'm still working on those." Derrick shot him a look. "This pretty much seals the deal on Chase being involved. I put out the word on any freelance jobs he might have commissioned. Nothing in the wind. He's been a good boy ever since he sold his string of clubs. However he's managing this, it's damned clever."

Danny sat down and put the list on his desk. "Maybe. This is a good start, but there's a piece missing. I'd love nothing better than to stick this whole thing on him, but I keep coming back to why. Once he lost in court, and I finished building, he backed off. I don't mean completely. He's still a pain in the ass, but what's happened lately to trigger this kind of attack?"

"Going to get Tony involved?"

"Yeah, I'll pass this information to him today. If it is Chase, maybe a visit from the sheriff's department will dampen his enthusiasm."

"Want us to recon the perimeter again tonight?"

"Can't babysit the parking lot forever. I've got a back-up plan for when the attendant takes breaks. That should discourage any more forays. Thanks for your help, though." He nudged the list in front of him. "Let me know if the other cars lead to anything interesting?"

Derrick stood and knocked on the edge of the desk. "Sure. I'll be around for another week or so. Call me if you need to. Same price as this time."

Danny smiled. "Appreciate it."

He got up and closed the door after Derrick left. He knew he'd have to tread softly where his neighbor was concerned. It would be his word against Chase's, but he wanted to go for it anyway. He called Tony's direct line.

"Mancusco."

"It's Danny. Any luck looking into Chase's past?"

Caution crept into Tony's voice. "Sounds like you have a new reason for asking. What's up?"

"The list of plates Derrick took from cars in my lot last night included Chase's."

"Shit."

"Thought that would be good news. An incentive for someone in the department to have a friendly chat with him."

"You'd think so, but the first request I sent upstairs came back faster than a bad alimony check. Don't know that a plate number on a list compiled by a friend of yours will improve our chances."

Danny let his anger seep in. "Derrick is an accredited, licensed investigator who's helped the sheriff's department on more than one occasion. But you're telling me Tahoe's finest isn't going to do squat without a smoking gun. Is that it?"

Tony sighed. "Okay, bad choice of words. This is a small town, and everybody in the department knows Derrick can be trusted. Let me see how creative I can get with another request."

Tony was doing his best with what he had to work with, so Danny backed off. "Sorry to sound ungrateful. This is all coming at a really bad time. I'll stay loose until I hear from you."

"Right." Which from Tony meant he expected the worst, so he didn't want to hear about it in advance.

Danny laughed. "No ninja raids, I promise." He ended the call.

A half hour into club paperwork, he was interrupted by a knock on his door. "Come in."

Bud eased around the door, a faded John Deere baseball cap curled in his hand. "Got some time?"

Danny had forgotten all about his friend. He smiled. "You bet. You've temporarily saved me from having to pay bills."

Bud's gaze took in the small office. "Elaine was having a hard time when you had your opening night. The place looks great."

It surprised Danny to realize Bud had never been in the club. He could see the man was nervous by the way he stood there, loose-limbed and out of his element. He tried to put him at ease. "Glad you like it. Want the investor's tour?"

Bud shook his head. "No, I need to talk about that money we invested."

Danny tried to keep his posture relaxed. "Have a seat."

Bud sat halfway into the chair. "How are things going? It looks pretty prosperous."

"And expensive," Danny said, pulling no punches. "The first six months of operation is always a settling-in period. We don't know if the take is a pattern or because we're new."

That information changed Bud's optimistic expression to the worn, hopeless visage that had developed since his wife was diagnosed. No way Danny could soften the blow.

"I can only guess how bad your situation is," he said uncomfortably. "And I wish I could give you some good news, but there isn't any way I can help you financially right now. If I could have, I would have come to you before this."

"I knew what the answer'd be before I came." Bud wrung the cap in his hands. "I was prepared for that."

Danny was confused. "Then what can I help you with?"

"You're the only one I know with *connections*," Bud began, his voice weakening on the last word.

He can't be this desperate. He broke in before Bud could continue. "Don't go there, Bud. Borrowing money at an unscrupulous rate is a really bad idea. I won't be responsible for getting you involved with the type of people you're looking to do business with."

The other man lifted his chin, his eyes feverish. "I haven't got a choice, and this isn't *business* we're talking about; it's my wife."

Danny started to apologize, but Bud waved his words away. "There's a treatment in Mexico I heard of, and if it'll help, we gotta try it. They only take cash, though, and my credit's all shot what with the hospital and doctor bills."

Danny felt sick to his stomach. "Have you considered the legitimacy of this treatment? How about Elaine? I thought she was too weak to travel."

Bud leaned forward, not hearing the cons. "That's

part of what the money'd be used for. A private air ambulance down there and back."

The whole thing was ludicrous, and Danny could only half believe his normally straight-thinking neighbor wanted to go through with the plan he'd outlined. He made another try at reasoning. "Have you talked to Elaine's oncologist, her radiologist? What do they think?"

"They're not going to approve of a treatment that won't line their pockets," Bud insisted, getting angry. "I'm a grown man, used to taking care of me and mine. After Elaine gets better, I'm going to sell the ranch, pay off the loans, and we'll get a small place in town. But I need the money *now*."

The next words were the hardest Danny had ever uttered. "The answer's still no. I won't help you bring more grief to yourself."

Bud's Adam's apple bobbled, and the corners of his mouth tightened as he stood. "I thought we were friends, but I guess that only works one way. I won't bother you again." He turned, clicking the door closed softly as he left.

Danny rubbed the heels of his hands in his eyes. That was the longest five minutes of his life. He reached for the phone and dialed. His brother answered.

"Dugan, can I talk to Dad?"

His dad came on the line. "Thought I might hear from you. How's Pallas?"

"She's fine. I need to talk to you about Bud."

Rick whistled softly. "He came to you about the Mexican cure scheme? I tried to reason with him, and he just got mad. Said he knew someone with connections who owed him."

"When did he stop listening to anyone?"

"After Elaine's last procedure failed. He's probably gone home to drink. Your mother went over there with hot food a couple days ago and said the house was trashed. Looked like he had done it in a rage." Rick huffed out a breath. "I'll give it a couple of hours and go over to see him."

"Thanks. Call me if there's anything I can do to help."

He hung up feeling only marginally better. Two of the nicest people he knew and their lives had taken a horrible turn. It made his own problems seem small.

Danny's thoughts turned to Pallas. She was due in about three hours. An hour on the books he'd been neglecting, then a long run might ease his frustrations. He smiled in spite of his day. Entertaining Pallas Mulroney was definitely something to look forward to.

Chapter Twenty-Five

Pallas struggled to concentrate on the cards in her hand. Her feelings toward Danny Tarantino wouldn't fade into the background, darn it. She told herself she was just indulging her biological urges, or she wanted to learn more about her father's ban, or that she was fascinated by the mystery that surrounded Danny. Throw in the fact that he was funny and sexy and...*stop*.

She blinked and scanned her competition. Two of them were watching her, ready to take advantage of her distraction.

The others had their own problems. Her earlier supposition that the Amarillo Slim look-a-like would be the next to drop out was very likely. She'd watched him approach the playing table and nonchalantly circle his chair before sitting down. An old superstition, and proof he was worried.

They were only an hour into the game. If she buckled down, she could overcome her sloppy start. Pallas shot a bland look at the two players watching her. Good, they glanced away.

Three hours later she threw in her last hand and reviewed her winnings. One day and two players left. If she kept her head, she'd be sitting at the finalists table on Friday.

The partnership was within her reach. Teasing

images seeped in. Seductive, hazy pictures of a classy office door with her name on it. The door stood partially open, and she could see a window framing a spectacular view of water and a mountainous opposite shoreline. That was odd. San Francisco Bay didn't have that kind of view. Then she realized her daydreaming had placed her smack in the middle of an office on the shores of Lake Tahoe. A chill climbed her spine.

She glanced at her watch. Yikes. It was six fifteen, and she was due at Danny's at seven thirty. She still had to shower, get ready, and pick up the food.

Sassy's husband, Pat, had mentioned a fantastic rib place, and Pallas decided ribs, potato salad, ginger ale, and Danny would be a terrific way to spend the evening.

Her years at Stanford, and since, had been spent putting in long hours to get and maintain an edge, first in her studies, then in working her way up to the position of principal. There hadn't been much time for, nor had she been interested in, pursuing casual sex. So here she was, about to go on a date where the expectations for how the evening would end were definitely understood.

She had called in her order to the restaurant so she'd have more time to get ready. When she caught herself freshening her lip gloss for the third time, she gave up and left.

The rib place had her order ready, and Pat was right. If it tasted anything like it smelled, the food would be great.

The rest of the drive to Over the Moon was practically by autopilot, so she mulled over the information she'd learned at Danny's folks. Her instincts about Ty had been right. The big question was why he'd lied about seeing her father palm that card twenty years ago.

She pulled into the parking lot, turned off the engine, and sat for a moment, trying to put the evening into perspective. She was a big girl and had known what she wanted since their first kiss three nights ago. So why did she feel like a quaking mass of uncertainty? Fear of disappointing Danny? Or just plain scared they would be so great together that she'd have to change the biggest decision she'd made so far in her life to accommodate falling in love?

She sighed as she gathered the dinner. She would do what she'd always done, give it all the heart she had.

He wasn't around when she came in, so Pallas went to the bar. Bru lifted an eyebrow at the bags she carried and walked out to meet her. "More commando clothes?"

She grinned. "Nope. I brought dinner. Got some ribs and potato salad from that little place by Suttons and ginger ale to wash it down."

Bru breathed out in longing. "Every man's dream. Meat to tear with your teeth and a beautiful woman to watch you."

Pallas suppressed a flustered giggle. Bru's reference to Danny's teeth brought to mind her own mental picture of what he could do with his sexy mouth.

"Speaking of meat," Bru continued. "Danny said to tell you he got called to the kitchen to calm down Henri, the chef. Half the filets that arrived for the dinner special are apparently not acceptable, and Danny is the only one that'll go near the guy when he's in a snit."

Pallas held out the sacks. "Hold these for me, would you? I'm going to sneak a look. This should be good."

Bru winked, and she walked to the kitchen to peek in. She stifled a giggle. Danny stood in front of a small man with a tiny mustache and large toque. He looked like a caricature of a French chef and was swearing in French and stabbing at a piece of meat on the counter with a sharp knife. As he started to lose steam, Danny held out his hand for the knife. He then proceeded to bend over the meat and give it a few good stabs of his own before returning the knife. He smiled and said something that elicited a smile from Henri. Pallas hurried back to the bar.

Danny emerged from the kitchen and huffed out a breath. She and Bru broke into polite applause. "He quitting again?" Bru asked.

"He wanted me to make the meat supplier allow him surprise inspection visits," Danny said. "Since we're such a small customer, I doubt that'll happen. I did agree to call Dugan. The O'Brien ranch sends some of its top-grade beef to that supplier. Dugan can request special attention for Over the Moon orders and make it stick. Henri claims he'll remain *vigilant*."

Despite his smile, Pallas saw the lines of strain around Danny's eyes and mouth. She wanted to smooth them with her fingers, then kiss them away. "Tough day?"

His smile sparked to life. "It just got better." He sniffed the air. "Are those ribs I smell? And did they come from where I think they did?"

Bru reached under the bar to bring up the bags reluctantly. Danny snagged them and headed for the door to his quarters. He slowed and looked at Pallas over his shoulder. "You want some, too?"

Before she could answer, Bru asked, "Hey, what if there's an emergency?"

Danny stopped and held out his other hand to Pallas. "Unless it involves fire, blood, or a national emergency, I'm not here."

Once inside the connecting hall between the club and his quarters, Danny turned and set the sack on the floor before locking the door. Pallas went into his arms. The kiss was slow and hot.

She still wasn't sure as she looked into his eyes if she wanted the return gaze to be one of love or just lust.

****

All the upheaval he had experienced in the last four hours faded. Pallas's warm, soft body and pliant mouth drove away everything but the moment.

She tilted her head back, wicked intentions in her eyes. "There's lots of sticky sauce."

He swallowed, heat and raw need charging his blood. He fished for his keys with clumsy fingers. "I have lots of suggestions for cleanup."

Once inside, Danny carried the sacks to the table he'd already set. "I'll get some ice. Do you want anything from the bar?"

She ripped into the bag that contained the ribs. "No. I brought cold ginger ale. You can get a serving spoon for the potato salad, though."

It didn't take much for him to imagine Pallas here permanently. When he'd worked with the architect, he'd made sure his place was spacious and comfortable. Room for a wife? He couldn't sort the feelings that swamped him.

They sat down to eat, and in no time their hands were covered in sticky sauce.

She stared out the big window. "Looks like a storm on the lake tonight."

"Sometimes it hangs over the water, and all we get on shore is wind."

They ate contently for a while until Danny caught her watching him. He wiped his hands. "What made you decide on ribs?"

"Pat's a big fan of this place. They slow bake them for hours, but it sounded at the bar like you already knew about them."

He nodded, completely relaxed. "Yeah. I haven't eaten there for over a year, though. This was my favorite meal when I worked at Suttons."

She showed surprise. "Really? I didn't know you'd worked there. What did you do?"

"Security. At first for the headliners, then I ran floor security for about three years. It mostly consisted of placating guests who were foolish enough to leave themselves open to having their purses or wallets lifted." He shrugged. "I did a stint at training spotters and employees running the games, too."

"Is that how you heard about what had happened to my father? The story must have taken on quite a status to have survived all those years."

He leaned in, the same overreaching need for her tugging as strongly as it had when she walked into his club three days ago. "Maybe the story is still around because people can't believe it's true."

"Thank you," she said, wiping at her mouth self-consciously. "Do I still have sauce on my face?"

He realized she'd caught him studying her mouth.

"Sorry, no. Didn't mean to stare. I was thinking of something else."

"Like when will the small talk be over?" she asked quietly.

He laughed. "Yes."

She stood and stacked her dishes. "One of the advantages to take out is the quick cleanup."

He grinned and started helping. "A good dishwasher doesn't hurt either."

They loaded the dishes, then Pallas walked over to the window. He came up behind her and wrapped his arms around her waist. They stood in the dimness, watching the flat light push under the storm clouds and illuminate the angry surface of the water. She shivered, and he didn't know if it was nerves or chills, but he rubbed the tops of her arms. He was about to ask about her luck in the tournament when a shrill beeping sound interrupted.

She jumped. "Oh God. Is that a smoke alarm?"

He couldn't believe it. Was this the worst timing ever, or was he still under attack? "Yes." He turned to run into the club. "And it better not be a joke on Bru's part."

Pallas was right behind him. Danny didn't know how bad the situation was, so he would deal with her safety when he found out.

The noise was much louder in the club, the bar all but deserted. Sprinklers erupted when they were halfway across the dining room, spraying them with cold water.

Black smoke rolled from the kitchen, and Bru stood shouting at someone inside through a wet bar towel.

Danny grabbed his shoulder and spun him around. "What happened? Who's in there?"

Bru coughed. "I think it's a grill fire. Henri came out yelling, followed by the rest of the kitchen staff. He started waving his arms, said something in French, and ran back in."

He slapped keys into Bru's free hand. "Open my office door, then go outside and wait for the fire department to show them where in the office to turn off the alarms."

Bru nodded and took off. Danny started to go into the kitchen when he felt a hard tug on the back of his shirt.

Pallas handed him a wet towel. "I'm going in with you."

Chapter Twenty-Six

Fear chilled his guts. He grabbed her upper arm and pulled her face within an inch of his. "No way. Go to the parking lot and help there if you can."

She wrenched her arm free. "I speak fluent French," she shouted. "Do you?"

In times of stress, the Frenchman lapsed into his native tongue, and right now Danny didn't have time to cajole him into speaking English. The smoke seemed to be lessening, and he heard sirens from emergency vehicles approaching. For all he knew Henri could be overcome by smoke and lying on the floor.

He spoke into Pallas's ear. "Breathe through the towel with one hand and hold onto my shirt with the other. Do not strike out on your own. Got it?"

She nodded and followed his lead as he went to his hands and knees. If it was a grill fire, Henri would be near the stove. Danny's eyes stung. He used one hand to guide him as he felt his way down the large stainless-steel work island in the middle of the room. He was turning the corner when he was hit in the face with some stiff material. "What the hell...?"

It was Henri's toque. The chef was duck-walking and flapping the air with his hat. He coughed hoarsely into a kitchen towel, then let loose a stream of rapid-fire French.

Pallas tugged on Danny's shirt. "He says the fire's

out, but he's choking on the smoke, and we should leave."

Danny nodded, grabbed the front of the chef's stained, wet coat, and swung him around to lead them out. They headed back in the direction they came from just as the alarm and water stopped, only to be replaced by the escalating noise of sirens.

In the parking lot, medics ran forward to help. Pallas and Henri were led to waiting aid cars, the little man mumbling, "*Je suis désolé*," between coughing spasms. Danny waved off the medics when he spotted Bru talking to the fire chief.

Bru turned to Danny. "The sous chef confirmed the fire started at the chef's grill. Henri was upset about the steaks and tried a new recipe with a brandy baste. When it accidentally splashed, the flames jumped and caught the towel at his shoulder on fire. He panicked and threw it down. Since he'd mopped up some brandy with it earlier, the fire spread to the work surface. He ordered everyone out, shouting he would 'rescue the situation.' "

Danny pointed to the medic who was tending Pallas and told the chief he would be over there. Pallas, wrapped in a blanket, held an oxygen mask over her nose and mouth while the medic put drops in her eyes. He shivered. The club blocked the biting wind a little, but it was still very cold outside. Clothes soaked with water made the chill worse.

The woman finished with Pallas and turned to Danny. She was the same one who'd responded to their call last night. "You're the most exciting thing to happen to this end of the lake in a long time. Sit down and have a shot of oxygen while I check you over. Any burns or vision problems?"

He shook his head, causing a fit of coughing, then allowed the woman to help him. Pallas opened her blanket and pulled it around his shoulder, leaning her head against his wet shirt. She reached over and slid her fingers between his.

The fire chief walked up as the first truck left. "The damage is confined to a fairly small area. It hadn't spread to any other parts of the building, so we canceled the alarms. We have a second eye witness who confirms what the first one said, so we're closing this as an accident unless you have reason to think otherwise."

Danny shook his head as the man walked away. Of all the piss-poor timing. This had to be it. His insurance company was already very unhappy about the ruined paint on the cars in his lot. This would send his premiums through the roof.

He stood and walked into the club, leading Pallas by the hand. Water soaked the sprinkler zone adjacent to the kitchen. It dripped onto the carpet from wet tablecloths and pooled in plates of soggy food.

Bru and Mandy were mopping up the end of the bar. He tossed Danny the keys to his office. "They reset the alarm and sprinkler systems."

"Thanks," Danny said and walked past his office to open the fire door that led to the gambling side of the club. He shook his head. Apparently, the die-hards had waited in the parking lot for the all clear. The lights had never gone off as his back-up generator had kicked in. The tables and slots were already half full. One of the cocktail waitresses approached.

"Can we fill drink orders?"

Danny tipped his head toward the bar. "Check with

Bru. He and Mandy will need time to clean up."

He spent a few minutes chatting with the pit bosses, then made his way back down the hall. Pallas stood in front of his office, still wrapped in the rescue blanket. Maybe there was just no damn way they were meant to get together.

He stroked her cheek. "I need to deal with the insurance company and hire a cleaning crew. You're going to freeze, even with your car heater going full blast. You can take a hot shower and run your clothes through the dryer in my place before you head back to Suttons."

She tried to smile through blue lips. "Thanks, but I'll stick around." Her eyes were red-rimmed and her teeth chattered.

He shook his head regretfully. "I'll be at least an hour, and I doubt I'd be very good company at the end of it."

She stuck her chin up. "You might need someone to talk to, so I'll stay." Her look softened. "Please?"

He couldn't think of a single thing to say to that, so he leaned close and kissed her. It was an odd sensation, kissing someone with chattering teeth, but he kinda liked it. "I need to make a few calls."

She nodded and wrapped the blanket tighter. "Sure." Then she headed for his quarters.

Inside his office Danny pulled out a phone book and went to the yellow pages. A large ad for a cleaning crew that responded within an hour and specialized in water damage caught his eye. The man who answered assured him they could easily handle his problem. Danny was relieved the service was available but stunned by the cost.

He dialed his insurance agent next, punching in the number to forward the call for emergencies. His agent picked up at home. "Mark, this is Danny Tarantino at Over the Moon. I've had a small kitchen fire, and there's water damage. I wanted you to know I've arranged for a cleanup crew to start immediately. Is there anything else I need to do?"

"Sorry to hear it. Was this due to vandals, too?"

Danny sighed. "No, it was an accident."

"Go ahead with the cleanup. I'll be there at eight tomorrow morning." The agent hesitated.

"Anything else?" Danny asked.

"Yeah. This may shift you into a high-risk category, and depending on the extent of the claim, even end your coverage with us."

The last words sucker-punched him. Not that he blamed his agent. They had to protect themselves from high payouts. He mumbled, "Guess it can't be helped," and ended the call.

He walked into his quarters, peeling off his wet shirt as he went. When he reached the bedroom and started taking off his pants, he heard someone clear their throat. Pallas stood in the doorway to his bathroom wrapped in a towel, her hands and face smudged with soot, her hair tangled and bedraggled.

She stared at his face. "My things will take a couple of rounds in the dryer. I, uh, wondered if you had something I could wear when I get out of the shower?"

His bedroom felt like the size of a closet. He muffled a cough and stepped to a mahogany dresser, sliding open the bottom drawer. He stood up and handed her some pajamas.

The look on her face as she held out her hand was like nothing he'd ever seen before. Considering the pajamas were pink and blue with tiny cherubs on floating clouds, he didn't blame her.

"Uh, these are Susan's," he said. "She and Dugan celebrated their fifth wedding anniversary here before I moved in. Susan brought them as a joke, and they were left behind unworn. I keep forgetting to return them. They'll fit you better than any of my things."

Pallas nodded, wide-eyed. "Thanks." Then she turned and closed the bathroom door.

He stood in the middle of the room, still wearing his wet jeans when she hurried out five minutes later. "It's all yours," she said.

****

She watched as he passed into the bathroom without speaking. Slow, hot tears flowed at the misery she'd seen on his face. He hadn't even commented on her appearance. Why she felt compelled to stay and try to help, she didn't know, but stay she would. If only to listen. To what? Where was the explosion, the letting off of steam? The fact that he hadn't let go was scary. No one could have that much control.

She rubbed at her hair with a towel. Still a little chilly, she went to his dresser and opened the top drawer. Boxers and cotton athletic socks. Great. Warm feet.

The dresser mirror reflected disaster. She'd gotten off the sooty smudges, and her lips were getting pink again, but her hair.

She nearly wailed. Usually a source of pride, it clung to her head like a wet rag.

Hopefully Danny wouldn't get a second look at her

in these pajamas. She was a good six inches taller than Susan, so the sleeves and pant legs were short to the point of silliness. So much for a making a good impression for the evening.

She was waiting in the living room when he came out dressed in sweatpants and a T-shirt. She saw his mood matched that of the storm. He glanced at her, then at the pajamas and shook his head. "Back in a minute." Then he left.

She toweled at her hair in frustration.

True to his word, he came back shortly. "Is there any more of that?"

Momentarily confused, she looked down. "Oh, you mean the coffee. Sure, let me get you some."

He sank onto the couch and hung his head, rubbing his neck. "The cleaning crew arrived in record time. They must be thrilled someone is actually going to pay for their offer of premium service. At a premium price, of course."

She sat the cup of coffee in front of him. "They threw you out?"

He rolled his shoulders. "That's about it. We're down to half-staff, and Bru's got everything at the bar under control." He laughed without humor. "This was supposed to be my first night off in a long time, so I'd already arranged for coverage in the casino."

She walked around behind him and massaged his neck. "It's not so bad, then?"

He leaned forward, breaking the contact. "Bad enough. My insurance deductible is high. Now I get to pay it twice. Once for the cars and once for the fire. This might put my books so far in the red I won't be able to recover." His voice was low and rough. "I'm sure that'll make someone happy."

She sighed. Any new business was a risk, but the losses and bad reputation Danny had suffered in the past week could be ruinous. Then there was the fact that a good chunk of his start-up capital was from friends and family. "You can recover."

"Easier said than done," he said, still not looking at her.

"I'm good with numbers," she offered. "We could look at your books. See if there's any place you could stretch your budget."

"I need to think things through." He stood and paced. "There are still a lot of unanswered questions."

"Like what? Maybe I could help."

He turned his full attention on her, his dark eyes intense. "Then help me understand why part of me still thinks you could be in on all this."

It hit her harder than anything ever had. "You think I could...?" She blinked, pain blossoming in her chest at his meaning. "Why? Because I wanted to play in your tournament? Because I happen to be here coincident with the attacks on the club?"

He didn't answer, so she continued, the pain now burned away by anger. "To what end? As a paid professional here to sink your business? Or maybe I'm here to provide a sexual distraction while my partner does the dirty work." She stepped up to him and poked his chest, hard, tears punctuating her words. "In which case, I failed. I'm sorry you cooked up this little blamefest starring me, but I only wanted to help."

Danny's face formed a tortured mask. He took a deep breath and shook his head, running his hand through his hair. "Tonight was too much. My brain is on overload. I don't understand why you're willing to give up what you've wanted so badly. You're so close. The only thing that makes sense is there has to be more to it." He dropped his arm. "What am I missing? Why would you give up so much without expecting something in return?"

Spent anger and confusion flickered in his eyes, and her anger subsided.

"Because I've never met anyone who cared as much about his dream as I do mine." She shrugged. "It took me about two seconds to decide it's better to save a dream that's already here than build one I've only begun to realize in the last few days."

He brushed back a damp curl that had dried and sprung forward to frame her face. "I couldn't stand the thought that you'd want to hurt me. It made me say stupid things. I'm so sorry." His voice was husky. "Forgive me?"

She studied him for a moment. He handled anger like she did. Burned bright and hard, then reason prevailed. She went into his arms. "Apology accepted."

Danny pulled her tight and kissed her temple. "Thank you."

Chapter Twenty-Seven

He kissed her long and tenderly.

Pallas had nothing to compare with the sensations reeling through her. She'd heard of couples fighting and making up in bed, but thought it had always been a convenient excuse. Whatever the motivation, she wanted Danny. Now.

Smoke. Her hair still stank. She pulled back. "Ten minutes for another shampoo and my kingdom for a hair dryer and a toothbrush."

He laughed. "Seven, since I've already waited this long. There's a hair dryer and spare toothbrush in the top drawer to the right of the sink."

She turned and practically sprinted into his bedroom. Five minutes later she was drying her hair with one hand and brushing her teeth with the other. Her hair was still damp as she pulled on the pajama top, deciding to leave it unbuttoned. She walked into the bedroom, taking a deep breath, the storm outside echoing her internal chaos.

He came up behind her and pushed her hair aside, his warm lips pressing against the soft skin below her ear. "You did save me, you know."

She turned and hugged his waist. She kissed the corner of his mouth, sliding the tip of her tongue to lap his smooth upper lip. He must have shaved before she came for dinner. She skimmed her hands under his T-shirt to roam over his chest. "We can talk about the money later."

He cupped her face with his hand, forcing her gaze to connect with his. "I'm not talking about money. I'm talking about me close to giving up, and you not letting me."

It was the hardest thing she'd ever done, but she set aside her physical desire, trembling with the effort. "I know what it's like to care so much about something and feel alone."

He tipped his head, his mouth only an inch from hers. "You're not alone now."

His words fell around her, completing a half-empty struggle to have someone understand what she'd wanted to do for her father. And for herself, if she were being honest.

She moved back into his kiss, letting go of everything but her body's needs.

He curved his thumbs into the lapels of her pajama top and started to slide his hands down the front. He stopped when he discovered the buttons undone and leaned back to look at her.

She took the end of the drawstring holding the pajama bottoms up and held it out to him.

He smiled a wicked smile, his eyes dark with passion as he untied the bow. "Two generous offers in one evening. My winning streak just surfaced."

It was true. She was offering herself to him, but nerves warred in her stomach with desire. What if what she wanted so much wouldn't be enough? And sometimes sex was just sex. But not this time.

When the slipknot gave way, the bottoms fell to her ankles.

Danny loosed the top off her shoulders, and she shook it off. He let out a huff of breath, then slid his hand slowly up her hip and around her belly, finally running a finger under her breast. "So beautiful."

Pallas wanted to believe him. Believe he didn't see all her freckles. Believe he didn't think her breasts were too small.

He bent to torture her, his mouth doing delightful things and causing a gasp to start in the back of her throat and die when she made a sound of need. Heat flared in her. The kind she knew could only be satisfied with him inside her.

She watched his face in the black and white snapshots the inconstant moonlight afforded her. All her imaginings over the last four days culminated, and she ached with wanting to please him.

Her hand skimmed the top of his sweats and dipped in. He stilled when she curled her hand around him. She took that as an invitation and tugged his sweatpants over his hips. He let go of her to shimmy them to the floor, then dropped to his knees in front of her.

She started to step back, but he took her ankles and steadied her. "Let me help with your socks."

First one foot, then the other was divested of its covering. He didn't stand back up immediately, but slipped one hand to the inside of her thigh, his fingers exploring.

"Danny?" His name came in a plea, her eyes closed and head hung back.

"Yes?" His warm breath exhaled very close to where his thumb was now stroking.

Her hand held onto his shoulders, but her brain refused to string words together coherently, to tell him she wanted him desperately. "I, um, think…"

She heard the smile in his voice.

"You think I should stop? You think I should leave? What?" he teased. "If you can still think, I'm not doing it right."

She wanted to tell him that wasn't true; he was doing everything right. But she couldn't connect the words. He could still speak in sentences, damn him. She would get him for that. Right after, *oh God*…

Her grip on his shoulders tightened, and she rose to her toes, hips arched forward as the first wave of release hit. He held her upright with one hand and did magic things with the other. Urgent, meaningless, embarrassing sounds escaped her.

The next thing she knew, he stood and scooped her into his arms, depositing her onto the middle of his bed.

She reached for him and panicked when he moved away. But he only leaned as far as the nightstand. It did, however, give her a chance to touch him again and nip his shoulder with her teeth.

He dropped the packet and sheathed himself before leaning over her. "Now you'll have to wait."

She laughed as the flats of her hands played a game of friction against his nipples and she arched into him.

"Enough," he said through his teeth. "You have the best hand."

She moved the backs of her fingers from his lower belly up his ribcage, loving it as his muscles trembled. "I call. Show me what you've got."

He moved over her, his thumb finding a heretofore neglected but sensitive spot at the top of her thigh. She shuddered, grabbing the bedspread with one hand and guiding him with the other.

She clenched her teeth as he slipped into her. It had been a while. Other times were mildly satisfying, but nothing over the top. *This* was Danny. A man she'd only known for four days but would never be sorry she'd given herself to.

"Relax," he said. "You're a little tight. Let me know if it hurts."

She shook her head as her hips rose to take him. She wanted the out-of-control feeling again. In a matter of seconds, his slow, easy strokes became urgent.

"There," he said. "You are so..."

She didn't hear the last word as the flash fire rekindled. She grasped at him blindly, somehow holding his mouth on hers hard, taking everything he gave.

He pulled back, only enough to gasp in her ear. "Pallas, honey, come with me now."

And she did. In a glorious, keening kaleidoscope of pure feeling.

He caught himself on one elbow beside her, his chest heaving. "Sorry."

She thought she hadn't heard right over the staccato of her heart. "For what?" she asked, pushing a shock of hair from his forehead.

"I wanted to give you more our first time together."

She brought her knees up and slid them back down, restlessly. "Are you kidding? It's going to take a week to uncurl my toes." She turned toward him, letting her hand slip between his thighs and trail upward. "Besides, we both had a lot of tension built up."

He grinned and brushed his thumb in that sensitive place again. "So since you have no shoes to wear and the first time was only meant to relax, how would you feel about a slower, more attentive pace?"

She laughed, and rolling him on his back, straddled him. "There's something I've always wanted to try."

Danny groaned in completion as they finished making love the second time. Pallas framed his face with her hands and kissed him, deeply. Without hesitation, she had given him all she had and taken in kind.

She snuggled in, warm and sated. "That was wonderful."

He hugged her, running his hand up and down her back. "It was okay if you like that sort of thing."

She laughed. "Liar. If it was any more okay, we'd have to call Sheila."

He frowned into the darkness. "Who's Sheila?"

"That EMT who's been here twice already."

"Oh, her. By the way, the dryer buzzed while we were otherwise engaged. Your clothes are done."

"I thought I heard something. But I just figured I won the prize behind door number two."

"You did. And you're never getting rid of me."

She tensed. Now was as good a time as any, she thought. "Then borrowing that money shouldn't be a problem."

He kept his hold on her. "We'll talk about it tomorrow."

Chapter Twenty-Eight

Pallas became aware of the loveliest sensation. She was wrapped in a cocoon, and warm hands caressed her back and hips. She frowned and made a disgruntled noise when something scratchy moved against her mouth. Then she remembered where she was and Danny's heavy stubble. She stretched her arms to encompass his neck, pressing her breasts against his chest in a move that brought them both murmurs of pleasure.

"Good morning," he said, kissing the end of her nose. "Sleep well?"

She opened one eye, then the other, in surprise. "It's still dark."

He laughed. "It'll be light soon. It's six thirty, but we have a long day ahead, and I didn't ask last night when you wanted to get up."

She'd never woken in a man's arms. It was delicious. "Do you have an iron and ironing board?"

He dipped an eyebrow. "I could borrow them from the employee locker area. Why?"

"Because," she said, wiggling against him, "that way, I could iron my wrinkled clothes instead of dampening them and running them through the dryer again. Which means I have a little time to spare."

"I don't see how that would save...oh."

****

Chocolate-colored satin trimmed in cream lace peeked from under the cherub pajama top. What had he done to deserve a view like that, Danny wondered as he snuck up behind Pallas while she ironed in his kitchen. He held back a chuckle when he saw she'd donned his athletic socks again.

She held her left arm up at a ninety-degree angle, showing him her wristwatch without turning. "Don't start something you don't have time to finish."

He swooped in anyway, slipping his arms around her waist and kissing the part of her neck he could reach around the tidy french braid. "Then don't walk around looking like that."

She squirmed and held up her sweater. "Unless a dry cleaner can get the smell out, I think it's ruined."

He was still kissing her neck. "I'll add the cost of your clothes to the insurance bill."

She turned in his arms and gave him a steady look. "Thank you. I know you have reservations about this whole thing about my dad, and you have a lot to do today, but could you remember to talk to Ty? Dad will be here early tomorrow, and I want to make arrangements for lunch."

"I'll ask him, but there's another angle I want to pursue."

She brightened. "Can I help?"

"Nope. This is a long shot, and it has to be run through more or less official channels. I'll let you know if it pans out."

She hugged him. "I'm grateful for any help."

He gave her his best wolfish look. "Grateful enough to let me play connect the dots?"

She pushed him away. "Down, boy. I'll have to

swear off you for a week to recover."

He felt instantly chagrined. "Pallas, I'm sorry." Then he saw the corners of her mouth quiver in a suppressed smile and grabbed for her.

She stepped out of his reach. "Your insurance agent will be here in ten minutes." She shot him a look. "And don't think I haven't noticed you've avoided discussing that loan."

He saw the determination in her beautiful eyes. "Waste of time."

"We'll see." She slipped the pajama top off and turned for her sweater.

He whistled as he got the full impact of the matching satin, chocolate-colored bra and all those freckles. "Damn, woman."

There had only been a couple of people in the club when Pallas left, but Danny could see she was a little embarrassed. Fortunately, she understood he couldn't take her back to Suttons.

His agent had just left when it hit Danny like a rock-solid punch. Pallas had offered to loan him her winnings but had never mentioned staying. Her vacation was over day after tomorrow. Even though night before last they had both conceded something great was building between them, she hadn't said anything about what she expected to happen next.

He rubbed his unshaven chin. Their comfort level with each other in his quarters reminded him of how easy his mom and dad were with each other. Yet he hadn't made any promises of permanence. Maybe if he started talking about that tonight after dinner, she wouldn't push the loan issue. Speaking of promises, there was his to help Pallas discover the reason her father had been falsely accused of cheating.

He reached for the phone and dialed.

"Jimmy G's."

"Jimmy. It's Danny Tarantino. I need a couple of favors, if you can."

"Sure. Sorry to hear about your fire. Was it deliberate?"

"Thanks. No, it was an accident at the chef's grill. I should be back in action for lunch and dinner, maybe by tomorrow."

"Insurance cover the cost? I can always scrape up some extra money…"

Danny smiled. Who said casino owners were hard-hearted? "It's all taken care of, but since my place is being cleaned, I wondered if you've seen Ty?"

"Yeah. The players stopped practicing as a group, but he's come in solo to sit in where he can in the afternoon."

"Okay, I'll be over shortly. The second favor involves your memory. Go back twenty years and tell me anything you remember about Jack Mulroney's ban."

"Ancient stuff. Why are you digging it up?"

Danny figured with their history it wouldn't hurt to confide in Jimmy. "That beautiful redhead you met a couple of days ago is one of his daughters. I'm helping her find out why it happened."

"I'll be damned, small world. I was just an errand boy at the time, but it took place at Suttons."

"That part I know. Anything else?"

"Uh, somebody with a lot of juice, and I don't know who, put out the word that the ban was not negotiable. It didn't matter if you owed Lucky Jack;

you couldn't buck the ban and let him gamble at your place. I didn't know the man, so I didn't care, but some of the others said Jack knew something he shouldn't. Course it was all speculation. Does that help?"

Danny mulled over Jimmy's theory as he tapped the desk with a pencil. He hadn't thought of that particular angle, but it made sense. Jack Mulroney may or may not have actually known anything that could hurt one of the casino owners, but he was smart enough to know the whole thing was a setup to get him out of the way.

Danny played a long shot. He called Tony.

"Mancusco."

"Any luck interviewing Chase?"

"Hello to you, too. Before we discuss your question or all the favors you're burning, what the hell happened last night?"

Danny sighed. "Purely accidental. Henri's grill area caught fire. Affected the kitchen and dining room. We had to evacuate."

"Everyone okay?" Tony asked.

"Smoke inhalation for a couple of the kitchen staff, but they'll be fine."

Tony paused before continuing. "What are you going to do? The guy threatening you has been quiet for a while, but that doesn't mean he's gone."

"Not much I can do right now, but I'm not giving up. The bastard will have to do his worst."

"Glad to hear you're hanging in there. Back to your question on Chase. The answer is yes, I did get to talk to him."

"How'd that go?"

"Something like this... 'Mr. Chase, are you aware

of the threats against the business owned by your neighbor, Mr. Tarantino?'

'No, and I resent this intrusion.'

'Sir. You were present three nights ago when Mr. Tarantino's customers' cars were damaged. Do you know of any reason for the attacks on his business?'

'No, and I resent this intrusion.'

'Mr. Chase, night before last your car was in Mr. Tarantino's parking lot. Could you tell me what business you had there or if you loaned your car to someone?'

'No. This interview is over.' "

Tony stopped. "You get the picture. Unless we have some hard evidence, he doesn't have to cooperate and he doesn't intend to. I was told to tread softly, and for all the information I got, I might as well have never been there. The only flicker I saw was when I mentioned his car being in your lot. He definitely looked surprised. I dug up a little interesting background, though. Thirty years ago, Chase was married, and they had a child."

Danny was taken aback. "Must've been very short lived. I never considered him the marrying kind."

Tony snorted. "Speaking of not being the marrying kind, how's the vacation romance with Ms. Mulroney?"

Danny kept his tone neutral. "Fine."

"Hey, you're supposed to laugh when I bring up marriage." A choking sound came through the receiver. "Don't tell me you're serious about her after what, four days?"

A shift of warmth crept in when he thought about Pallas. But Tony was right. It had only been four days. "Just keeping my options open. By the way, I need another favor."

"Nice segue," Tony said dryly. "What kind of favor?"

"Not big. How long would it take to scan your department computer records and find out about any major incidents that happened around April, twenty years ago, give or take a month?"

"Like what?"

"Like casino robbery, arson, murder, that kind of thing."

"Short list. Is this official or unofficial?"

"It's a hunch."

"I won't even ask, then. It'll take about ten minutes. Want me to call you back as soon as I get the results?"

"Yeah, thanks."

Danny was about to make another call when someone knocked on his door. "Come in."

He wouldn't have been more surprised if the Rockettes' entire chorus line had kicked through his doorway. There stood Henri in brand new overalls and a freshly starched toque. A bright red kerchief tied at his throat finished the ensemble.

Danny looked him up and down. "Uh, the kitchen won't be in working order until tomorrow. Didn't you get a call?"

The chef nodded. "*Oui*. I have brought food for the workers and staff. I will use a table to set up in the dining room."

Danny could see there was no deterring the man. "Thank you, very much. I appreciate the thought, but you didn't have to go to all this trouble. I'm keeping everyone on full pay."

Henri loosened his stiff posture. *"Oui.* I understand. It is the least I can do."

Danny felt another rush of warmth. He'd known the chef was temperamental and emotional. He was now learning the little man was also generous. "Well, thanks again."

Henri nodded and left, closing the door.

Danny starting working on the questionnaire Mark had left, but his mind was on the search Tony was running. He snatched up the phone halfway through the first ring. "Tarantino."

"You are not gonna believe what I found," Tony said. "What I want to know is how the hell you came up with this?"

Chapter Twenty-Nine

Danny gripped his cell phone. "What have you got?"

"In April, twenty years ago, there was one murder and a couple of missing persons."

"Which would I be interested in?"

"The murder victim owed lots of money to lots of people and wasn't prompt about repaying it. The male half of the two missing persons was Jonathan Chase's partner at Suttons."

Half the air left Danny's lungs. "Jonathan Chase isn't associated with Suttons. I worked there for years."

Tony continued. "He isn't now. He sold it thirteen years ago to the current owners. Made a bundle. Chase was the quiet partner. Al Hart was the front man. Although casino ownership is public record, most people thought it was owned by Hart. Chase cooperated during the interviews after Hart's disappearance."

"I suppose he had an alibi for the time."

"He didn't need one. He gave a statement on his whereabouts, and Hart's never been found, so there were no charges filed."

"So Hart was declared legally dead after seven years, and Chase sold the club as full owner. Did Hart have any family?"

Keys tapped in the silence. "Yeah. A wife who raised a big stink. She's the one who reported him missing and claimed entitlement to income from the casino until Hart showed up or she could collect on his life insurance.

"When Hart disappeared, he only owned about twenty percent of Suttons, which still added up to a tidy take. He and Chase also had an airtight personal contract, which not only included a surviving-partner insurance policy but *any* eventuality—coma, lost at sea, *anything.* The wife got a minimal stipend and the rumor that her husband ran off with a showgirl. The girl being the other reported missing person.

"Hart also had a brother in Atlantic City. It seems casinos ran in the family. He set up a sizable reward in return for any information leading to his brother's whereabouts, but no one ever came forward. The reward is still active."

Danny made some mental stretches and didn't like the results. "That gives me a lot to think about. Thanks."

"You still haven't answered my question," Tony said. "What made you think of April, twenty years ago?"

"Keep it to yourself for a while?"

Tony paused. "Unless it involves information on an open case."

"Not sure yet. Twenty years ago in April, Pallas's father, Lucky Jack Mulroney, was banned from gambling in any Tahoe casino for a year. He'd been caught cheating at Suttons. Yesterday, Pallas and I found out my dad had played an unwitting part in the setup."

"You think it was a setup? Why?"

"That's what I'm helping her find out. It's possible

Lucky Jack knew something he shouldn't, or somebody thought he did. Whether he did or not, for some reason, he took the ban without squawking. During that same time, Chase's partner disappears. It's a little too coincidental."

Tony interrupted. "Okay. This is all very interesting and might be worth pursuing, but some lunatic is trying to shut you down, and you're chasing a twenty-year-old gambling ban nobody cares about except the redhead. Is her issue worth losing your club over? Because that might happen unless you start focusing."

Danny's gut wrenched. Tony's attitude shift pissed him off. "I am focusing. I think there's a connection between the events of twenty years ago and what's happening to me today."

"And has it occurred to you that the beautiful redhead has been around as long as your problem? That she conveniently showed up to claim a tournament slot caused by the near-fatal accident, that she was the only one that got sick, that she could *be* your problem?"

"Yes," Danny said, not covering the edge in his voice. "All of that's occurred to me."

Tony sighed. "I'm sorry. I'll back off, for the time being. What's next?"

"Jack Mulroney will be in town tomorrow. We're going to have a chat with him and Ty Addison."

"We, meaning you and Pallas?"

Danny thought of her standing there in that ludicrous pajama top this morning, reminding him to talk to Ty. "She only needs to know if her father was innocent. No way is she in the equation if there's a connection and this whole thing turns sour." He swallowed, his throat dry. "Besides, she goes back to San Francisco day after tomorrow."

"Which should leave us time to concentrate on the guy threatening you before she comes back."

Warmth spread outward from his solar plexus. "Who said she's coming back?"

Tony's voice dropped. "If she's involved, she'll be back because it isn't over. If not, she'll be back for you."

"Maybe, maybe not. She has a whole other very successful life two hundred miles away."

"Doesn't matter, if she's as hooked on you as you are on her. Just keep your head. Okay?"

"Sure," Danny said and meant it. "Change of subject. It's been a couple of days since we turned over the drink that made Pallas sick. Do you have any lab results yet?"

"Expected back late today or tomorrow morning. Let me know if you find out anything interesting from Jack Mulroney. I wouldn't put much credence in what Ty Addison has to say."

"I know. He's having a hard time of it. If he agrees to meet with us tomorrow, Jack may be able to trigger some memories. I'll let you know. Thanks for the update."

"Right. See you."

Danny ended the call and frowned. Tony hadn't been very subtle in his suspicions about Pallas's involvement in his club's problems. He scrubbed his face with his hands. He'd come close to losing her last night. A thought that terrified him.

He took a deep breath. In any case, he was on the short road to crazy. That might make him stupid, but he only cared if she was at the other end.

Right now, a dozen questions fought for his concentration. He needed more answers to put the pieces together, and he would probably get a few of them, but not until tomorrow.

He smiled and called Suttons. "Room 617, please."

"Hello." Then came a sleep-softened moan like she was stretching.

Danny envisioned her lying in bed wearing the turquoise silk wrap and not much else. He shifted in his chair. "That's a very sexy way to answer the phone. Sorry to wake you. I thought I'd wish you luck for this afternoon."

"Uh, huh, thank you," she murmured.

"No. Thank *you*. Want to meet at my place for dinner again?"

"Should I stop for ribs?"

"Nope. Between the food going unused in the kitchen and some stuff Henri brought over, there should be plenty. Besides, the only ribs I'm interested in are freckled."

He could almost feel the heat in her Cheshire Cat smile and see those heavy-lidded beautiful blue eyes.

"Then I'll bring dessert," she said.

He shifted again. Talk about literally feeding a fantasy. "All right. See you at seven."

"Wait a minute. Are we dressing up or down?"

"I have tux duty in the casino from three to seven. Wear something complicated at your own risk."

"I'll take it under advisement."

He still had the grin on his face a few minutes later when Bru strolled into his office.

Danny checked his watch. "You're a couple of

hours early."

"Yeah. Some water seeped under the door in the storeroom, and the cardboard boxes holding the bar stock got soaked. Mandy and I are going to clean in there when she gets here. That door's always locked, and we totally forgot about it, so the crew you hired didn't get to it." He cocked his head at Danny. "You were max stressed last night. Looks like you got plenty of relaxing sleep." He peered closer, pretending to study Danny's face. "No, not sleep. You got plenty of relaxing something, though. Where is she?"

Danny rolled his eyes. "Where's who?"

Bru wiggled his eyebrows. "Pallas, I'm assuming. Did you know anybody leaving your quarters has to go right past the bar? Unless she left by boat, she was still with you when I went home at two."

"It's gratifying to know my personal life is so interesting. Nevertheless, it *is* personal."

The bartender made a rude noise. "Testy, testy. Is she coming for dinner again?"

"And we're having lunch tomorrow and dinner tomorrow night. Will keeping track of our whereabouts interfere with your work?"

Bru pulled back, frowning. Danny'd gone too far.

"Sorry."

His friend lifted a shoulder. "No big. I just didn't think it would happen so fast. Where's the terror, the dry heaves? My social circle reduced by one important friend in less than a week." He shuddered. "That means it could happen to me, too. I mean Pallas is great and everything…"

Laughter bubbled up in Danny. A combination of the thought of him and Pallas as a couple and Bru's look of horror. "It's all about you, dude. I'll still be here every day. You're not getting rid of me that easy."

The horror started to fade a little, so Danny reassured him. "It's not communicable."

Bru twitched. "Anything new on the mad note writer?"

Danny filled him in on his talk with Tony and his hunches about Jonathan Chase.

Chapter Thirty

Pallas lay awake after Danny's sweet call. Their night together crowded everything else out of her mind. Gone was the notion that they might not be sexually compatible. Gone, too, were her reservations that had her holding on to her life in San Francisco. There was no mistaking the raw desire in Danny's eyes when they made love. All the pieces of a real and lasting relationship were coalescing. And the partnership had taken a back seat the minute she'd offered him her tournament winnings.

That left the other reason she was here. Her father's ban. No denying the sights she'd set on her future had shifted, but she wouldn't give up that goal.

She got up and dressed, wanting to get to the tournament early. The competition had dwindled considerably. Most of the remaining tables would have only two or three players left. There would be three hours of elimination play, then the final challenge round where the top winner from each table was invited to an hour of no-holds-barred draw poker. She wanted to be in that final challenge and intended to size up her possible competitors.

When she got downstairs, she scanned the room and saw Ty Addison talking to another man. Her promise to Danny had been not to approach the players at Jimmy G's. She saw no reason not to talk to Ty about lunch now. She crossed to him and waited. As Ty turned her way, she held out her hand. "Do you remember me, Mr. Addison? I'm Jack Mulroney's daughter, Pallas. We met at Over the Moon a few days ago."

The older man was visibly shaken. He took her hand, then released it immediately. "Uh, sure. How's your dad doing?" His pale color and unwillingness to look her in the eyes were dead giveaways. He didn't want to have anything to do with her.

"He's fine. As a matter of fact, he'll be in town tomorrow and…"

"Tell him I said hello. I don't want to be rude, but I've got to be going. I'm late for the practice hands at Jimmy G's. Nice to see you again." He left hastily. At the doorway he cut a quick look behind him.

She stood there wondering about his reaction. This was the second time he'd panicked after they'd only exchanged a few sentences. And this time he'd outright lied. Danny'd told her the group was no longer practicing there. It had to be something else, but she had the feeling asking him directly wouldn't net her any more than what he'd just given her. Maybe he thought she blamed him for her father's ban. That wasn't at all true, but it looked like she would have to wait and see if Danny could talk him into joining them for lunch.

She sighed. The room had filled with players, and she had a job to do. She'd held her own so far, but as the winnings were posted each day, she could see the competition would be stiff. Her day job involved risk-taking but of a wildly different kind. She cleared her mind and sat down to focus.

Her skill and luck held. She won the money she'd

come for, plus more than enough to pay her expenses. The other young player at her table topped her overall winnings by six thousand dollars. The leanest margin between first and second place at the tournament. Her smile was genuine when she signed her final winnings card. She now had a much better plan for her money and headed for the sponsor's table.

She nodded at the fifty-something guy. "Hi. I'm Pallas Mulroney. I was sitting at table six."

The man gave her an undisguised look of yearning. "Yes, I know. What can I personally do for you?"

"I saw your schedule of tournaments when I signed the contract. Are there any spots left on the next one?"

The tournament promoter blinked at her question. "Playing at your level takes a toll on a person. Sure you want to get into another tournament so soon? With your ranking here, I can get you in a slot in one starting in Reno in ten days. Give you time to rest." He winked broadly. "Won't hurt the feelings of the camera crew, either."

She took the crude compliment in stride. "I'm interested in something sooner. Are there any openings or not?"

He handed her a card. "Two, starting in a couple of days," he said, shifting in his chair. "Wanna be added to the list? We'll need the entry fee within twenty-four hours."

Spreading herself thin, she thought. Sassy's christening for baby Chloe, lunch with her dad and Ty, if he would come, to discuss the ban. And of course, Danny. Well, damn. Her list hadn't included her possible partnership. What kind of Freudian slip was that?

She bit her lower lip and nodded. Danny would have no reason to turn her down now. She *could* have it all.

****

Danny walked through the door at Jimmy G's a few minutes before two. He figured he could talk to Ty about lunch tomorrow and still have plenty of time to get back to the club and change into his tux. As soon as his eyes became accustomed to the light, however, he saw Ty wasn't there.

Jimmy walked toward him. "Everything okay?"

Danny shook his head. "Okay's a loaded word. Getting closer to finding out who's attacking the club, though. Thing is it may be connected to the gambling ban imposed on Pallas's dad twenty years ago."

The older man grinned. "Sounds like the redhead might stick around a while."

Danny nodded. "Working on it. There's the little matter of her hugely successful new partnership in San Francisco. That's the sticking point."

"You'll figure it out. So Ty's part of your solution? That's why you're looking for him?"

"He could be. Seems to be making himself scarce." He took in the big, open room. "If he comes in, ask him to contact me, will you?"

"Sure." Jimmy nodded, his gaze steady. "Ty's had a lot to overcome, you know. His whole slide into the bottle wasn't just gambling debt. He'd lost his family because of it, too."

Danny hadn't known. "No pressure. Just want to jiggle his memory. If he gets uncomfortable, we'll let it go."

"Hope he's able to help. Speaking of help. You still

okay for money? Offer stays open."

Danny smiled. "You're as bad as the redhead. She keeps trying to bail me out, too."

The tall man held up his hands in surrender. "Too much woman for me." He tipped his head toward the casino's door. "Good luck finding Ty."

Outside, Danny stood in the lot, thinking. The motel Ty had listed as his residence on the tournament contract was within walking distance of Jimmy's.

A few minutes later he was knocking on a faded blue door. Ty opened it, his lips pulled in. He looked more resigned than surprised.

"Can I come in?" Danny asked.

Ty turned back into the room, leaving the doorway empty.

Danny stepped in and closed the door. He noticed a small, battered suitcase on the bed. "Taking a trip?"

The older man glanced at the suitcase. "Thought I'd go to Vegas for a while." He paused, then looked sidelong at Danny. "Unless the trouble at your club's over. That why you're here?"

He was sad at the hollow hope of Ty's words. "Uh, no. I came to ask you a favor."

Ty shrugged, still not making eye contact. "I guess I owe you."

He shook his head. "You don't owe me anything. The decision is entirely up to you. Can we sit down?"

A flush of red circled Ty's neck above his collar. "Sure." He walked to a table with two plastic chairs.

Danny had always preferred straightforward talk and figured Ty did, too. "Twenty years ago you were involved in Lucky Jack Mulroney's ban. He'll be in town tomorrow, and it means a lot to his daughter to know what happened. Can you join Jack and us for lunch at my place around noon?"

Ty's hand jerked spasmodically, so he slid it off the table. He took a deep breath and gave a wobbly smile. "Guess it's about time. I'll be there."

Danny tried to put him at ease. "No one's laying blame, just trying to put some pieces of information together. You know my father was the dealer that afternoon. He thinks the whole thing was a setup, and you and he were drawn in to make it look legitimate. There also might be bigger issues here than Jack's ban, so if you'd rather not get involved, we'll understand."

The older man shrugged. "I'd better unpack and get over to Jimmy's. See if I can find a profitable game."

Danny stood and held out his hand. Ty's grip was firm, and he met Danny's gaze.

****

The black dress she put on was the closest thing to wanton Pallas had ever purchased. She'd bought it on a whim and hadn't had the courage to wear it to any of her company's evening functions. Very little distinguished it from a silk slip except for the heart shape of jet beading that drew the eye from her décolletage to the daringly long slit up the front.

She intended to use every ounce of her womanly wiles to get Danny to accept her loan. *Not to mention getting him out of his tux. Not that that would be a problem.* She topped the dress with a short, faux curly lamb jacket. The looks she received when getting off the elevator and crossing the lobby at Suttons proved she'd made the right choice.

The thrum of expectation had been building in her belly since she had gotten in her car and was getting stronger the closer she got to Over the Moon. It was going to take an inordinate amount of willpower to concentrate on convincing Danny of her sincerity in wanting to loan him the money, but she could do it. After all, she'd talked industrial giants into investing their money in high-risk ventures. *You weren't head over heels in love and lust with any of them, Mulroney.*

It was a couple of minutes past seven when she arrived. A quick scan told her he wasn't in the gaming area. She knew there were hard-core gamblers out there, so the crowd of people who showed up in spite of the slight smell of smoke and cleaning solution didn't surprise her.

During the short walk to the dining room, she wondered if he would still look at her with an all-consuming possession as he had when she left this morning. She hoped so because she had it so bad for him she was beginning to doubt her sanity.

She reached for the button on her jacket. Luckily, it was bolero style, and there was only one. She managed to undo it and shake the coat off without dropping it or her beaded clutch.

Danny stood facing the half-empty bar, talking to a cocktail waitress. The girl nodded at him, then gave Pallas an open appraisal.

Bru spotted her next and grinned. He tipped his head toward her and said something to Danny. When Danny turned his full attention on her, the air whooshed out of her lungs. It was all there—the heat, the need, the same wanting she knew was as plain as day on her own face. Her gaze focused on his mouth, and her skin flushed warm remembering the deliciously wicked things he had done to her with it last night. Things she'd begged him to do again and again.

He took a couple of steps to meet her, leaning in to kiss her chastely and whispering, "Please tell me you've never worn that dress for anyone else."

She shook her head, not trusting her voice.

"Good," he said, taking her free hand and running his thumb back and forth over her knuckles. "Dinner's warming in my kitchen. Potluck okay?"

"Fine." She hoped there was lots of water because she couldn't have spit to save herself.

As they started past the bar, Bru walked down to them. "Lookin' fine, Pallas. Can I fix you a Moon Goddess to go?"

She grinned, the warmth of Danny's touch traveling up her arm. "Uh, no, thanks. I'm already under the influence."

Bru was momentarily speechless, then recovered. "Sprinkler system working in your place, boss?"

Danny glowered at him, but she looked at Bru curiously. He wiggled his eyebrows. "Heat."

She pressed her lips together, her blush returning as Danny opened the door to the enclosed hallway. He dropped her hand and started to unlock the second door.

"What, no stopping to kiss?" she said, half joking.

He turned and gave her a look that stripped away any last doubt she might have harbored about his need. "I'm afraid you'll have to wait," he said. "The floor in this hall can't be all that comfortable, but it's exactly where we'd be if I started kissing you."

She looked down, blinking and gauging the thickness of the sculpted carpet. "Oh."

He took her hand again, pulling her gently through the door and closing it behind them. They walked part way into his quarters before Danny held out his other hand. "Let me take your things."

She gave him her jacket and purse. He tossed them on the couch but didn't go farther into the room. Instead, he removed his coat and tie, unbuttoned the top two buttons on his shirt, popped his cufflinks, and put them in his pockets so he could roll up his sleeves.

"Might as well be comfortable for dinner." He walked behind her then, his hands coming to rest on her hips as he stopped to press his lips to the nape of her neck. "I like your hair up. It exposes possibilities."

Pallas trembled as his fingers slid up and down the soft flesh in front of her hipbones. "Thanks. Are we going to talk?"

"What's your hurry?" he asked, continuing his trail of kisses along her shoulder to the dress strap. "About this dress. It has some amazing structural engineering. Kind of like the things showgirls wear under their costumes."

She wondered for an instant how he knew what showgirls wore under their costumes, but decided it didn't matter. She would play it his way. "Actually, that's true, but it's very comfortable. I don't even need a bra."

He stopped mid-kiss. "Evil woman." Then he pulled her into his arms. She looped her arms around his neck, pressing herself into his chest and hips. He maneuvered her close to the living room wall, his hands slipping to her waist.

Pallas broke the kiss and rubbed her nose against his. "You promised we'd talk."

"Then talk," he said, dark eyes challenging her.

She put her palms against his chest. "About the

237

loan."

"Are you hungry?"

"Not really," she said, intent on pursuing her subject.

"Good," he answered, his tongue now following the groove of her collarbone. "Neither am I."

"Danny, stop."

He lifted his face and held his mouth within inches of hers, putting his hands against the wall of either side of her head. "Persuade me."

She squirmed. The onslaught her body was expecting, was crying out for, had ceased. Her breasts ached, and liquid torture swirled in her belly. His desire hammered at her through the beating of his heart beneath her fingers. She bunched her hands but could not keep her body from leaning in. What had happened to the power of her womanly wiles and the speech she'd rehearsed to make him understand how much she wanted to help?

He stared at her mouth.

"I did well today," she breathed.

He nodded, a hot light in his eyes. "You do everything well."

Her disloyal knees bent toward him. She had to get out what she wanted to say. "Anyway, it occurred to me that if I loaned you the money I won and I could negotiate the timeframe for buying the partnership, if that's what I still wanted, I could always come back and win it again. I mean, I know I can do it, and...well, I actually signed on for another tournament and the buy-in's due tomorrow."

"Yes," he said, interrupting her.

"What?"

"I said yes, I'll let you loan me some money. Now can I have your mouth back?"

Part of her brain registered disbelief at how easy it had been to convince him, but the part that wanted him naked, well, that part won. She closed the gap between their lips and sighed into his kiss.

Danny proceeded to kiss her senseless, and when she thought her knees would give way, she felt the rasp of her zipper being pulled down. Bare-skinned in a dark bedroom was one thing, but in a lighted living room with a man who was still dressed, Pallas should have felt self-conscious. But all she felt was joy and giddiness and yes, power.

Chapter Thirty-One

Danny thought he could go slow, make it sweet and aching for her, but when he pulled the straps of Pallas's dress forward and it fell it to the floor, it took a reserve he didn't think he possessed to keep from taking her in a very ungentlemanly way.

She reached for his shirt buttons, not saying a word. Afraid if he touched her, heat would make sparks fly from her skin, he started pulling pins from her hair, freeing it to fall over her shoulders. She shook her head, and having finished with his buttons, slid her hands inside his waistband to tug at his shirt.

He wondered if he could have a heart attack at thirty from sheer lust. She peeled off his shirt and ran her mouth across his chest while her fingernails made witchy tracks over his back. He stood it for all of thirty seconds before picking her up and pulling her legs around him to head for the bedroom.

"Food later," he mumbled.

She nipped the corner of his mouth. "Picked out what I want."

He toed the heels of his shoes and kicked them off somewhere in the living room, vaguely aware that hers had fallen off, too. When they reached his bed, a waning moon cast enough light for him to go to his knees, sitting her on the edge.

He gently pulled her arms from his shoulders and

stood to take off his tux pants. His own discomfort was growing by the second, but he refused to give in. The longer he held out, the more enjoyment she would have. When she started to unhook her silky black stockings, he stopped her. They met on their knees in the middle of the bed.

She reached for him. "My turn."

He shook his head and cradled her to her back. "Next time, I promise," and slipped inside her.

He waded through the heat of her passion as she made sounds of pleasure and satisfaction. They ended on one gasp.

As their heartbeats slowed, Danny quashed the remnant of belief that he'd experienced the best lovemaking ever last night.

He grinned when she pulled his wrists over his head and lay on top of him, rubbing against his length while she kissed him. His grinning stopped, and he propped himself on his elbows when she knelt and nipped at his thighs with her teeth.

"That's going to cost you," he said.

"Mulroneys always pay their debts." She giggled as she ran her fingers over the arch of his foot, making him jump.

"No fair tickling." He laughed, diving for her.

Pallas turned to him when she could speak again. "Did you mean what you said?"

He gave her his best arched eyebrow hitch. The money again. She was stubborn in her efforts to help him. "Are you holding me responsible for rash promises I made while you had your way with me?" he asked.

She plucked at his lower lip. "As I recall, you had

all your mental faculties when you said you would let me loan you the money."

He licked his finger and made a circle at the top of her breast. "I never have all my mental faculties with you in reach."

"Danny?" Her tone turned impatient.

He wanted to keep the subject light without flat refusing. "Oh, sure. The money. I thought for a minute there was some other promise you'd witched out of me. Pretty unfair considering I would have signed over the deed to the homestead to have you again."

She laughed and grabbed him in a fierce hug. "How about dinner, Casino Boy? Just so I can regain some strength."

He kissed the tip of her nose and rolled to the edge of the bed, reaching to click on the bedside lamp. "One crumpled dress coming up." He turned. "Unless, of course, you wouldn't mind eating in those black stockings and that pajama top from last night. I'm beginning to like cherubs."

She looked exasperated. "Darn. I was so nervous when I got here I left the change of clothes I brought in the car."

He stood and walked around to her side of the bed to sit beside her, then lifted her chin. "You were nervous to be with me? Is that why you wore that drop-dead sexy dress? To impress me?"

This close, he saw the answer in her eyes before she spoke. There was no guile or false modesty.

"I was sure, but I wasn't sure about, you know, whether last night was maybe a sort of tension breaker, a way of scratching an itch we both had."

He barked a laugh. "Honey, you could have worn

sackcloth and duct tape, and I would have still gotten hard. If that's what you thought, then this is going to be the longest one-night stand in history. In gambling parlance, 'we're a natural.' " He leaned to nuzzle her neck. "And not just in bed."

She laid her hand on the side of his face, smiling. "Big talk. Now please go get my clothes while I clean up and see if anything in the kitchen is salvageable."

He headed into his dressing room. Any other woman and he would have balked at following orders. He called over his shoulder, "I'm assuming your keys are in your bag. I'm certain they're not anywhere on your person."

"Very funny Tarantino. Yes. They're in my bag."

He pulled on some soft jeans and a sweatshirt, then stopped in the doorway to his dressing room, watching in fascination as she stretched and grinned. *A redhead, of all things, I've fallen in love with a gorgeous redheaded financial whiz and demon poker player. One who wants to save me and my dream, maybe at the expense of hers. What magic feat am I going to have to perform to deserve this?*

He stepped into the room. "Thought you were going to check on dinner while I got your clothes?"

She started, then scrunched her face. "Oh, all right. I suppose it's better than marching through the club *en dishabille.*"

A pang of remorse went through him. "Sorry about your dress. I'll hang it up before I leave."

She smiled. "I don't think either of us thought much about the condition of our clothes this evening."

He knelt by the bed again, sliding one hand under the covers around her waist and one to cradle her neck.

"Get used to it," he said as he pulled her toward him for a kiss.

He cut the kiss short out of sheer self-preservation and got to his feet. Having this woman in his life forever was a growing possibility.

She trailed her fingers up his arm. "Let's talk more about that loan over dinner."

When he walked out of his quarters to the bar, Bru nearly dropped the bottle he'd been juggling. The bartender gave him the once over. "You get any more relaxed, you'll need a cane."

Danny shook his head. He was too happy to take the bait. "I'll pick up a couple of ginger ales on my way back in."

He walked through the casino and out to the rental Pallas was using. A small, nylon carryall lay on the front seat. He retrieved the bag and was headed back when he heard a woman's piercing scream. It came from the nearly empty lot on the dining room side of the club. Danny cursed and took off at a dead run. The grisly sight that greeted him when he came around the corner pulled him up short.

One of his cocktail waitresses, Shelby, stood by her car door, staring at a scene illuminated by her headlights. The car was still running. The lights showed Elliot Kerr slumped against a tree on the other side of the shrubs bounding Jonathan Chase's property. Kerr was pinned to the tree with an arrow through his upper chest. It was impossible to see how bad he was bleeding since his jacket was black. The guard dogs growled and sniffed but didn't maul him.

He looked dead.

Danny got as close to the scene as he could. He

squinted and blinked. "Shit."

With his pale face hanging forward and the headlight illuminating his thinning hair, Kerr bore a striking resemblance to Jonathan Chase. What the hell was going on? Was Kerr related to Chase? Had he been hanging around Over the Moon to gather information?

Then Danny noticed the fletching on the arrow. *Damn.*

The lot attendant showed up in seconds. Followed by Bru. "Jeez, isn't that the guy from your tournament?"

Danny nodded and took the arm of the attendant. "Don't let anyone from here off my property. Those dogs are dangerous. I'm calling the sheriff."

Bru followed Danny into the club. "What can I do?"

"Send Mandy out to calm Shelby down but don't move her car until the sheriff's office says it's okay. Then call Jonathan Chase and have him come get his damn dogs so the medics can get in there."

Bru tipped his head in the direction of the parking lot. "Uh, that arrow…"

"Yeah, I know. It looks like one of mine."

Danny opened the door to his quarters and headed for the phone. Pallas came out of the kitchen carrying a steaming dish to the table. She wore the pajama top, her black stockings, and a grin.

The grin died when she saw him. "What's wrong?"

He motioned her over as the number rang on speakerphone, connecting him to the 911 operator. "There's a seriously hurt man at 720 Lake Road. He's pinned to a tree behind the house by an arrow. There are guard dogs, so we can't get close enough to tell how bad it is. I'm calling from the business next door." He listened to the woman's questions as Pallas set down the dish and gripped his wrist, her face pale. "Danny Tarantino, 555-1190. Yes, I know the man. His name is Elliott Kerr, and he's around thirty. Can you send an ambulance right away? Yes, I'll stay on the line until an officer arrives."

He put his free hand over the mouthpiece and spoke to Pallas. "My cell phone's on the nightstand. Would you get it for me?"

She hurried into the bedroom, returning and handing him the small unit.

He handed over her bag, then looked at her worry-etched face. "Do you trust me?"

Pallas tipped her head. "Of course, why?"

He hugged her, wanting to back up time and keep her in his bed and his arms. Wanting to tell her how much she'd come to mean to him in five short days. "Get dressed, please. I may need you for an alibi."

She drew a sharp breath but took the bag and hurried into the bedroom.

He punched a speed dial number on his cell, then muted his desk phone, holding the cell phone to his other ear. He breathed a silent prayer of thanks when Tony answered.

"Hello."

"One of my former tournament players, a man named Elliott Kerr, is pinned to a tree on Chase's property by what looks like one of my arrows."

"Shit."

He let out a pent-up breath as he heard sirens approaching. "My word, exactly, but I have a very good alibi, if you're wondering. I've also got the feeling this is the end of the threats against the club. For one thing, I realize now why Kerr looked familiar. For another, Chase's dogs aren't ripping the guy to shreds. Maybe because he isn't a stranger to them."

Tony sighed. "I didn't want to watch the NBA playoffs anyway. Meet me at the station and bring your alibi." He paused. "You realize as your friend, I won't be assigned the case."

"I know. Just show up as moral support?"

"On my way."

"Thanks." Danny punched the End button.

Pallas came back into the room as someone knocked on the door. Danny nodded to her, so she answered it, taking a half step back. Pat Murphy filled the doorway.

He could see the surprise on the deputy's face at finding his sister-in-law here. He held the phone toward the big man. "Dispatch on the line."

The deputy took the phone. "Murphy. Yes, the ambulance's arrived." Another spell of silence passed while he listened, taking Danny's measure as he did. "I'm sure he won't mind coming in to give a statement."

After he hung up, he turned to Danny, a neutral expression in his eyes. "Man's still alive, for the time being, but not by much. Got enough life left to accuse you of shooting him."

Danny knew he hadn't shot Kerr, knew Pallas would back him up, but a hard knot of dread formed in his stomach anyway.

She slipped her hand into his. "That's ridiculous, Pat. Danny was on duty in the casino until seven. Then we came in here for dinner. I've been with him since then."

Danny watched her glance follow her brother-in-law's to take in the discarded clothing and shoes and the dishes still full of food on the table.

As bad as things were, he almost laughed at the fiery flush that crept up her cheeks. She held it together, though, sticking out her chin and pinning the deputy with a haughty look. "We had some personal business to discuss first."

Deputy Murphy gave it right back to her. "Then you'd best tidy up the leavings of your personal business, but touch nothing else." He gave a short nod. "I'll wait and call backup. Being as we're related, I can't be involved in this investigation."

Her mouth formed an O, and she looked around the room. "I'm sorry, Pat. Being defensive comes natural when you're the youngest of four girls. I'm rarely seen as old enough to make my own decisions."

Her brother-in-law stood by silently as Danny helped Pallas tidy up.

Danny held out her purse. "Do you want to go with me or follow?"

She looked at the tiny evening bag, then down at her jeans. "With you."

"Okay. You'd better bring ID." He turned to Pat Murphy. "Tony Mancusco is meeting us at the station. We'll wait if you'd like to check."

The deputy shook his head. "I have some details to finish here. I trust you'll go straight there."

Pallas hugged him. "Thanks, Pat." Then she stepped away, a curious look on her face. "How come you're here? I thought you worked days."

The big man grinned. "I traded shifts. Tomorrow's

little Chloe's christening and the arrival of your folks."

Danny saw the reality of their situation cross her features.

"Would you mind if I told Sassy and Mom and Dad about this?" she asked her brother-in-law.

Steady green eyes regarded her. "I'd prefer it."

"Thanks, again," she said. "You're the best."

Danny locked his quarters after them, stopping at the bar and waiting for Bru to finish a mixed drink. "Any help you can give the deputies, do it. Pallas and I will be with Tony at the station."

Bru nodded.

Outside, the crime scene was even more grisly as lights had been set up to aid the emergency technicians and investigators. Kerr lay on a stretcher, the arrow having been cut at the tree, still protruding. The technicians had set up an intravenous drip and wrapped as much of his torso as they could in blankets. Pallas gasped and turned her face away.

They got in the car and drove to the cruiser blocking the driveway. Danny approached the officer and spoke through the window, handing him two IDs. "I'm the owner, Danny Tarantino. We're on our way to the station to give a statement."

The officer got on his radio to confirm, then backed his car up.

Pallas stayed silent until they were on their way, but her hands twisted in her lap.

"Change your mind about coming?"

She blinked and turned to look at him. "No. I'm trying to make sense out of this. What does Elliott Kerr have to do with the attacks on your club?"

He didn't answer until they came to a stoplight,

then gave her his full attention. "The arrow looked like one of mine."

To his surprise, she nodded. "That makes sense. Nothing else they've tried worked, so they had to do something extreme. They even picked a time when you were off-duty. What I don't get is why him?"

"I have a theory," he said as they continued. "I think Kerr and Chase are related, and this whole mess is somehow connected to your father's ban."

She turned her head sharply. "How?"

He nodded. "In the right light, Kerr looks like a younger version of Jonathan Chase. He had a child about thirty years ago. It took me a while to figure out, but that's what I think. As for this being connected to the ban, I don't mean your father had anything to do with the attacks against the club. I mean your father may know something from a long time ago that not only had to do with his ban, but the stuff that's cropped up this past week."

She pulled her upper lip against her teeth. A habit, he was learning, that showed she was concentrating. "You think this whole mess could be cleared in a few days with Dad's help?"

"Possibly. I need more information from Tony, though."

She was quiet for another minute, then spoke softly. "Like finding out what was put in my drink?"

He reached for her hand as they pulled into the parking lot. "That's part of it."

The station was busy, which was not surprising for a Friday night in a town boasting round-the-clock entertainment.

Tony stood when they entered, giving Pallas a

discreet once-over.

Danny stopped in front of his desk. "Pallas, this is Tony Mancusco, a good friend and righter of wrongs."

She shook the hand he offered. "Nice to meet you. I appreciate the help you've been able to give Danny."

Tony smiled. "I've only helped so far because I hadn't met you yet. Is it too late to say bad things about him so you'll consider other, more sincere offers?"

She blushed and laughed. "I'm afraid so. He's stuck with me for the long run."

Danny glanced at her, warmed by her comment. Damn, she was beautiful, even in jeans and a long-sleeved tee and under the harsh fluorescent lights. He could see he would have to pace himself in the future. She looked beddable anywhere.

Tony had said something and was turning away.

"What?" Danny asked.

Tony spoke over his shoulder. "I said, we can go into an empty interview room. The duty guy is at the tail end of an investigation. He'll be back soon. I'm being allowed to start the paperwork, and that's all."

As they walked toward a series of hallway doors, one opened, and Jonathan Chase walked out followed by a deputy and an expensively suited man with a briefcase. Chase saw Danny and turned livid, pointing at him. "That's him. He tried to murder my son. You have the evidence."

Chapter Thirty-Two

So Kerr *was* his son. Things were beginning to fall into place. Danny stepped toward the older man and spoke quietly. "They don't have *my* evidence. Yet."

Chase blinked, then his skin turned ashen. He reached into his pocket and took out a vial, opening it and tipping a tiny white tablet under his tongue. He spoke to the man in the suit. "Get me some water."

With his cane blocking the narrow hallway, Chase took some slow breaths, and color returned to his face. His glance flicked to Pallas. "Your alibi? Paid by the hour?"

She made a tsking sound. "I'm not a member of that profession, but if I were, I could afford to be choosey." She took his measure from head to toe and back. "A shriveled up old nothing like you wouldn't be worth my time."

Chase's eyes bugged, and he knocked the paper cup of water out of the hand of his lawyer in his haste to cut around them.

"Looks like you hit a nerve," Tony said, trying unsuccessfully to hide a smile. "That also confirms the theory that he and Kerr are related. I wonder why he felt the need to bring in Troy Silvers, a top criminal lawyer, for a simple deposition." He crooked his finger at the young officer who'd accompanied Chase and his lawyer out of the room. "Is that Mr. Chase's statement?"

The man nodded. "He said he wasn't feeling well and wanted to visit his son in the hospital. He'd come in tomorrow and sign the typed version."

Tony held out a hand. "I'd like to read it. It might be associated with an ongoing investigation."

The deputy shrugged and thrust the pages at Tony. To Danny's consternation, he also grinned and gave Pallas a none-too-subtle appraisal. "Not enough time to enter it into the system tonight, anyway." He glanced at his watch, giving Pallas a sidelong glance. "I was off-shift as of about an hour ago. Can you leave it on my desk when you're done?"

Tony nodded and preceded them into a small room furnished with a table strewn with a legal pad and some pencils. Four chairs surrounded it.

Pallas turned to Tony before he even closed the door. "Danny was in the casino or with me the entire time." She shot her chin out, challenging Tony to say otherwise. "If you're his friend, you know he couldn't have done anything that barbaric."

"Don't sit down," he said mildly. "I need to get your statement but in another room. We're going to keep this as clean as possible."

She glanced at Danny and smiled. "Guess we can't compare notes."

Tony shook his head and guided her out the door. He was back in a couple of minutes. "I had doubts, but you are one lucky son of a bitch."

Danny shrugged, not quite understanding. "She is beautiful."

His friend shook his head. "I don't mean that, although she certainly is." He pinned Danny with a look of disbelief. "Ms. Mulroney stopped me in the hall and asked if 'engaged in sexual relations' was an acceptable phrase. She blushed to the roots of her hair when she said it. If I ever find a woman willing to stand up for me that way and she'll have me, I'm a goner."

Danny slouched in his chair, smug and satisfied. That was it in a nutshell. He was a goner and couldn't be happier about it. And all the reasons Pallas and he had the real thing kept piling up. No way he could or would deny his feelings for her. He gave a wry smile. "Yeah, it's amazing. I keep thinking I'm going to screw up and she'll bolt. I guess if being suspected of attempted murder doesn't do it, there's not much chance."

Tony sat across from Danny, laying Jonathan Chase's statement on the table. "I want to see what Chase had to say."

Danny watched his friend scan the pages, a line of worry developing. "What's the matter?"

"Chase claims you found out Elliott Kerr was his son and tried to kill him. Primarily because of all the money Chase cost you in lawsuits. He said you've threatened him before, and this was your way of finally getting back at him."

The knot in Danny's stomach tightened. "Hell, I've never threatened Chase. If I'd wanted to harm him, I would've done it a hundred and fifty thousand dollars ago. Besides, it only clicked that they were related when I saw Kerr slumped at the base of that tree. His face was pale, and the headlights emphasized his thinning hair. That's..." Danny stood, his metal chair screeching against the floor.

Tony sat back. "What is it?"

Danny scrubbed his face with his hands, then leaned them on the table. "If I'm right, it's another reason for me to have tried to kill Kerr."

"What is?"

"The notes. If Kerr wrote the threatening notes, we can compare the handwriting to his signature on the contract he filled out for the tournament."

Tony whistled and shook his head. "Revenge and money. Two very good motives for attempted murder. You also can't prove you didn't discover Kerr's identity before tonight." He held up a hand at Danny's startled look. "I'm only bringing up the obvious. Switching subjects. What about the arrow? Could it have been stolen or copied? Who besides you is good enough to have hit his target in the dark?"

Danny had known the question was coming. He tried to keep his expression neutral. "I'll have to dig around. Check to see if the storage shed has been broken into and if any of my arrows are missing. Someone could have used an arrow similar to mine. I'd have to examine it to be sure."

Tony's gaze was steady. "The department will do the comparison examination. Just to make it aboveboard. How many arrows do you keep in the shed?"

"Twenty."

Tony slapped the pad and pencil. "I'll take your statement, the key to the storage shed, and send someone over for that contract. We're going to need written permission to take those items into evidence. Avoids having to get a warrant. We also need to be notified immediately if you *stumble* across any evidence or information. Can't have some three-hundred-dollar-an-hour suit claiming tampering or corruption of the chain of evidence."

He nodded. Tony's point was well-taken. If Kerr died and it went to trial, a good attorney could sway the jury with only a couple of pieces of circumstantial evidence. And no matter how much Pallas talked about standing up for him, asking her to tell a courtroom full of gawking strangers she was having sex with him while a murder was being attempted from his property was a last resort. The realization of how hard that would be hadn't hit her yet, but it would.

He stood and brought a small key ring out of his pocket. "Here's the key to the shed. There's a back-up on a hook in the tack room. You know where that is. Get the permission in here, and I'll sign it."

Tony accepted the key and got up. "Write down everything from about six until Kerr was discovered. I'll see how Ms. Mulroney is doing and whether the lieutenant on duty is back."

He started to leave and turned. "One more thing. The question you so neatly sidestepped about who had access to your equipment and the ability to make a shot like that in almost full darkness. There can't be more than a couple."

Danny wished himself anywhere but here. He sighed. "There's only one. And right now, he's at rock bottom and not thinking clearly. I wanted to talk to him first."

"The answer's no. You know that. If you do find him, contact us."

Danny lifted a shoulder, avoiding Tony's gaze. "It doesn't make sense for Chase to hire someone to kill his son, just to frame me. And why was Kerr crouched by that tree?"

"Good points." Tony nodded. "But the answers have to come from the investigation." A look of understanding suddenly lit his face, and he snapped his fingers. "You're talking about your dad's neighbor, aren't you? Bud McKee. I've been to a couple of your matches. He's an expert shot, and you use the same practice range."

His stomach sank. "Damn it, Tony. His wife's in the hospital dying of cancer."

Tony made a fist around the key. "And what about the attempted murder investigation aimed straight at you?"

Danny locked his jaw. "All right, I've got it. Only keep his circumstances in mind, okay?"

His friend nodded and sighed. "Okay. Listen, Toxicology found nitroglycerine in the drink that made Pallas sick. Really throw even a healthy person for a loop for a short while, but nothing long term."

"That's used by people with heart problems, right? Like Chase?"

"And about a million others."

Danny pushed out a breath. "I'll let her know there won't be any permanent effects."

Tony turned to leave again, then spoke over his shoulder. "Your life has certainly gotten exciting since she showed up."

****

Pallas reread her words for the third time. Short of writing *Danny Tarantino is innocent* in all caps across the top, she'd made it embarrassingly clear that he was with her from seven until a few minutes before the victim was discovered.

She looked up as Tony walked in. She liked Danny's friend. He was obviously honest and wanted to help without compromising his or Danny's ethics. He was dark-haired like Danny but rangy rather than solid. His kind brown eyes had twinkled when she'd asked the question on wording her statement.

"Done?" he asked.

"Yes. Can I leave?"

Tony held out his hand for her papers. "Danny says he can bring you in sometime tomorrow to sign the typed version. Is that all right with you?"

She sighed as they walked back down the hall to the room where Danny waited. "Going to be a busy day. My parents are arriving, then we have lunch and Chloe's christening. Maybe I'll come in early and sign it."

Danny stood, an odd expression on his face. "Ready?"

They said good-bye to Tony and left. When they reached the car, Danny pulled her into his arms for a passionate kiss.

"Not that that wasn't very nice," she said, snuggling close, "but was there any particular reason?"

He kissed her cheekbones and the tip of her nose. "You reminded me how busy we'll be tomorrow, then Sunday you'll be gone. For good unless you're called back to testify. Something I hope isn't going to be necessary. In any case, I'm going to kiss you every chance I get until you leave."

"I'm not leaving."

Chapter Thirty-Three

Danny held her at arm's length. "What do you mean, you're not leaving?"

She focused on his eyes, shadowed by the parking lot light. She lifted a shoulder. "I decided to loan you the money *and* have enough for the partnership. I told you I already signed up for the next tournament. I'm going to get enough, and I'm not going back. Not now, anyway."

His blank expression wasn't what she'd expected when she told him her decision. She'd hoped for at least a hint of a smile. "What's the matter?"

"I said you could loan me *some* money. I don't want to be responsible if you lose the partnership. I also don't want you to be around if this situation gets uglier. It would be better all-around for you to go back to San Francisco as planned."

She shook out of his hold. Five days' acquaintance and some amazing sex did not mean he could tell her what to do. "Really? I'm hearing what you want. Now you're going to hear what I want.

"You may try and weasel out of that loan, but you know damn well I meant all of my winnings, no strings attached." She paced away from him. "If I wanted the partnership more than I wanted to loan you the money, I wouldn't have offered, would I?" She jabbed a finger toward the station. "This *situation* is almost over, and you know it. Elliott Kerr lied when he accused you, and if they do their jobs right, they'll find that out. I love it that you want to protect me, but as far as running back to San Francisco, not gonna happen."

He walked toward her, head down. "All of that makes sense, but I won't have you dragged…"

She held up her hand, palm out. "I'm over the legal age, barely sane, because you make me crazy, but I'm staying. Got it?"

His head snapped up, and he stopped. "Is that so?"

Her heart lurched like a trip hammer, and now that they were outside the circle of light, she couldn't read his eyes. "Depends on your comeback."

He stepped closer. "You're stubborn and impulsive, and I don't think you're controllable."

She put fisted hands on her hips. "What's the downside?"

He sighed with resignation. "God help me, even with everything I know, I want you to stay." He held out his arms. "As for that other part, I'm not sure crazy comes close to describing it."

Tears burned her eyelids, and she went into his embrace. "It's not going to be easy."

He nuzzled her neck. "I've always liked a challenge."

She swallowed and hugged his waist. "As someone mentioned earlier this evening, 'Get used to it.' "

His kiss made her a promise, heated her blood, and swept away everything but the two of them. She reveled in it.

He was quiet on the way back to the club as Pallas turned tonight's event over in her mind. When they estimated the time of assault on Elliott Kerr, she could be Danny's only hard witness, although Bru or the other bartender might step forward and testify they only saw him leave the one time, to get her clothes. It was a sobering thought.

"About the lunch meeting tomorrow," she said, turning to him. "We could cancel. The accusation against you is more important."

He glanced at her and shook his head. "Nope. I think your instincts about your dad's ban are right on. We still need to get him and Ty together. I meant to tell you earlier I found Ty at his motel. He was packed to leave town."

She jerked her gaze to his. "What happened?"

"I think he's carrying some guilt attached to your father's ban. Maybe he was set up like my dad. Might also be because they both saw something they didn't attach any importance to, and the one who did wanted to make sure they weren't around to make a connection. This whole thing is going to bust wide open in the next day or two. Sure you don't want to change your mind and go home? Could be some nasty fallout."

She put her hand on his forearm and grinned. "Not in a million years. I've never felt this high."

He laughed. "Well, this week hasn't been typical. Life with me is generally pretty ordinary." His gaze stayed straight ahead. "Think you could get used to ordinary?"

She was lightheaded with joy. It sounded like he was asking her to stay forever. Her answer came from her heart. "I'm looking forward to it."

The lot on the dining room side of the club still had a few official vehicles in it when they got back. Danny took her hand. "Still hungry?"

She grinned. "I'm not falling for that one again."

"Regretting where you wound up?"

Pallas curled her hand around his neck, pulled him to her, and kissed him soundly. "No."

When they got to the bar, Danny handed her his keys. "Would you go on in and see if any of the food is worth saving? I need to check the casino and see how bad this little misadventure hurt the take."

"Okay."

She went into his quarters and found the serving dishes, even though covered, held dried-out food. She dumped them and looked around. The events of the week brought her up short every time she went down the road of them as a serious couple. How serious? She was well and truly head over heels for a man who was almost a complete stranger, yet the thought presented barely a ripple.

He returned a few minutes later.

"Everything okay out there?" she asked.

He shook his head. "I'll never cease to be astounded by hard-core gamblers."

She laughed. "Let me guess? Barely a ripple."

"Amazing," he agreed.

"Good. Because I'm about to eat more of your profits."

He glanced at the empty table. "I was afraid heating it twice, then letting it sit would be too much. Want to go into the big kitchen and see what's available?"

She hugged him hard. "I'm happy things are working out, and in case I don't get to see you alone much in the blur of activities the next few days, meeting you has been a highlight of my life."

He hugged her back. "I like the way you conduct meetings. You know, my dad won't ever let me forget he sent me my future last Monday."

She tipped her head back and held his face between her hands. "I do love you, you know."

"I know," he said and kissed her thoroughly.

Her heart sank. He didn't say he loved her, too. Had she made a mistake, professed her feelings too early? He felt the same—she was sure of it. She just had to be patient.

His cell rang, and they both groaned. Danny pulled it out and answered it. "That's the house ring. I told Bru no calls unless it was urgent."

****

He gritted his teeth and hoped whatever Bru considered urgent was easily solved. "Hello."

Bru's strained voice responded. "Your neighbor, Bud, is here demanding to see you. He's very drunk and abusive. I didn't want to throw him out without checking first."

Danny closed his eyes. Would it be too much to ask for a half hour to tell Pallas he loved her and talk about their future? He huffed out a breath. Obviously, it would. Besides, Bud was a friend in a world of hurt. "Tell him I'm on my way. While I'm talking to him, call Tony. Got that?"

Pallas frowned as he hung up. "Tony? Your friend the lieutenant?"

He smiled casually and knew it probably wouldn't work since he'd already said it was an emergency. "Wait here? I'll be right back."

She eyed him suspiciously, then nodded. "I'll just walk out with you and scare us up some food while you're handling whatever."

"Not okay. Bud's out there raising a stink. He's mad as hell and wants to see me."

She looked confused. "Why would he be angry…?" A light dawned, and her eyes showed fear. "You think he shot Kerr, don't you?"

He held out his hands. "I honestly don't know, but it's a possibility, and I don't want you out there while I'm dealing with him."

She set her shoulders. "People don't do things they regret when they're faced with calm opposition. I'll be the calm one."

He laughed out loud. She probably did think she could be calm. He doubted she'd stay that way long though, once her ire was raised. "All right," he said. "We go out, and I—with a capital I—try to get him to see reason. You, on the other hand, do not jump in, please."

She headed for the door. "That's sensible."

He caught up and took her arm. "I'm glad you think so."

He heard Bud from the hallway. When they approached the bar, he stood in front of Bru, weaving and poking him in the chest. "…and as part owner of this place, I want to see Danny, right now."

"Bud."

The older man turned, tremendous pain in his eyes. "What's happened?"

The older man flung up his arm. "Nothing that would cause a blip on your radar, you son of a bitch. You killed her is all." His lips trembled, and he focused on Pallas. "You better pray it never happens to her. Because she wouldn't be the only one eaten from the inside out."

The words shocked and hurt, no matter how much Danny believed it was the alcohol talking. He steeled himself to hear what he didn't want to. "Is it Elaine?"

Pallas gasped as Bud lurched toward him.

"What do you care?"

"Elaine and I are friends," Danny said. "I like her very much."

Bud pointed a shaking finger in Danny's face. "Damn straight. Too bad you didn't remember that when I asked you for that favor. Friends take care of each other. I've known you since you were a snot-nosed kid, and you couldn't bring yourself to do the one thing that might have saved her."

Danny sucked in a breath through a knotted chest as Bud used the past tense when referring to his wife. No wonder his friend was out of his mind. Better to let him ramble on than drive anywhere in his condition. Hopefully Tony was on his way.

"I'm sorry, Bud. She was a fine woman and my friend, too. I can't imagine... Is there anyone we can call for you?"

Bud half-shouted, "You don't get it. There is no one else. I lost my friend and my wife in the space of two days. I can't even go home."

Danny saw Pallas inching into Bud's range and moved an arm to hold her back.

Bud eyed the two of them belligerently. "Don't look at me with pity." He raised his hand a couple of inches above his head. "I've had it up to here with pity."

The gesture threw him slightly off balance, and Danny reached out, thinking he might fall. He was wrong. The feint to one side was a calculated move to get him closer. Bud yelled a furious, "No," then brought his fist up at an angle intended to catch Danny in the jaw.

Danny saw it coming and started to pull out of the way. The blow caught the top of his shoulder and glanced off the side of his head. He staggered into Pallas as Bud spun and ran for the door.

In the ensuing confusion, no one went after him. By the time Danny disentangled himself from helping hands and assured everyone he was fine, Bud was gone. Danny swore and waved Bru over. "Did you call Tony?"

Bru tipped his head toward the door. "He should be here any minute. You okay, man?"

Danny expelled a big breath. "Crap. Life sucks. They didn't deserve this."

Pallas stood to one side, her hand soft on his back.

Bru set two ginger ales on the bar as Tony walked in.

The lieutenant looked around. "McKee gone?"

"Just left," Danny said. "He was blind drunk and out of his mind with grief. Took a swing at me."

"Why would he do that?"

Danny rubbed the side of his head above his ear. "I think his wife died today, or he's finally accepted there's no hope for her. He had this crazy plan to fly her to Mexico for a cancer treatment he heard about. Wanted me to help him find a loan shark so he could borrow the money. I wouldn't do it."

Tony whistled. "Tough thing to go through, but we still need to talk to him."

"When you find him, can you bring in a counselor

or someone?"

"We have a chaplain on call," Tony said. "I'll arrange it."

Danny rubbed his head again. "I don't know what else to do."

Tony peered at him. "You keep rubbing your head. Did McKee connect? Are you hurt?"

His tone was wry. "Only the part he hit. His upper body is pretty strong from working his bow. I'm mostly embarrassed he was able to tag me at all. Listen. Can you call me when he's brought in? And when you hear about Kerr's condition?"

Tony hesitated. "What I said before about your involvement still stands."

"Yeah, I know," Danny said. "I want to make sure Bud's all right."

"As long as that's it," Tony replied. "I'll get on it. It's going to be a long night."

"I owe you."

Tony looked at Pallas. "You have any single sisters?"

She smiled. "Two. Flight attendants out of San Diego. I'd say Gina is your type."

"Gina, huh?" Tony mumbled and left, talking to himself about needing a haircut.

Danny took Pallas's hand. "I'm going to call my dad. Can you finish getting us something to eat? Nothing fancy."

She gave him a fierce hug. "I'm so sorry."

He kissed her forehead. "I'm glad you're here."

She handed him the ginger ales. "Go talk to your dad. I'll take care of the food."

He watched her go into the kitchen and wanted

nothing more than to make love to her until he couldn't think, then fall asleep in her arms. Instead, he went into his quarters and pulled out his cell phone.

"Hello."

"It's Danny."

"Hey," his dad said. "What's up?"

"Too much. Somebody pinned one of my former tournament players to a tree in Jonathan Chase's yard. Turns out the guy was Chase's son, and it looks like one of my arrows was used."

"Your arrow? They don't think you shot him."

"That's what he claims. He's also more than likely the guy who's been threatening me. I went to the station and gave a statement. Pallas was with me, so she went, too."

"That should settle it, then. Anything I can do?"

Danny loved it that his dad didn't think for an instant the shooter could have been him. "Cops are on their way to gather evidence. You could monitor the road that goes out to the range. Don't let anyone use it, and don't let anyone touch or go near the equipment shed until they get there."

"Okay. I'll roll one of the trucks across the road so they need to come here for clearance. What else?"

Danny rubbed his thumb and middle finger across his forehead. "Bud just left blind drunk, and he's really hurting. He didn't say so, but I think Elaine died today."

Rick huffed out a breath. "Poor bastard. No matter how much you're prepared for it, bad news is still bad news."

"There's more. The sheriff's department is looking for him in connection with the shooting since he had access to my arrows."

"Damn. I'll keep an eye out for him."

"Yeah. Let Tony know if you see him. And Bud might need someone to talk to when they catch up to him. Are you available?"

"I'll be here."

"Uh, Dad. Do you think we could bail him out, too?"

"Sure. If the victim's still alive, he could get minimum bail if he needs to take care of Elaine's arrangements."

"That would help. Talk to you later."

Pallas walked in with a tray. She motioned him over. "I'm a strong believer in keeping your strength up. Sit."

Danny ate mechanically, not tasting much.

She finished and sat back, looking at her watch. "Less than an hour ago I said, 'None of this is going to be easy.' Remind me to keep those little forecasts to myself."

He scooted his chair back and waved her to his lap. He put his arms around her and rubbed his chin against her shoulder. "If you want to go back to your hotel, I'll understand."

She yawned. "Can we go to bed and cuddle until we fall asleep? I'm toast."

"Yes. And thanks."

Chapter Thirty-Four

Pallas awoke in the deepest part of the night. The heat at her back felt like she'd fallen asleep in front of a fire, but it was Danny. He slept curled against her, his arm flung across her waist. She opened her eyes and looked out the window at the moon, discerning its silvery movement over the choppy surface of the lake.

The heat of Danny turned to want and traveled through her skin to suffuse her whole body. She laid her hand on his and slid it under her breast.

His breathing changed to an irregular sighing, and he raised his head to bring his mouth close to her ear. "Yes."

She smiled a cat smile in the dark and turned to his arms, needing to give everything she had. Knowing she gave, Pallas felt she had the right and the power to take. Her pajama top slipped over her head without a single button coming undone. She flattened herself against his chest, fitting her belly against his arousal.

No one could touch them here, could take this away.

When Danny entered her, their passion took on a perfect rhythm, each motion a cycle fulfilling and creating a greater need.

She tried to hold back, wait for him, but she was too far gone. Her fierce call of his name was met with his own chant of hers.

As their breathing slowed, he kissed her shoulder. "I wanted to make love to you last night."

She rolled on her side and brushed her fingers through the hair at his temple. "I might have been dreaming, but didn't we do that? At least twice?"

"I mean after the whole drama of the attack on Kerr, the thing at the station with Chase, and Bud's visit. I wanted to take you until all I could feel was your arms and legs around me and me deep inside you."

She exhaled, her blood sluggish in her veins. "And you waited?"

He nodded. "I wanted to wait until I could tell you something, but it was all pretty overwhelming. Now at the risk of being accused of making a commitment in the heat of the moment, I love you, too."

She already knew it, but hearing him say it shifted her whole world.

He pulled his head back to look at her. "Uh, you're not saying anything. Have you changed your mind?"

"No, I'm wondering how my knees got weak when I'm not even standing."

"Oh, that. I plan for that to happen a lot."

Waking a second day in Danny's arms made Pallas a happy woman, despite the events of last night. She breathed against his shoulder and actually felt possessive toward a man for the first time ever. She had seen the way some female patrons in the club and even a few of the pretty women working for him looked at Danny Tarantino. She grinned into the darkness. But he was stuck with *her* for the long haul.

That edgy, *damn, I can't believe this is all mine and getting better every minute* feeling just kept growing. She'd wanted him and made no secret about it a few hours ago, then took everything he gave until the breath left her boneless body. She couldn't imagine ever needing anything else.

She scrunched under the covers, her mind clearing from the heated fog that had enveloped her. What would the partners think? Charles had already tried to poison their thinking, and their offices were located in San Francisco, over two hundred miles away. If they offered her the partnership and she explained her situation, they might say thanks but no thanks and be happy to have dodged a bullet. A candidate who was nuts enough to go on vacation for a week and decide to stay because of a physical attraction sounded weak. Maybe her credentials and personality would be strong enough to convince them she could work at home. She sighed. Chances were not good.

She frowned at the clock display while Danny snored lightly. It was a little after six, and since Tony, his friend at the police station, said he would call if they brought in Bud and no call had come, Danny's neighbor was still out there. She went cold. *Or he's gone.*

Poor Danny. His new club was being threatened, he was being accused of attempted murder, and his insurance company was one event away from cancelling his business insurance. In addition, she was pushing him to attend her family function, meet her parents for the first time, and help her unravel the mystery of her father's ban. He was strong-minded, but things were going to have to land in his favor soon. She would help where she could. Maybe save delving into her problem for later.

She nuzzled Danny's neck. "Wake up, Sleeping Beauty. We have things to do, places to go, people to see, and mysteries to solve."

****

Danny laughed, and kissed the tip of her nose. "Okay. If goddesses can get out of bed, so can I. Your folks will be here in a couple of hours, and you probably want to get back to the hotel and primp before you show at your sister's."

His laughter turned to a roar when both her eyes widened and she rolled away and out of bed. "Maybe I was too hasty," he mumbled as he watched the bathroom light go on and that great derriere over those long silky legs disappeared inside.

"I'm using your spare toothbrush again," she called out.

"After three uses, it's yours," he responded, then scooted across the bed and made a grab for her when she poked her head around the jamb and stuck her tongue out at him.

She squeaked and slammed the door, shouting through it, "I saw that look, Tarantino. And we don't have time."

"Then don't tempt me with that tongue of yours, woman."

"I'll remember that," she said as the shower started. "Be out in a few."

They parted an hour later, and Danny promised to meet her and her father in his club quarters for lunch. He'd called the station while she was in the shower and learned that Bud still had not been picked up. He grabbed his keys, and on a hunch, headed for the practice range, Bud's second home.

A heavy ground fog slowed his progress, enveloping his car as he drove first down Bud's long driveway, then around back to nothing more than a rutted shortcut to the range between the two ranches. His hunch paid off when he rounded the last curve, his lights picking out Bud's truck. He slowed to see the older man slumped over the steering wheel. A dry, bitter taste rose in Danny's throat. Bud had said he had nothing left.

He approached the driver's door slowly, afraid of what he'd find. His hope was that Bud had only passed out and was as all right as a man could be who had lost a much-loved wife. Danny tapped on the truck window, and Bud shifted. Danny released a held breath and tapped harder. Bud turned to face him and shook his head.

"We have to talk," Danny shouted.

Bud grimaced and squeezed his eyes shut, then shook his head again.

Danny crossed his arms. "You were wrong last night about losing a friend. It takes two to end a friendship. I'm not going to let ours go."

Tears ran down the older man's face. He gripped the top of the steering wheel and rested his forehead against his knuckles.

Danny tried the door. It was unlocked. He opened it and took a half-step back. Bud had thrown up in the footwell. "Come get in my car. It's warm."

Bud looked at him and shrugged. "I screwed up. I'm weak, and I screwed it all up. Turned to booze when she needed me. Blamed everyone I could when she didn't get well. Tried to get you in trouble by using one of your arrows." He laughed without humor and held up a length of hose and some duct tape. "Hell, I couldn't even die decently. I passed out before I could talk myself into it."

Danny didn't comment on the helpless gesture, but his guts felt icy at the implication of the hose. He glanced back at the tailpipe where the other end of the hose was taped. He shook his head. "A week ago I wouldn't have understood. Now I do."

Bud ran the back of his hand across his mouth, a tremulous, crooked smile in place. "Got it bad for the redhead? She feel the same way?"

Danny nodded.

"Then I hope you're together seventy years." Bud climbed down from the cab. "Sorry I hit you last night. I'll go in later and explain about the arrow to your friend on the force. Guess they'll be looking for me for killing that dog, too. I feel like a shit. I love dogs, and it didn't do anything to deserve being shot."

He held out his hand to stop Bud. "You were aiming for one of the guard dogs?"

Bud wobbled in place a bit, then looked at Danny in surprise. "Yeah. Stupid, I know. But I hit it, didn't I? I mean I saw the area blocked off with tape when I came to your place later. I was supposed to do it tonight, but I knew if I didn't do it when I was drunk, I wouldn't be able to work up the nerve again." He hung his head. "I thought the money would help."

Danny sucked in a breath. His supposition that things were getting better tanked. "Somebody paid you to use one of my arrows to kill Chase's dog? It wasn't your idea?"

Bud looked at him blankly. "No. When I was there a couple of days ago, I stopped at the bar on my way out." His gaze lowered. "Bad idea, I know, but I got to talking to a guy there about how much I needed money, and I thought you owed me. He followed me out to the parking lot and offered me the money for the ambulance airlift to Mexico if I'd take one of your arrows and shoot one of Chase's dogs. Said you'd get in trouble." He shrugged half-heartedly. "It was already too late for Elaine, but I didn't think so at the time."

Danny had failed his friend. He should have tried harder to reach out to Bud earlier. And not just because it had resulted in Bud's attempt to make him look bad. He'd do what he could to help now, but he needed answers. "Have you seen him since?" Danny asked quietly. "Would you recognize him?"

Bud shook his head. "Everything for the past couple of days is pretty much a drunken blur. Surprised I haven't totaled my truck."

Bud's confession answered Danny's question about why Elliott Kerr was shot. He brought up the scene in his mind's eye. It had been cold and dark outside, and Kerr was wearing a black distressed leather jacket with a brown suede collar. And he was hunched down. Probably spying on the club. In Bud's condition, he could have mistaken the moving shape for one of Chase's Dobermans. Elliott Kerr had been the victim of his own scheme.

Danny sighed. "You have to go talk to Tony now."

Bud took a step away, waving his hand in denial. "I can't. I ran out of the hospital yesterday when Elaine died. I have to go back and fill out the paperwork." He swiped at tears with the back of his dirty hand. "She'll just lay there unclaimed because I've been such a jackass. We have to go there first. The…mortuary details need finalizing."

Danny put his hand on Bud's shoulder. Tony

would have to wait. "We'll go to the hospital, then. I'll call Tony from there, and by the time the paperwork's done, he should be ready for you."

Bud straightened and wiped his hands on his shirt. "Okay."

Danny didn't have the heart to tell him about Kerr. He hadn't heard from Tony about the man's condition, so he assumed Kerr was still alive.

****

Pallas saw her parents' car when she pulled up to Pat and Sassy's. It had been six months since she'd seen them, and she itched to have them meet Danny. Especially her dad. She paused before getting out.

As for her being his alibi during an attempted murder, maybe she would save that for lunch with her father and Ty. That way, her father could break it to her mother at a more suitable time.

Coward, she thought, opening the car door.

Pat stood talking to her parents, and she barely had time to give each a kiss and hug before she was towed to the girls' bedroom by Sassy. Her sister shooed her daughters to the living room to spend time with their grandparents. "Okay, spill. What's been going on with you and the gorgeous Tarantino man?"

Pallas rolled her eyes. She should have expected this based on Sassy's earlier demands for details. She sucked in a big breath.

"I *knew* it," Sassy exclaimed.

She laughed. "Knew what? I haven't said anything."

Her sister smirked. "Don't have to. You have 'rolled around naked' oozing out of your pores."

Panic lit her insides. If it was that obvious, could

her parents see it, too? "Please tell me Mom and Dad won't be able to…"

Sassy flapped her hand. "No prob. I'll distract them with Chloe. But for pity's sake, turn down the wattage."

"Can't. It's crazy, I know. The man checks every one of my boxes and has added a couple I didn't know I wanted."

Her sister tipped her head. "Happy for you. However, didn't you come here to win the money for that prized partnership? What's going to happen there?"

Pallas lifted a shoulder. "Up in the air. Signed up for another tournament next week. Danny needs my help financially and…"

Sassy held up her hand. "You're loaning him a big pile of money? Are you sure about this?"

Annoyance crept into her voice. "Not his idea. And I still haven't convinced him. Remind me. What do I do for a living? Oh, that's right. I find solid investments for people. And this is a solid investment."

Sassy stepped in and hugged her hard. "I want to be you when I grow up."

Pallas laughed and hugged her back. "I love it that we're going to be spending a lot more time together."

****

It was another half hour before she could get her father alone. She took him into the kitchen.

Pallas looked at the tall, red-haired man she had worshiped as a little girl. Nothing had ever ruffled him, although she and her sisters had tested his patience plenty of times. "I made a lunch date for us. A place called Over the Moon at noon. Mom said she'd be happy staying here and fixing lunch for Pat and Sassy and the girls. There's, uh, someone I want you to meet."

Her father's eyes registered mild surprise. "You've met this someone this week?"

She called her parents every Sunday, so her relationship with Danny would be news. She nodded. "He means a lot to me."

Jack Mulroney grinned down at her. "I assume he feels the same."

"Yes."

"You're breaking your old dad's heart."

She hugged him hard. "I promise you'll like him, but that's not all."

Now that the time had come to tell her father what she'd been up to, she got nervous. "Ty Addison is going to be at the lunch, too."

He held her at arm's length. "This isn't leading up to that obsession for digging around that twenty-year-old ban, is it?"

She rubbed her index finger against her thumb and tried to distract. "It's really gotten interesting. We think there may be a crime associated with it."

"We?"

"Danny and I. Danny Tarantino. He owns Over the Moon."

Her father's eyebrows slanted upward. "Let me get this straight. You're involved with a man who's getting you caught up in the criminal element, and you want me to give my blessing?"

She leveled her chin. "He tried to make me stay away, even go back to San Francisco. This was my idea." She lifted a shoulder. "It might help him, too."

He laughed. "He can't know you all that well if he tried to get you to do something you were determined not to do."

She smiled. "He'll learn."

Her father sighed. "If we have this meeting and nothing comes of it, will you call it finished?"

Indecision twitched inside her. She knew they were close to finding an answer to the question that had haunted her for so many years.

"Pallas?"

"All right," she conceded. "But if something does come of it, you'll help?"

Her father paused, then nodded. "That's fair." He looked at his watch. "Let's get back to the others. You can fill me in on the rest at lunch."

She threw her arms around his neck and gave him a kiss. "Thank you, Dad."

He shrugged philosophically. "We'll both be in trouble if we're late for the christening. Why don't I meet you at this place? I'll ask Pat for directions."

Chapter Thirty-Five

Danny felt uncomfortable when the doctor and chaplain came out to talk to Bud at the hospital. "I'll call Tony and be back in a half hour, okay?"

Bud was already wrapped in his own misery. He nodded.

Danny went to the information desk, but they wouldn't give Kerr's status to anyone but family.

He couldn't use his cell phone in this area of the hospital, so he went outside to call Tony. As he followed the exit signs from the hospital chapel, he turned down a short hallway and saw a man he'd gone through UNLV Police Sciences with standing outside a door. He was wearing an Eldorado County Sheriff's Department uniform. "Hey, Jerry, visiting someone?"

The man grinned and stuck out his hand. "Nope. I'm back from Vegas. Didn't like it there, so I waited for an opening here." He looked behind Danny. "Hope no one in your family's sick."

Danny shook his head. "No. I gave a friend a ride."

Someone walked up behind him, and before Danny could turn, a hand gripped his upper arm, jerking at him.

Jonathan Chase sputtered, "This is a brazen attempt to get at my son again. I'll have you arrested, here and now."

He twisted his arm free and turned, immediately

alarmed at the unhealthy color of his neighbor's face. "I'm here with a friend who lost his wife yesterday. I wasn't responsible for what happened last night." He tipped his head toward the deputy. "I recognized a friend and stopped to say hello. I didn't even know this was your son's room." He nodded at Jerry and started toward the door to the outside when Chase grabbed him again.

"You're not leaving." He flapped his hand at the deputy. "I want this man detained for questioning. He's suspected of shooting the patient you're guarding."

Jerry looked concerned. "Sir, you don't seem well. If you'll calm down, I'm sure we can sort this out."

Chase pointed a finger in his face. "You're his friend. You're in this with him. I'll have your badge, too." Then he gave a strangled groan and brought up his right arm to claw at his pocket. His left arm dangled at his side.

He and the deputy grabbed for him as Chase started to slide to the floor.

Danny yelled over his shoulder, "Get someone down here. We have an emergency."

A nurse stepped around the corner, taking in the situation.

"He has a bad heart," Danny said, loosening Chase's collar as the older man's head lolled from side to side. The motion caused the vial Danny had seen him use at the police station to slide out of his pocket.

The nurse spun on her heel, and a few seconds later a woman's voice came over the PA system loud and clear, "Code Blue, East One."

The hospital staff swung into action. A doctor and two orderlies dragged a crash cart and gurney into place and started working on Chase. Danny glanced at the label on the vial. He held it out. "He was reaching for this when he went down."

The doctor grabbed it, read it, and slipped it into his pocket before they wheeled Chase away.

"That was harsh," Jerry said. "The guy was out of control. Did you really shoot his son? Like in self-defense or something?"

"No, but he has his own reasons for wanting to convince the law I did." He stepped outside and got a call through to Tony. "I'm at the hospital with Bud. I took a chance this morning and found him passed out in his truck at the range. I brought him here to take care of the paperwork on his wife. He's willing to talk to you now."

Tony sighed. "That's one of the first places I checked. He must've come out later. I'll dispatch a car to pick him up. Did he say anything about last night?"

Danny had the beginnings of a headache. "He was paid to shoot one of the guard dogs with one of my arrows. He thinks he did, so I didn't tell him about Kerr. I said he'd have to talk to you. Elaine was already gone when he showed at the club the first time, but in his mind he was getting even with me for not helping find someone to lend him the money for that ambulance flight to Mexico."

"Hope I never get that nuts over anyone."

Danny rubbed his forehead. "No, you don't. And speaking of nuts, I was on my way to make this call when I ran into Jerry Morris. I stopped to say hello, and Chase saw me. He went ballistic. I had no idea it was Kerr's room Morris was guarding. Anyway, Chase wouldn't let it go and ended up having an attack of some kind. He's probably in intensive care or an operating room by now."

Tony whistled. "Man's half a deck short."

"Think about it. Chase isn't just an ordinary cranky neighbor who doesn't like noise. His reactions have always been negative in the extreme. When you add in that his partner disappeared twenty years ago and he ended up with the whole enchilada, the pieces start to come together. For one thing, all of the harassment directed at me has been centered around my property. It started virtually the day after I filed my intent to build. Man, I think that's where the body's buried. Literally. And the threat's been dredged up again by Kerr's actions. Chase is going over the edge because he knows how close he's coming to being exposed."

"That'd really be something if you could prove it," Tony said slowly. "Especially since Chase has never had so much as a littering charge."

"Pallas and I are talking to Lucky Jack and Ty Addison at lunch today. We're going to try and get to the reason for her father's ban. I think it's all tied together."

"Call me if you get anything."

"Fill you in when I come in to sign my statement this afternoon. Break the news to Bud easy that he actually shot a man, okay?"

"Sure. Can you stay with him until the car gets there?"

"Yeah."

****

Danny got back to the club around ten and learned his kitchen was done and passed inspection. He called the kitchen and dining room staffs, hoping to get his dining room up and running as soon as possible. Henri insisted on coming in immediately.

Danny had intended to have lunch brought in from another restaurant but wanted to impress Pallas's father. "Henri, could you prepare a nice lunch by noon? I'm having some people over and..."

"*Certainement*, but I will have to hurry. My kitchen has been in the hands of strangers and one can only imagine what has become of my *arrangements*. I will bring only the best ingredients."

"Uh, thank you, Henri. Call any sous chefs you need to help you."

Next, Danny went to his quarters. He swallowed a couple of aspirin, flopped down on his bed, and smiled. He would have to get used to Pallas's fragrance hanging lightly in the air throughout his quarters. Maybe in fifty years or so it wouldn't make him want her all the time.

He looked at his watch. Ninety minutes until lunch. If the attraction between him and Pallas was as evident as Bru and Tony said, he should be on his best behavior around her father. Lucky Jack was likely to be protective of his headstrong, youngest daughter.

By the time he put on a jacket and tie, Henri had invaded the dining area in his quarters and had a vase of flowers sitting among the gleaming china and cutlery. If Danny had hoped for simple, he was going to be sadly disappointed.

The chef gasped, nodded, and hurried past as Danny opened the door to admit Pallas and her father. Danny knew how much this meeting meant to her, so when he saw her in a pale gray suit that looked like emotional armor, he nearly took her in his arms.

She must have sensed his intent because her eyes went wide, and she reached behind her to bring her father into the room. "Dad, this is Danny Tarantino."

The older man gave him a subtle once over and smiled. "Nice to meet you."

He stuck out his hand. "Welcome. Nice to meet you, too."

Jack Mulroney shook his hand warmly. "Great place."

"Thank you. Come in and make yourselves comfortable. Pallas told you we're expecting Ty Addison?"

"Yes. She also tells me my being thrown out of any Tahoe casino for a year may be tied to a crime."

Danny could tell Pallas was her father's daughter. Jack Mulroney came right to the point. "Yes, sir. I'm afraid it might be tied to a series of problems that have recently developed here at the club."

Jack nodded. "Then let's get to it."

Pallas's father had a reasonable attitude about the situation, good. Danny held out the mistress's chair for Pallas and the master's chair for her father. He sat between them.

Pallas started filling the water glasses when someone knocked on the door. It was Ty, with Henri close on his heels carrying a soup tureen.

He set the soup on Jack's left and reached for his bowl, nodding at Danny. "The bread is in your warming oven, *Monsieur*."

Before Danny could react, Pallas scooted back her chair and reached for the carafe. "I'll get it. We need more water, too."

Jack's glance followed his daughter's direct path to

Danny's kitchen, then gazed knowingly at him for just a fraction of a second.

He couldn't help squirming and loosened his tie a little.

After a slight hesitation, Ty walked over to Jack and extended his hand. "Long time."

An expression of real pleasure crossed Jack's features. "Good to see you, Ty."

Danny felt grateful toward the old gambler. Until now he wasn't sure if Ty would show. He'd spruced up with a well-worn western suit and bolo tie. Even his boots were polished and his hair slicked down.

Lunch proceeded amiably with comments on the weather and Jack's description of his recent trip to Atlantic City.

Her father grinned at Pallas. "It was enough of a success that I've decided to take your mother back to Monaco. And as long as we're traveling, I've always wanted to play in South Africa. We'll be gone at least a month."

"That's wonderful, Dad," Pallas said.

Danny waited for a break in the conversation, then leaned forward, addressing Jack. "This past week there have been a series of attacks against my club, its poker tournament players, and patrons. Pallas and I think these incidents might be connected to your ban twenty years ago. That's why we asked the two of you here today."

Jack Mulroney's gaze passed from Danny to Pallas and Ty, then back. "Attacks?"

Danny saw Jack's unease and realized he was getting ahead of himself. "Yes, sir."

He outlined everything from the threatening notes

to his father's involvement as the young dealer called on to verify the missing cards. He finished by weaving in his own guesses about how Elliot Kerr and Jonathan Chase's relationship fit in. He was very careful not to plant the idea that Chase murdered his partner.

"What we'd like to know is anything either of you might have witnessed that could've led to the cheating accusation and the ban."

Jack shrugged. "I thought about the events of the day a thousand times for the first few months afterward, and the only conclusion was I'd unknowingly stepped on some important toes." He hesitated for a beat. "The ban wasn't handled legally. I do know that."

Danny's pulse kicked up, and the hair on his neck prickled. "Exactly how was it handled?"

Jack sighed. "I assume you know the protocol when someone's caught cheating?"

Danny nodded. "Perp is escorted to a security office, evidence is collected, police are called, and state gaming commission gets involved."

Jack tipped his head. "Didn't go that way. Ever wonder why the ban was just for Tahoe and not the whole state like it's supposed to be?"

Danny blinked. "No." He looked at Pallas, then covered her hand with his. "I didn't know they had that discretion."

"They didn't," Jack said. "I was escorted to a small office and told the terms of my ban. If I didn't go along, well, I had a young wife and four daughters. That was that. I decided there were lots of other places I could play and left."

Pallas sucked in an audible breath. "They threatened you!"

Jack smiled. "No, they threatened *you*."

She was indignant. "You didn't cheat. I know it."

"No, I didn't," her father said. "But they wanted me gone, and I obliged."

Danny's thoughts raced. No police, no gaming commission agents. Just a quiet talk in a back room with veiled or outright threats having to do with his family. How would he react in the same situation? He shook his head and held out his hand. "You did the right thing, but I'd like to help set the record straight."

"That's not necessary," Jack said.

"Yes, it is," Pallas spoke up, color returning to her face. "Now that we know you were set up, we need to find out what the connection is. You promised you'd try."

Her father nodded and turned to Ty. "You think of anything that could help?"

Ty held his hands palms out. "I hardly remember what happened that day. I had markers all over town, and when a man I didn't know offered to pay them off if I'd, you know, make that accusation…" His voice grew soft, and he looked at Jack. "He kept saying you'd be fine. You were a really good player, and you'd land on your feet anywhere. I grabbed onto that."

"I was way past angry to begin with," Jack said. "They were talking about my wife and daughters' health like it was so much casual conversation. I'd have stomped you into the ground if I'd had time to look for you. But I was too busy getting my family out of town."

Ty took a deep breath. "I didn't have anyone to depend on me. It didn't occur to my alcohol-soaked sponge of a brain that they'd involve your family." His hand slid up and down the water glass, trembling. "Just so's you know. It never sat easy, and I hope someday you can forgive me."

Jack clapped Ty's shoulder. "You paid a much bigger price."

Danny was glad the two men were mending fences. He could tell by Pallas's face she was, too.

"Don't think about that day," Danny said. "Think about the days or weeks before that. Did either of you witness anything unusual? See any people that shouldn't have been together? Overhear an argument or threat?"

Ty shrugged. "I'd been buttonholing people for weeks. Trying to float a loan or two. Even resorted to waiting in parking lots for friends who'd been avoiding me. I owed everyone."

Danny waited patiently. "Maybe you saw something that wouldn't be thought of as unusual or damning until later."

Jack frowned. "Now that you mention parking lots, I remember something that involved Jonathan Chase and his partner. A couple of days before Suttons threw me out."

Pallas squeezed Danny's hand.

Ty actually grinned. "Yeah, that was back before they built on, and there was a small parking lot on the north side. Lots of privacy and the door was easy to slip through without being seen. Tapped a couple of people for loans there."

Jack chuckled. "You scared ten years off me, walking out of the dark like that."

"I was scared myself," Ty said. "Or I'd have never had the nerve to hit you up twice in one week." He shook his head. "That was a cold night. Not many people outside."

Jack sat up straight. "Sure. And while we talked, Al Hart and some woman came out. They weren't paying attention to anything but each other until Chase followed and caught up with them. They all got into a car and took off. Chase was driving. His lights picked us out as he left the lot."

"That was right before I got the offer to clear all my markers," Ty said. "Does that help?"

Danny's breathing quickened. He nodded. "It makes sense. Hart left late one night with his girlfriend, and neither was ever seen again. Rumor had it he'd finally left his wife for the showgirl he was seeing. That he'd just walked away from it all. The police bought it since there wasn't any evidence to the contrary."

Ty and Jack sat back in their chairs, shaking their heads.

"I heard about it in Vegas later," Jack said. "But it never occurred that there was a connection. I was too busy getting my family settled and looking over my shoulder."

Pallas crumpled her napkin, red spots of anger high on her cheekbones. "All the shame and anger because Jonathan Chase wanted to make you look untrustworthy. That's so awful."

"Whoa, hold on," Danny said. "We can't prove it was Chase just because he was seen leaving Suttons with Hart and the girl. Yes, there's enough circumstantial evidence to pursue his part, if any, in their disappearances. But Chase is still powerful. Do we want him knowing these two men have remembered the details from that night?"

"No," she said, sighing. "You're right. But if we

turn this over to Tony, will he investigate?"

"He's already asked to be informed of anything that comes to light," Danny said. "Does that make you feel better?"

Tears rolled down her face, and Danny stood to take her in his arms. "Hey. You did it. You hung in there until you found out. You should be happy." He held her away from him. "Or is this one of those 'I'm so relieved I could cry' things?"

She took his handkerchief and nodded. She looked over his shoulder and gave her father a watery smile.

At that moment, Henri sailed into the room with a dessert cart. He looked at Pallas dabbing at her tears and smiling. He clutched his fists to his chest. "*Mon Dieu.* I have interrupted the happy news. Congratulations. I myself will cater the wedding as my own personal gift!" He proceeded to sweep the toque from his head and bend over her hand.

Her face turned a dark rose with embarrassment as Danny lifted her chin with his finger. Here was his custom-made opening, and there was no way he was turning back. "How about it? You can't possibly turn down an offer like that. Marry me?"

Chapter Thirty-Six

Danny locked his knees in panic. He'd seen love and trust in her eyes and overwhelming passion. What he saw there now was not joy, or even nervousness, but stark fear. Worse than three nights ago when she'd drunk the Moon Goddess and realized something was terribly wrong.

"I'm sorry," he said. "I discussed an event with Henri, and he got the timing a little off. It's still a great idea."

Her breath tightened, and the color drained from her face as she swallowed and looked around the room in a sort of wild expectation. "Excuse me," she said and ran into his bedroom, closing the door.

He wet his lips and looked at the other men in the room. "Guess I caught her off guard." He privately wondered if the French Foreign Legion still existed.

Jack Mulroney seemed to be inordinately amused as he sat there grinning with one eyebrow cocked. Ty had turned red but looked as if he were enjoying himself.

Henri took the whole thing in stride. "Women," he said with a Gallic shrug. As if that explained everything.

After a few torturous minutes, Pallas opened the door a crack. "Danny, could I speak to you?" Then she disappeared back inside.

Jack stood. "How about I meet the two of you at the church? I'll let you explain the timing if you're late." He nodded toward the bedroom door, then leveled a gaze at Danny. "That's my baby in there. If you hurt her, I'll know. And you won't like the consequences." He smiled at Ty. "Let's go decide where we're going to play poker tomorrow."

Danny took a deep breath and walked to the door, easing it open. Pallas was sitting on the side of his bed.

What if she were getting up the nerve to say, "No. Don't be silly. We've only known each other for six days," or something equally rational? What if his rash proposal had scared her away permanently?

"Pallas, honey, are you okay? Look, I'm really sorry."

"Did you mean it?"

"Mean that I wanted to marry you? Yes." His hope took off.

"Why?"

He wasn't exactly sure what she was looking for here. "Well, besides the fact that my instincts are never wrong, you are beautiful and smart and sexy as hell, and I would be foolish to let you get away." He cupped her face. "You're my dream. Sometime in the past few days, everything I had and stood to lose was replaced by you."

"That's it. That last part. It's exactly how I feel."

His pulse sang in his ears and cotton filled his mouth. "Does that mean yes?"

She nodded, more tears filling her eyes. "I've been so scared it was too fast and too perfect, too everything."

He took her in his arms and kissed her, pulling her

down on the bed with him. "Can I tell you what I wanted to do to you when you came in wearing that suit?"

She slipped her hand inside his jacket and hugged him fiercely, showering kisses over his face. "You can show me."

He laughed. "I know this makes me sound stupid, but what about your niece's christening?"

Puffy but still gorgeous blue eyes flew open as she struggled to sit up. "Oh, my God, the christening. Sassy will kill me." She ran into the bathroom. "Could you get my purse while I clean up?"

He grinned. "Not even married yet, and I'm reduced to the rank of purse holder."

****

They made good time, and everyone gathered in the church for the ceremony. Pallas's gaze kept straying to Danny. What would babies with him look like? Were dark or red hair genes stronger? She didn't care. As far as she was concerned, being with him was all that mattered. The Tarantino family was a bonus. Everyone there had treated her warmly and like she already belonged.

Her father had given them a hard-assessing gaze when they arrived, but didn't mention what had transpired at the club. That didn't last long, however. Back at Pat and Sassy's house, Jack Mulroney cornered them in the kitchen. "Are you happy, girl?"

Pallas laid a hand on her father's chest and held out the other one to lace fingers with Danny. "Very." She winked and slipped into a brogue. "And did you be after knowing his mother is an O'Brien?"

Jack laughed. "Good to know. I think there's an

O'Brien hiding somewhere in your mother's family tree. By the way, she's been hinting about the way the two of you are looking at one another. Will you be making an announcement?"

She shook her head. "I'll make sure Mom has the whole story tomorrow. Well before you leave for Monaco."

"You'd best do that. She'll want to be privy to all the arrangements. Help pick out invitations, colors, and flowers and such."

At this, reality reared its giant, scary head. Invitations? Flowers? She stared at her father's grinning face. Way more to this than she had thought just a minute ago.

Danny apparently thought it was funny, too. He laughed and squeezed her hand. "The kitchen at the club is back in business, and I'm the on-call guy tonight. I have to get back and check everything out. Why don't you have your family dinner there about seven? My treat. I'm not expecting a large crowd to show the first night we're open. It'll take a few days to build trade back up again." He glanced at his watch. "We have to stop and sign those statements, too."

She nodded. "Give me two minutes. I'll go tell Sassy."

She caught her sister coming down the hallway toward her, but before she could say anything, Sassy grabbed her in a hug. "I'm so happy for you."

She returned the hug. "You are?"

Sassy took her by the shoulders, her eyes shining. "Of course. When are you moving to Tahoe? Are you going to live with him? Can you wait to get married until I lose ten pounds so I can look good as matron of honor? Oh God, matron sounds so old. Can both my daughters be flower girls? You can't have only one. The other would be so hurt."

She threw up her hands and rolled her eyes. Would she even have to call her other two sisters, or would they have plucked the news out of thin air as Sassy had? "Soon, I don't know, and how long would that take? And yes, we can have two flower girls."

Her sister squealed. "My diet starts right after dinner."

"Speaking of dinner," Pallas said, still amazed at her sister's divining abilities, "Danny would like the family to celebrate at his club. Dinner at seven. And keep your lucky guesses about the two of us to yourself. This is Chloe's day. My news can come later."

Sassy squealed again. "Mom and I don't have to cook for the whole tribe? And I get to have dinner at a beautiful club? Pinch me."

Pallas shook her head. "You are so easy. See you at dinner."

Danny drove her to pick up her car at the club. "You're awful quiet. Still on board to marry me?"

She nodded. "Trying to stay on my feet after the reality slap. The last six days have been a wild ride, and I still don't know how I'm going to handle the partnership offer."

He pulled her hand to his mouth for a kiss. "One step at a time."

Chapter Thirty-Seven

They drove to the sheriff's department to sign their statements. Tony wasn't in, so Danny left him a message, and they went back to Suttons.

Pallas flopped on the bed and let out a big sigh. "Where to start? I need to find a place to live, maybe a job, and a warmer wardrobe."

He stretched out beside her, happy to have some time alone with his new fiancée. "My place, my place, and I'll keep you warm at my place."

She turned and found his mouth for a kiss. "That's very generous, but I can't live with you until we're married, and how am I supposed to work at your place?" She wiggled against him. "I do like the part about you keeping me warm, though."

He ran the flat of his palm over her hip. "We'll get married in a civil ceremony while your parents are still here and have whatever size wedding you want later. You can change one of the spare bedrooms into an office while you sort out what you want to do about a job, and I'll keep you hot." He licked the whorl of her ear. "By the way, I'm partial to Tarantino Financial Services, Ltd. What do you think?"

****

He changed into his tuxedo for his first walk through of the evening. With the club in full operation again, he needed to reallocate his budget to cover his losses as best he could. He grinned. There was a beautiful woman he could ask for help.

Bru gave him the high sign, so he stopped at the bar.

"Hey, man, you're not going to believe this, but Henri claims you and Pallas are getting married."

He nodded. "True story."

A wide grin split Bru's face. "No kidding. That's amazing. When did this happen?"

Danny couldn't wipe the smile off his face. "The opportunity popped up at lunch, and I couldn't let her get away."

Bru shook his head. "You didn't even see it coming. I hope if it ever happens to me, it's that quick and painless."

Mandy came up beside them. "Congratulations, Danny. She's beautiful and nice, from what I hear." She turned to Bru. "As for you, I hope it's long and excruciating and ends in misery." With that, she spun and walked back down the bar.

He laughed at the puzzled expression on Bru's face. "Know thine enemies and would-be lovers."

Bru's eyebrows lifted in comprehension. "Mandy?"

"Been sharing that all along, pal."

His next stop was his office. He had about a half hour to deal with mail before Pallas and her family showed. He was well into it when the phone rang. "Danny Tarantino."

"It's Tony. Got a minute to tell me what happened at lunch?"

"Sure. But first, what's Kerr's status? They wouldn't tell me at the hospital."

299

"Actually, it's pretty good. The arrow missed any vitals, and after they got a couple of pints of blood into him, he started improving. That'll help Bud. He's still stunned he shot a man instead of a dog."

"Have you talked to Kerr at all?"

"Once, as follow-up to the incident. He's feeling cornered, and that's made him nasty and uncommunicative. I have Bud's statement that he was hired to shoot one of the guard dogs with one of your arrows, though. We showed him a picture lineup, but he couldn't pick out Kerr as the guy who hired him. We did find some of that high-end stationery at Kerr's apartment. He used a pair of scissors to cut off his father's monogram. There was a nick in the blade that's as good as a fingerprint. He's not going anywhere."

Danny took a deep breath. He was happy Bud wouldn't be facing manslaughter charges. Attempting to kill a dog was bad enough. It also looked more and more like Chase either had known or was involved in Kerr's actions against his club. "Does Chase know about any of this?"

"He says not. He's in the hospital recuperating from a mild attack of angina. What else have *you* got?"

Danny outlined his talk with Jack Mulroney and Ty.

Tony whistled. "We need to get that in writing."

"I know. I don't trust Chase, though. Even if he's in the hospital, he can still create trouble. I let Jack and Ty know you'd be following up, but it needs to be as confidential as possible until some concrete proof is established. Mulroney's leaving for Monaco soon, and Ty can make himself scarce with my help. However, this is my property, and we can dig all we want. Who knows what we'll find? If there happens to be a body or two, you could start building your case from there."

"I think we need to sew Chase up so tight you couldn't see a chink of daylight. Kerr may be the weak link once we present him with all the evidence against him."

"There is one other thing. I'm marrying Pallas. Want to be the ring bearer?"

"What? After knowing her less than a week? Are you sure this isn't a sex-induced overreaction?"

He laughed out loud. "I'm sure. I had all my clothes on and all synapses were firing when I asked her. Besides, she's giving up way more than I could ever ask. It's what we both want."

"Oh," Tony said. "In that case, will her sisters be there?"

"If that's what it'll take to get you into a tux."

"Saying congratulations before the wedding is bad luck, so I'll just say you are one fortunate dog."

"Thanks."

Henri outdid himself and to everyone's surprise entertained Sassy's girls while Danny gave tours of the club to his almost-in-laws. Everyone left at last, and by ten he was toast and knew he faced another set of circumstances in the morning. He hadn't told his family about his proposal to Pallas and wanted to do that face-to-face. The ranch house was so big that they might have room for Pallas until they got married. His parents, especially his mother, were going to love this.

His eyes tried to focus when he entered his bedroom in the half dark, then he grinned. Sometime in the past couple of hours Pallas had come back and lay sleeping in his bed. He went into the living room, got undressed, and returned to slip in behind her. She stirred and tucked herself in to fit him. Danny fell asleep almost instantly.

Three hours later his cell phone jangled. He reached for it with his eyes still closed. "Hello."

"It's a boy," Dugan shouted.

Danny grinned and sat up, a jolt of adrenaline clearing his head. He rubbed his eyes open. "All right! Congratulations, bro. How is everyone?"

"Susan and Donovan O'Brien Tarantino are both fine. If you leave now, you can see him when they wake him up for Susan to feed. I'll wait for you by the side door near the staff lot."

"Uh, can I bring someone if she wants to come?"

Danny heard the grin in his brother's voice. "Does the someone have beautiful red hair and blue eyes?"

"Yeah."

"Sure. The more the merrier. Mom and Dad just left."

Pallas rolled over and snuggled against his neck, making sleepy noises.

He kissed her shoulder and blew in her ear. "Pallas, we've got a new nephew."

She shook her head. "Sassy's got girls."

"Dugan and Susan, honey. A boy. Do you want to go see him?"

Her eyes fluttered open. "Is it early?"

He kissed her nose. "Very. It's one a.m."

She burrowed into her pillow. "I'll meet you in the car."

He laughed. "Liar. Okay, I'll be back in an hour."

"I'm coming, I'm coming." She rolled to a sitting position.

Chapter Thirty-Eight

The parking lot was nearly empty when they pulled in. Pallas was still yawning, and she looked about seventeen. Her hair was up in a ponytail, and complete lack of makeup accentuated her cream-colored skin and pale freckles. She shivered and pulled her chin into her jacket collar as they walked toward the building. "When does it warm up around here?" she asked.

He put his arm around her. "Pretty short summer season. We're over six thousand feet, so even with a lot of sun, it stays cool. Change your mind about living here?"

She burrowed against him and sighed. "As long as we can occasionally vacation in the tropics."

"Agreed. Want to honeymoon in Borneo?"

She giggled. "Or Fiji. Hot jungle sex all tangled up in a mosquito net."

Danny stopped, and his mouth dropped open as he watched her walk away, exaggerating her hip swing. "Fiji it is," he managed.

Visiting hours for the maternity ward didn't start until ten a.m., but as they approached the side door, Dugan was waiting.

He kissed Pallas on the cheek and handed Danny a cigar. "Seven pounds, four ounces. All fingers and toes accounted for. Great set of lungs."

When they entered the room and neared the crib,

Dugan made cooing noises even though his son was asleep. Susan gave them a three-finger wave from the bed and yawned. Low lighting showed the infant bundled in a blanket with wisps of dark hair escaping his tiny knit hat.

Pallas peered at the baby and whispered, "He's beautiful."

Danny reached for her hand and squeezed it. "An uncle twice in less than a day," he murmured.

His brother caught the words and turned to him. "Something you want to tell me?"

Danny nodded. "I asked Pallas to marry me at lunch yesterday. Haven't had time to make it formal or tell Mom and Dad."

Dugan grinned and turned to Pallas. "I didn't think he was that smart. Don't tell me you accepted this lunkhead?"

Pallas nodded and returned the grin. She got another kiss. This one smack on the lips.

Dugan pulled out another cigar and handed it to her. "Welcome to the family."

"We'll save these for later," Danny said. "You better get back to bed."

Dugan glanced at his watch. "It's almost feeding time. Come back later today and visit for longer."

Danny nodded and tugged on Pallas's hand. "The door down here leads to the same parking lot."

They walked the corridor quietly and turned the corner. A patient in a wheelchair moved slowly in front of them. As they started to walk past, the hair on Danny's neck stood up. The man in the chair was Jonathan Chase.

Danny let go of her hand and put out an arm to

block Pallas with his body.

"What's the matter?" she asked.

Chase turned at the sound of her voice. A look of irritation, then recognition crossed his face.

Danny was not prepared for what happened next.

Chase smiled. "I don't imagine you're here to visit me. But it's an opening I'd be a fool to let pass."

Danny pushed at Pallas, and she got the message, slowly backing away.

Chase cranked his wheelchair ninety degrees with a dexterity Danny hadn't figured on. The older man brought a gun from the folds of his robe and aimed it at Danny while speaking to Pallas. "Please stay. Or I'll be forced to shoot Mr. Tarantino."

Pallas whimpered, and Danny heard her take a step in their direction.

"That's better," Chase said. "The doctors have told me that even with excellent care, my heart will fail completely within the year. I have no intention of spending whatever time I have left in and out of courtrooms or in prison." He waved the gun. "I had a loyal employee procure this and some highly effective barbiturates."

The nine-millimeter Luger in Chase's hand scared the hell out of Danny. The round-nosed bullets it contained would go right through him at this range. And Pallas was behind him.

"I intended to kill that stupid useless son of mine for coming back and interfering, but killing the two of you, her first, will be much more gratifying."

Icy fear drained into Danny's stomach. He had nothing to lose and everything to gain. All he needed was a split-second diversion.

Pallas must have read his mind. A ring of keys hit the floor and slid toward the wheelchair. The gun wavered, and Danny lunged, attempting to knock it aside. He heard the report and felt the searing tear as a round split the web of his right hand. His left fist connected with Chase's jaw.

Hospital staff came running as he pulled the gun out of Chase's stilled hand, laid it on the floor, and kicked it away.

Pallas threw her arms around his neck, trembling hard and holding him tightly. "I was so scared." She leaned back and patted at him. "Are you okay?"

He closed his eyes and pulled her to him, ignoring the pain in his hand. "I am now."

Ten minutes later, he was sitting on a bed in an emergency room enclosure when Tony walked in and flashed his badge at the doctor.

"Pallas told me what happened. She obviously didn't have any idea what kind of damage that Luger could have done to both of you." He glanced at the wound. "You got off lucky. Chase is an old man on medication. If his reflexes were a half second faster, you'd be permanently prone."

Danny hissed as the young doctor tugged a stitch into place, focused on the conversation. "Thanks for the vote of confidence. Did she also tell you she threw a ring of keys on the floor to distract him?"

Tony shrugged and grinned. "Just saying. This's the second time in three days you've been tagged by an older guy. Guess your prime's over. Oh, and as I said earlier, you are one lucky dog."

Chapter Thirty-Nine

Pallas and Danny sat in his parents' kitchen two days later. Mary and Rick Tarantino were already treating Pallas like one of the family. They insisted she move in with them until a justice of the peace came out to marry them the upcoming Saturday. Danny's mother waited on him hand and foot and wouldn't let Pallas lift a finger.

They were discussing a quick week's honeymoon in the tropics somewhere, then a longer one in Italy in the fall, when Tony called.

"Did Pallas kiss it all better?"

"Wherever she could," Danny responded.

Tony groaned. "I've got to stop setting myself up like that. Thought you'd want to know we wrapped it up today, and it's not pretty. Elliott Kerr watched his father bury Hart and the showgirl on the far side of your property twenty years ago, and since he was only ten, was too afraid to say anything. Shortly afterward, his parents split, and as the years went on, Chase basically ignored him. There was no response when his mother remarried and the stepfather wanted to adopt him.

"Kerr's been in and out of trouble for years. Two months ago he won seventy-two thousand dollars in the trifecta at Santa Anita. He figured that would earn him Chase's good will. When Daddy didn't want anything to do with him, Elliott sprang the news about his eyewitness to the disposal of the bodies. Said the information was documented in a safety deposit box. Chase agreed to a hundred thousand dollar pay off. But instead of leaving town, our boy Kerr took a nearby apartment and started dropping by for regular visits. He figured the old man might be even more generous if he was able to get rid of you.

"He got really chatty when he heard his old man was on his way to kill him when he ran into you."

Danny whistled. "So Chase knew nothing about Kerr's campaign?"

"He found out early yesterday morning when he spent some time alone with his son. That's when he also learned you were cleared. He was on his way back to his son's room when he saw you and had the meltdown that led to a bigger heart attack."

"I'm sure he'll use the state of his health to his advantage."

"Yeah. His attorney's already claiming Chase was in fear of his life, and the stress of his son's brush with death made him temporarily unbalanced. The attorney also said Chase's condition should preclude any jail time."

Danny sighed. "At least he'll be out of my hair. That counts for a lot."

"I know you have plans to make and everything, but I wanted you to know. If we find and identify the bodies as Hart and his mistress, by rights the reward's yours."

Danny rubbed his forehead. "None of this last part would have happened without Bud shooting Kerr, so in a convoluted way, he deserves a share."

Tony's tone was wry. "He'll no doubt need money

for a good attorney. I'll see what I can to about getting creative again."

"Thanks. By the way, the civil ceremony for Pallas and me is this Saturday at one. My folks' house. Can you make it? We're going to have the white tie and tails bit later."

"What's the hurry?" Tony asked.

"You're setting yourself up again."

"Oh, all right. Do I get to kiss the bride?"

"Under supervision."

Tony laughed. "I'll be there."

****

Pallas cooked a simple steak and salad for them in his quarters that night. She got a chuckle and kiss when she handed him the plate with his meat already cut up.

"You look dashing in your tuxedo with that bandage. Very mysterious," she said.

He rubbed his hand on the edge of the table. "It itches like crazy, but maybe I should keep it on after the stitches are gone. The story's been great for business." He glanced over.

Her eyes sparkled, and she sat on the edge of her seat.

He set down his fork and gave her his full attention. "What is it?"

She fairly quivered with excitement. "I quit my job today. I also told the new firm I was turning down the partnership."

That didn't quite gel with her appearance. It looked like she was having a hard time staying in her chair.

He shook his head. "Are you still okay about that? Losing out on the partnership and everything?"

Her grin was infectious. "Actually, the new firm is

thinking about opening an office in Nevada, based here. They have this idea that it could be very rewarding. Especially if it was run by a partner."

He shook his head, returning her grin. "They didn't want to let you go. I know the feeling. Will you be allowed to invest for relatives?"

"Close relatives?"

He stood and came around the table to take her in his arms. "This close."

Pallas kissed him and whispered a suggestion in his ear.

Danny raised an eyebrow. "Can goddesses do that?"

A word about the author...

DeeAnna is a freelance editor and travel agent for happy endings (romantic suspense, women's fiction, children's picture books, and mystery author). She writes and teaches for the love of it, has never met a dog she did not want to pet or a pie she did not want to taste. She tries to live life without props.

~*~

Find DeeAnna online at:
http://deeannagalbraith.com

Stratford-upon-Avon and
SHAKESPEARE'S COUNTRY

painted by A. R. Quinton
described by A. G. Bradley
with drawings by Gordon C. Home

BELOW BREDON HILL

SALMON

Published by
J Salmon Limited
100 London Road, Sevenoaks,
Kent TN13 1BB

First edition 1995

Designed by the Salmon Studio

Copyright © 1995 J Salmon Limited
Drawings by Gordon C. Home by
permission of A.& C. Black Ltd.

ISBN 1 898435 34 0

Printed in England by
J Salmon Limited, Tubs Hill Works
Sevenoaks, Kent

THE BELL TOWER, EVESHAM

Coloured Illustrations

Black and White Illustrations

STRATFORD-UPON-AVON

If any little town in England could be called self-conscious it is surely Stratford-upon-Avon. There is no other in any way occupying the quite peculiar position that Stratford occupies in the public eye. If it were not for the author of its glory the name of Stratford would in all probability mean just as little or just as much to the ear of a person in Hampshire or Yorkshire today as does that of Alcester or Henley-in-Arden: I think, moreover, one would have it so. It is a most felicitous example of the little English agricultural country town with its roots in the past and, save for the signs of Shakespeare worship, as slightly unaffected by modern changes as any such place could well be.

Its immediate neighbourhood is purely agricultural and pastoral, and so far as any part of England, being the most beautiful country in the world, can be described as commonplace, this may without offence be fairly called so. Nor is there any paradox in the suggestion that, so much the more, its unassuming atmosphere seems in harmony with England's greatest genius. One feels that this heart of England is the very setting one would ask for the personality of Shakespeare and is altogether more appropriate than an atmosphere of exalted natural beauty. It is a mere commonplace that a typical bit of rural England like this corner of Warwickshire, above all at such a period, is the best background for Shakespeare.

If Shakespeare's association with the place had been limited merely to his birth and youth and had he then wandered away for ever, after the more common fashion of great men, Stratford would still be famous. But the "return of the native" to a yet more intimate connection with his old home in middle life, his honours thick upon him and, so far as we may judge, an honest pride in becoming a leading burgess and owner in his own obscure town is unique. It gives Stratford far more than the interest of a mere birthplace and nursing mother and amply justifies the character of a national shrine into which the little town has been exalted. That the typical ordinary English countryside should have had this magnetic power over so illustrious a man makes surely for the greater fascination in these Shakespearean associations of Stratford.

Certainly Stratford is unique. Almost everyone, in person or through illustration, knows the appearance of Shakespeare's church as seen from the bridge, lifting its tall, tapering spire with such distinction above its leafy precincts on the banks of the Avon, which here as at Evesham has been artificially widened to the great artistic advantage of the old town whose bounds it washes.

Stratford Church consists of a nave over 100 feet long with north and south aisles, a north porch, transepts, chancels, and a central tower with battlements and corner turrets carrying an eighteenth century spire, 83 feet in height. Though some earlier Norman work is embodied in the tower and elsewhere, practically none is visible. Otherwise the transepts, tower, and north aisle, all of Early English date though a good deal altered from the original, comprise the oldest part of the building which, on entering displays a fine, spacious, and handsome interior richly decorated.

Just within the altar rails are a number of flat stones indicating the Shakespeare graves. The one nearest the north wall is that of Anne Shakespeare, wife of the poet, The next one covers the remains of Shakespeare himself, with the well-known lines cursing anyone who ventures to interfere with his bones – no superfluous precaution in those days when remains that came in the way of later interments were treated with such scant reverence. At some height up, on the north wall, is the famous bust of the poet, fashioned in the

The Site of New Place
& the Guild Chapel

The Guildhall
& Grammar School

year 1623. As Shakespeare's family were all alive when it was executed there must be some sort of likeness to the original, whatever its merits as a work of art. It is thought to have been taken from a mask after death and any clues which help us to realise what the man was like is very much more important than the abstract quality of the sculptor's performance. The mere colouring alone, the blue eyes and auburn hair and beard, though repainted, is valuable.

Old Stratford is skirted by a margin of modern roads and avenues, just the ordinary residential quarter that springs up around country towns. But old Stratford alone concerns us here, and the main street, which, under different names, is of a considerable length, contains the chief objects of interest that are not modern, always excepting the Birthplace, which stands in Henley Street.

It seems almost banal to expend a few lines on a building, every stone and beam and window of which has been the text of many pamphlets as well as the bone of many controversies. But it is singularly felicitous that two half-timbered houses of mid-sixteenth-century date, knocked into one and which certainly belonged to Shakespeare's father, should have survived. What precise restoration this ancient building has undergone may be read in many local books. It is enough that Shakespeare's father, a yeoman, became prosperous by successful trading, was able to buy first one and later on the other of these two adjoining houses, and became mayor or high bailiff of the little town that had only recently been incorporated and promoted to such civic honours. That John Shakespeare fell later into difficulties and so brought his name more than once upon the town records, adds at any rate to the slender stock of the family history that is preserved for us.

The two united houses, in one of which the poet's father lived and in which he himself was born, now known as the Birthplace, and the other historically designated the "Woolshop," from the fact that John Shakespeare used it for that purpose, passed through the ownership of William to that of his sister and daughter Joan Hart and Susanna Hall. Possibly also Shakespeare went to live with his father at the Birthplace after his early marriage to Anne Hathaway.

The Birthplace is a good specimen of a sixteenth-century house, and has of course a quite unique importance, but the grammar school where Shakespeare, according to tradition, was educated, together with the guild-chapel and guild-hall all connected, make an exceedingly striking group in that southerly extension of the High Street known as Church Street. The guild-hall, a fine old room, probably rebuilt in 1417, was the scene of great feasting in pre-Tudor times. In the great days of Elizabeth the hall was placed at the disposal of travelling companies of actors and it is on the records that John Shakespeare, the poet's father, doubtless while mayor or high bailiff, presided at an entertainment of this character in 1569. At the upper end of the hall a door leads to the big schoolroom itself, formerly two rooms where Shakespeare supposedly acquired knowledge. At any rate it has been decided which was his desk, for this is now preserved in the Birthplace Museum.

The old guild-chapel adjoining the grammar school fronts upon the street, and is one of the most prominent objects in the town. Sir Hugh Clopton rebuilt it in the time of Henry VII on the site of an old Augustinian chapel of 1296. Close by, with nothing in fact but a by-street between them, are the gardens of New Place where once stood the house in which Shakespeare lived after his final return to Stratford as an owner of land and tenements and apparently happy in being the leading citizen of his native town.

There are some traces of the foundations of the original house and also of its well, still left in the garden. The story of the vanished

CLOPTON BRIDGE

A Garden View
of the Birthplace.

house is rather curious and at the same time not a little distressing. Built originally in the time of Henry VII by Sir Hugh Clopton, of that well-known local family, as "a pretty house of brick and timber," it was probably the most important in the town and was known as the Great House. It passed from the hands of the Cloptons and was eventually purchased by William Shakespeare in 1597 for £60 which is thought to indicate that the place must have been in a state of dilapidation. Shakespeare at any rate repaired it and called it New Place and in the deed of sale it is described as "one messuage, two barns and two gardens." The poet was at this time thirty-three and not nearly prepared as yet to retire into private life, so the town clerk became for a time its tenant. On Shakespeare's retirement from London in 1609 he settled here with his family and died in the house seven years later.

In the course of time New Place passed out of the possession of Shakespeare's descendants, falling again curiously enough into the hands of the Cloptons, who after over a century of ownerships sold it to a certain Francis Gastrell, vicar of Frodsham in Cheshire. Tourists of some sort must even this early have haunted Stratford, for a mulberry tree planted by Shakespeare in 1609 became so much sought after by visitors that the recent and reverend owner hewed it down in a moment of spleen for the trouble they gave him. But this was nothing to the after-performances of this preposterous parson. He had apparently to reside at Lichfield, perhaps as a canon, for part of the year and was so infuriated at having to pay the poor rates in Stratford while absent, that he razed his house to the ground.

It is not inappropriate that one of the oldest and most picturesque houses in Stratford should have been the residence of the mother of John Harvard, the founder of that famous American university. It is a beautiful little specimen of the half-timbered Elizabethan style, a single gable fronting the street, of three stories, with a single long, mullioned, latticed window almost filling the space in each. On the woodwork are carved the bear of the Beauchamps, the bull of the Warwicks, and other badges and under the middle window T. R. 1596 A. R., for Thomas and Alice Rogers, the parents of Katherine Harvard. At the corner of Bridge Street and High Street, though wearing a modern front, the house is still standing where Shakespeare's daughter Judith and her husband Quiney, a vintner, lived. The old parts of it can be traced back in the town records to the fourteenth century. There are many other old houses, but without any particular associations attaching to them, and they are more or less scattered about the town, in Sheep Steet and elsewhere.

All about the river Stratford wears a singularly pleasant air, and breathes a fine sense of space; Bridge Street itself being of quite uncommon width. Then there are the two well-known bridges quite near together, the one road bridge of sixteen arche, built by Hugh Clopton, Lord Mayor of London, in the early sixteenth century, the other the old tramway bridge built in brick in the 1820's. The Avon being here expanded to a considerable width and deepened by a lock and weir below the town makes a most picturesque stretch of water, gay in summer-time with boats and on its farther margin fringed by willows and playing fields.

In the western environs of the town is Shottery, a village boasting the world-famous cottage of Anne Hathaway, with its lovely old-fashioned garden and orchard; this was the early home of Shakespeare's wife, Anne Hathaway. Woven around it are countless romantic stories of the poet's youthful courtship. Venerable in age and appearance, it is a property unique in its picturesque and architectural appeal, at the same time possessing associations which for generations have made it a scene of pilgrimage. The Cottage was

The Garden view
of 'Anne Hathaway's
Cottage'

originally a spacious farmhouse, the home of the Hathaways who were a family of yeoman farmers. The oldest part of the structure dates from the fifteenth century and inside may be seen a pair of curved oak timbers or "crucks" pegged together at the top. The timber-framed walls consist mostly of wattle and daub, with some brick panels of later date.

The interior abounds in interesting architectural features and curious reminders of former days. It is preserved in a furnished state and contains furniture, utensils and possessions acquired and used in the property by successive generations of the Hathaways. Apart from the kitchen with its old bake-oven still intact and the buttery with its stone paved floor and quaint dairy utensils, the room usually referred to as the "best room", was originally the "hall" and is so noticed in an inventory of 1581. The most striking feature of this room is its large open chimney with bacon cupboard and tinder holes. Near to the hearth stands the famous 'courting settle', on which tradition says that Shakespeare's wooing took place.

Of all the buildings associated with Shakespeare and his family, Mary Arden's House, the home of the poet's mother at the nearby hamlet of Wilmote, is the least known and yet perhaps the most picturesque and interesting. Seen from the road this grand half-timbered farmhouse of early sixteenth-century date is of striking size and proportions, while the view from the rear is extremely fine by reason of the irregular lines of the building and the uneven, moss-covered roof, which blend with the weathered grey stone, brick and timbers into a delicate patchwork of colour. The Ardens came of an old and leading county family of yeoman farmers and an inventory of Robert Arden's goods taken after his death in 1556 makes it clear that the house was substantially and comfortably furnished according to the standards of the day. It is well worth a visit.

The home of Mary Arden -
Shakespeare's mother at
Wilmcote.

HOLY TRINITY CHURCH FROM THE AVON

SHAKESPEARE'S BIRTHPLACE, HENLEY STREET

THE KNOTT GARDEN, NEW PLACE

ANNE HATHAWAY'S COTTAGE, SHOTTERY

WARWICK

The ancient town of Warwick has beyond all question an air of great distinction. Its pose is admirable, clustering as it does on a ridge lifted up considerably above a virtually flat country.

The view of the castle, with its noble array of grey towers and walls springing high above the rich luxuriance of grove and lawn and stream, can barely be suggested by description. The little Avon, is cunningly magnified to much more than its natural dimensions by the mill-dam just below. Boats flit upon its surface, between the tall mantling foliage and the hoary castle walls so imposingly upreared.

But as a matter of fact, this magnificent specimen of baronial pomp and pride, set in the heart of England, does not speak very loudly of storm and siege. To me at least it suggests rather the "celebrity at home," the gorgeous festivals, the wassail and the revelry of the highly placed, in the varying fashion of succeeding epochs.

Ethelfleda, the daughter of Alfred the Great, raised a fortification here on an artificial mound within the area of the present castle. Various earls of Warwick did a good deal more in the building way after the Conquest; but whatever this may have amounted to seems to have been wiped out, for certain walls and some of the towers were raised in the time of the second and third Edwards.

Henry V was entertained here by Richard de Beauchamp. Edward IV was brought to Warwick as prisoner by the famous Richard Neville the King-maker. Richard III was here twice; and in Edward VI's reign the property was given to the Dudleys. Ambrose Dudley entertained Elizabeth, Gloriana, on two occasions in the castle, but after his death it reverted to the Crown. Of royal and noble persons Warwick in truth has had its fill, and it is as a residence rather than a fortress that it makes its historic appeal.

WARWICK CASTLE FROM THE AVON

LORD LEYCESTER HOSPITAL, WARWICK

MILL LANE, WARWICK

KENILWORTH CASTLE

The ruins of Kenilworth are among the largest and stateliest in England. The richness of their colouring, too, adds no little to their beauty. The keep, the original portion built at the end of the twelfth century, is known as Cæsar's Tower. It is a very large, four-sided block of masonry, three stories high and flanked at each angle with massive towers. Higher up the slope to the west most of the buildings are two centuries later, reared in place of earlier ones and among them are the remains of the great hall. Opposite Cæsar's Tower and on the south side, conspicuous with its Tudor windows, is the large block of buildings built by Robert Dudley, Earl of Leicester and named after him. The outer walls of the great court are fairly perfect. Beyond them lie the meadows which formed the bottom of the great lake which, until the Commonwealth, extended round two sides of the castle and the extent of which can be easily traced.

Though Kenilworth has nothing like the martial record of many castles of far less size and fame, its intimate associations with so many sovereigns, their triumphs and their trials, give ample food for reflection as one wanders around the intricate mass of stately red ruins, here perfect to the height of their vanished battlements, there little more than the foundations of chambers once echoing to the sounds of life and gaiety. What would one give to listen for half an hour to the table-talk in the great banqueting-hall in the days, let us say, of Henry VII, or again in those of Robert Dudley entertaining his Royal mistress; to the tones of voice and accent, the subjects of conversation, the external attitude of men and women to one another, and a thousand things to which the contemporary pen can give us no clue. The pageant manager of today may reproduce the dresses, but anything else, ah, who can say?

KENILWORTH CASTLE

CHARLECOTE PARK

Charlecote, lying in a large level park sprinkled with fine trees and watered both by the Avon and its tributary the Wellesbourne brook, which rises on the battlefield of Edgehill, though greatly altered and added to, is still a noble specimen of a Tudor house. It is open to the public and indeed is worth an inspection; also to recall Justice Shallow, who long ago intimidated rural wrongdoers, including Shakespeare himself, within its walls, or to watch the deer that might be the lineal descendants of the very buck which is supposed to have had a hand in shaping the Bard of Avon's destiny. There is a hitch, however, in that it seems practically certain that there were then no deer at Charlecote. But Shakespearean authorities are agreed that the poet, for some reason or other, revenged himself on Squire Lucy by the portrayal of Justice Shallow.

The Lucys have been a prodigiously long time at Charlecote, for the village was granted by no less remote a notability than Simon de Montfort to one Walter de Charlecote, whose people may have been conspicuous for Heaven knows how long before that. It was he who first took that name of Lucy which has been so absolute here.

Charlecote was completed in the year of the great Elizabeth's accession and the beautiful gatehouse, it is said, was hurriedly completed to do honour to the State visit she paid here. Like many other famous Tudor houses, the mellow red brick of which this one is built lends additional charm to the glorious mass of gables and turrets. Although it has been much restored Charlecote stands out nobly, as it should do, at the end of a magnificent avenue, in the midst of a green deer-park that no plough has touched for centuries and where deer wander beneath trees that were shedding their leaves no doubt when guns were thundering at Edgehill over yonder in October, 1642.

CHARLECOTE PARK FROM THE AVON

THE AVON FROM BREDON HILL

SHAKESPEARE'S AVON

Winding in sweeping loops through some of the prettiest and most abundant countryside in England, Shakespeare's Avon flows gently from Stratford in Warwickshire to Tewkesbury in Gloucestershire. This is the landscape which Shakespeare loved and knew so well; a landscape of quaint villages, hoary timber-framed cottages and blossomed orchards, with the peaceful river quietly flowing finally to unite its waters with the more dramatic Severn tide.

From Stratford to Evesham, a matter of some twelve miles, the main road pursues a pleasant course along the low northern slope of the Avon valley and nowhere is it much out of touch with the meandering stream. Most of the picturesque villages which line the valley upon both sides are set back upon its bordering slopes, or farther still. Some squat upon the highway, others amid the network of flowery lanes with which this country is so abundantly interlaced.

Some four miles below Stratford is Welford-on-Avon. Here a double stone bridge of thirteen arches above and an ancient mill below bound the great loop of river which encompasses the village. At Bidford, the "Drunken Bidford" of Shakespeare's jingle which commemorates the poet's convivial drinking party supposedly held at the Falcon Inn, another stone bridge spans the widening stream; this is a river of fine bridges and Bidford Bridge is one of the finest.

Evesham, a pleasant and sightly little town, forms as it were the half-way staging post between Stratford and Tewkesbury. Down the broad, straight course of the Avon below the bridge a pleasant meadow slopes to its stream with shaded public gardens on the farther shore. Overlooking this delightful prospect is Evesham's most famous landmark, the beautiful Tudor Bell Tower, fashioned in three stories, each containing four stages of Perpendicular trefoil-

31

BY THE LYCH-GATE, WELFORD-ON-AVON

headed arcading and standing in stately isolation, sole relic of a once-famous abbey.

Now gaining breadth the river flows by Hampton Ferry through a widening landscape to Fladbury, a place of brimming glassy waters, of lawns and sunny walls, a mill and tumbling weir, perhaps the most delectable of riverside studies in which the Avon excels. Past Cropthorne, beloved by artists, and Wyre Piddle perched high above the flood where village gardens adorn the steeply rising bank, the river slips quietly under the Old Bridge at Pershore, time mellowed arches of brick and stone, while the town clustered around its abbey church, is slightly raised above the meadows.

Below Pershore Shakespeare's river meanders in great serpentine loops around the high, rounded distinctive bulk of Bredon Hill, that isolated outlier of the Cotswolds. Here truly is the heart of old England, a group of villages about its flanks within a mile or two of one another. Eckington and Bredon by the river, the two Combertons and Elmley Castle more immediately under the hill. Nearly one thousand feet high, Bredon is by far the most conspicuous physical fact in the whole Avon valley giving glorious views across the Vale of Evesham to the distant Malvern Hills.

Approaching Tewkesbury, the wide meadow flats which mark the surroundings of the confluence of Avon and Severn seem to make for the better setting and greater glory of the noble Norman tower of the great Abbey church that rises high above the ancient town. Tewkesbury boasts of more half-timbered Tudor houses for its size than any other town in this region of England which is so distinguished for them. Entering beneath the old brick King John's Bridge the river skirts close behind the shops and houses the length of the town and leaves to join the Severn, beneath the great brick and white-painted weather-board structure of the Abbey Mill.

A FARMHOUSE AT WELFORD-ON-AVON

SPRING BLOSSOM AT DORSINGTON

FORD ACROSS THE AVON AT HARVINGTON

LILAC AND APPLE BLOSSOM AT HARVINGTON

PLAYTIME AT NORTON

AN OLD CORNER, PEBWORTH

THE GREEN, BROADWAY

HAMPTON FERRY, RIVER AVON NEAR EVESHAM

THE CARRIER'S CART AT WICK

THE OLD POST OFFICE, CROPTHORNE

THE OLD BRIDGE, RIVER AVON, PERSHORE

COTTAGES AT GREAT COMBERTON

EVENING AT ELMLEY CASTLE

THE CROSS, ECKINGTON

KING JOHN'S BRIDGE, RIVER AVON, TEWKESBURY